Dear Romance Reader,

Welcome to a world of breathtaking passion and never-ending romance.

Welcome to *Precious Gem Romances.*

It is our pleasure to present *Precious Gem Romances,* a wonderful new line of romance books by some of America's best-loved authors. Let these thrilling historical and contemporary romances sweep you away to far-off times and places in stories that will dazzle your senses and melt your heart.

Sparkling with joy, laughter, and love, each *Precious Gem Romance* glows with all the passion and excitement you expect from the very best in romance. Offered at a great affordable price, these books are an irresistible value—and an essential addition to your romance collection. Tender love stories you will want to read again and again, *Precious Gem Romances* are books you will treasure forever.

Look for fabulous new *Precious Gem Romances* each month—available only at Wal★Mart.

Kate Duffy
Editorial Director

Hopelessly Compromised

Susan Swift

Zebra Books
Kensington Publishing Corp.
http://www.zebrabooks.com

ZEBRA BOOKS are published by

Kensington Publishing Corp.
850 Third Avenue
New York, NY 10022

First Printing: April, 2000
10 9 8 7 6 5 4 3 2 1

Printed in the United States of America

To Bruce,
who taught me everything I know
about romance

One

"God, help me!"

Kate Scoville kicked and flailed her feet, struggling to grip the tower wall with her oversized boots. She whispered a hasty prayer in the chance that the Almighty paid attention to her small corner of His world. Wearing clumsy, borrowed gloves, she grasped the rope tied to the attic window and pushed her boots against the side of the tower, seeking purchase on the wall.

At last, her toes found a mortared joint between two massive blocks of stone. Kate breathed deeply until her racing pulse steadied. The chill air knifed her lungs. She could see her breath—small puffy clouds—when she exhaled.

She looked down and gulped. Three far stories below her, the slate roof of the abbey gleamed, pale and frosty in the moonlight.

She tried not to utter curses damning her wretched uncle, whose treachery had brought her to such desperate straits. First he'd torn Kate away from her beloved home in Somerset. Then he'd nagged her to marry his beef-witted son, Osborn, until she thought he'd drive her quite out of her mind. Locking her in an icy tower attic until she cooperated had been the proverbial last straw.

Kate inched her boots down the tower wall. The short sword she wore on her belt beat against her side with every halting step as her cape flapped around her knees. She finally attained her immediate goal: the second-story roof of the abbey. Still clasping the rope, she crept across the slippery slates. If she reached the edge of the roof without mishap, she'd climb down to the ground by way of a convenient vine or tree.

At the end of the rope, Kate released it with a shaky, nervous hand. A few steps later, her feet flew out from under her. Yelping, she fell with a bump to slide down the pitched roof, scrabbling for a hold.

Scant feet from the brink, Kate plunged into a black gap. Her cape caught on the rough edges and timbers of the roof, breaking her fall. Despite her clinging garb, she plummeted through the hole, too shocked and frightened to scream.

"Oof!" Kate landed on a wooden floor, which emitted a massive boom as she hit. She whimpered in mingled fear and pain as her body clenched; fortunately, she had not fallen on her sword. She rubbed her left side through her doublet. She'd be bruised the next day, but she didn't have time to sit and bemoan her aches and pains.

Heat from her exertions flooded her body as Kate controlled her trembling. She stood, then looked about, recognizing the ballroom on the second floor of the abbey. She adjusted her borrowed clothing, the costume of a Tudor boy she'd found in the attic.

She'd donned it knowing that a doublet, hose, boots, and cape were more practical garb for escaping from a locked tower room than her usual bulky gown and soft shoes.

She prayed that no one had been awakened by her noisy advent into the cavernous ballroom. The entire household should have been roused by the din she'd made. Perhaps God did listen.

Kate smoothed her hair back with a quivering hand as she considered her situation. She was tired, sore, and frightened, but she was now only one floor away from freedom. She could leave through any of the large windows lining the ballroom to climb down to the ground. She wasn't sufficiently bold to use the front door.

Kate twisted the latch of the nearest window, pushing it outward. The hinges squealed, kicking up her heartbeat to a gallop.

But still, no one was roused. No one raised an alarm. With relief, Kate remembered the sordid habits of her uncle and his whelp. Herbert and Osborn were undoubtedly sleeping off last night's libations. The servants, as undisciplined as their masters, were doubtless in no better condition.

How could her grandfather have made such a foolish choice? She'd lived with him since the death of her parents, and surely he must have been aware of Herbert's predilections. The odd arrangement her grandfather had created in his will left Kate in her uncle's custody until her coming-out, but had made her the ward of an earl in faraway London, an older fellow she'd met but once. "Grandfather must have gone dotty at the end," she muttered.

She cast aside her fruitless reflections. Stepping

through the open window to the terrace outside, Kate flipped a leg over the balustrade near a pillar, which was covered by a sturdy ivy vine. Digging a boot between its twining, woody stems, she used it as her ladder to reach the snowy ground below.

She dashed over the snow without a backward look, hoping that no one from the house observed her, a dark shape stumbling over the bright, white snow. The front gate was locked, but Kate found a spot where the current earl had neglected the upkeep of the walls. Kate grinned when she saw the tumble-down stones, which proved to be an easy climb.

She headed for the tollgate near Derbeck. All coaches and stages traveling west to Bath or east to London would stop there.

But where would she go?

Kate hesitated as she regarded the imposing door fronting the Earl of Devere's Berkeley Square town house. She hoped that her guardian could relieve her anxiety. She'd felt little else since she'd embarked upon her current perilous course by setting her boots against the frosty stone wall of the tower attic of Badham Abbey.

She drew her hood back. Her hair, unattended for days, threatened to slip from its ribbon. Kate pushed it out of her face. Lifting the heavy brass knocker, she let it fall. Its boom echoed the frightened pounding of her heart.

However, the mien of the butler who opened the door didn't impress her. Small and withered with age, the fellow squinted with frank curiosity at Kate, who threw back her shoulders and glowered at his stare.

"Good day, sir." Kate knew she sounded like one of the *ton* despite her outlandish appearance. "Is this the residence of the Earl of Devere?" She wanted to be certain. It wouldn't do to invade the wrong house.

"Ye-es," the butler said. "Er, I am not sure if the earl is receiving." He eyed her again, disapproval pervading his features. "Who may I say is calling?"

"Lady Katherine Scoville."

"Indeed?" The butler, moving onto the doorstep, looked up and down the street as if searching for an equipage or a chaperone.

Kate decided to take matters into her own hands. She hadn't come this far to be intimidated by a servant who, judging by his poor vision, probably had trouble finding the door, let alone deciding who should enter and who should not. She slipped past him into the marble-floored entry. A staircase led upward to the first floor, and Kate could see an open upper hallway, trimmed with carved balustrades.

"Now see here—" His voice raised, the butler grabbed Kate's arm as she espied a uniformed footman, holding a silver salver, leaving an upstairs room. Shutting the door behind him, the footman looked down at her for a moment, then turned toward the back portion of the house, where Kate presumed the servants' stairs lay.

Her destination clear, Kate tore her arm from the butler's grasp, inadvertently knocking into a small piecrust table which stood in the entry. The delicate table teetered, then fell with a crash, shattering a vase that had been sitting on it.

A bell sounded as a man shouted from upstairs. "Bartram! What the devil is going on? You know full well that I don't allow racket in the house before noon!''

Kate, tussling with Bartram, took advantage of the butler's temporary distraction to leap up the stairs. Perhaps the owner of the voice would help her in her quest for her guardian. She pushed into the room from whence the shout had issued.

Her eyes widened. She had never seen a man in his nightshirt. For a moment, time stood still as they stared at each other.

Kate felt the blood drain from her face as she looked around, deeply cognizant of the impropriety of her situation. Good God. She was in a man's bedroom. A large bed, complete with four elaborately carved posters and rumpled sheets, stood to her right. Dressed only in a nightshirt and cap, the occupant of the bedchamber looked at her in the same hungry way a fox targeted a coney for dinner.

The chap did greatly resemble a fox, or perhaps an English setter. Tall and thin, he was a veritable Duke of Limbs. His lank, reddish hair stuck out from a white nightcap which slid down over his forehead. He had a Roman nose and pale, unshaven skin spattered with freckles, which furthered his resemblance to a spotted white dog. His wide mouth and large, soulful brown eyes completed the comparison.

He had a very nice smile, she concluded, as did all the setters she knew. She grinned back at him.

"Forgive me," Kate said in her sweetest tones. "I do regret bursting in upon you so abruptly. And forgive my appearance. I realize I must present a strange sight. But, as they say, needs must when the devil drives, and I have certainly been driven by a devil to this guise.''

The man continued to smile at her. "A young lady. Curious. A rather unusual female," he mused aloud, "but not at all unwelcome, despite her peculiar appearance." He sipped from a china cup. A full tea service sat on the table in front of him near a window overlooking Berkeley Square.

Whoever this young man might be, he apparently had a taste for the ladies. With her wealth of experience managing her late grandfather's roistering friends, Kate's anxiety eased a trifle. She could manipulate the situation quite well, thank you.

"Good day, sir." Scraping together the remains of her dignity, Kate bowed, for a curtsey would be ridiculous in her present attire. "Can you, er, direct me to the Earl of Devere?"

"Yes," he said, "I believe I can direct you to the Earl of Devere."

Kate heard a door open behind her.

"Ah, Bartram!" the young man said. "Do tell me, who is this delightful young person, and how comes she into my bedchamber?"

A dry voice spoke from behind her. "My Lord, may I present to you Lady Katherine Scoville."

The chap's brows lifted as he babbled, "Kate! Bonny Kate, Kate, the prettiest Kate in Christendom. Kate of Kate-hall, my super-dainty Kate. Hearing thy mildness praised in every town, thy virtues spoke of, and thy beauty sounded—"

Katherine reddened as she recognized lines from *The Taming of the Shrew*. Leaning back into his chair, the man cast his gaze up and down her person as he continued.

"Kate, like the hazel-twig is straight and slender— Oh! Let me see thee walk!" He blatantly examined her legs, exposed by the short doublet and the revealing hose.

"Walk out, most like!" she snapped. "I seek the Earl of Devere. Please direct me to him at once."

"You have found him. I am Quinn Tyndale, the current Earl of Devere."

"I beg your pardon?" Kate stared. "Is not the Earl of Devere an older gentleman?"

"I fear not—or at least, not yet. I gather, sweet Kate, that no one has told you that my father died this past year. I inherited his title and his responsibilities, including your guardianship."

"Ah, er, please accept my most sincere condolences." Kate struggled to maintain her composure as enlightenment dawned. Good heavens. Grandfather had made even more of a muddle of things than she'd previously imagined. The memory of a red-headed devil-boy leaped into her mind as she recalled Quinn's visit to her home in Somerset with his father ten long years ago. At age thirteen, Quinn had lorded it over her, taunting and teasing until she thought he'd drive her quite out of her mind.

But now her childhood enemy held her fate in the palm of his hand! What would happen if he held their past against her?

Quinn's next words dashed the slight hope that he'd forgotten. "I must say, it's a pleasure to see you, dear Kate. Kate, the pest who put frogs in my short-sheeted bed and added pepper to my soup! Dear, sweet Kate!" He looked her over yet again and laughed.

Kate, aware of the uncertainties of the situation, refrained from reminding the wretch that he'd peeked during blind man's bluff and used her favorite doll for archery practice—as his target. Pressing her lips together, she maintained a calm demeanor, though her thoughts tumbled like a brook in spring.

"Bartram, take our super-dainty Kate to the drawing room and get her some tea. I'll attend her shortly. Malcolm!" The earl shouted unexpectedly, and Kate flinched. A small dark man entered, so quickly that Kate suspected he'd been listening at the door. "Dress me at once! Can't you see we have a guest?"

Quinn winked at Kate as Bartram hustled her out.

Quinn couldn't restrain his mirth as he expertly tied his cravat. As Malcolm assisted him into his midnight-blue jacket, the valet asked about the source of Quinn's fine humor.

"Did you see that creature who was just in my rooms? Wasn't she a prime 'un?"

"She, my lord?" asked the valet in his Scottish burr.

"Aye, then," mocked Quinn, in a teasing imitation of Malcolm's accent. "My ward. I wonder what she is doing here."

"Mayhap something's amiss in Wiltshire."

"And what do you know of that, my fine sir?" Quinn narrowed his eyes at his servant, who shrugged.

"Gossip of your lordship's new status as guardian to the heiress of Badham Abbey shot through the servants like scandal at a *ton* party."

"Do tell." Quinn was ever impressed by the ability of servants to know their employers' every move. "So what can the lady want?"

"Who knows the wants of women, especially one as young as that?" Malcolm tugged at Quinn's sleeves.

"Hmph. She comes to ask a favor. I'd lay a monkey on it."

"And will you give it to her, my lord?"

"I'd give her much more than a favor, if she weren't my ward." Quinn gave a final tweak to his lapel before proceeding out the door. "Pity she's practically family. Can't play blanket hornpipe with her sweet self!"

Quinn had been surprised by the arousal he'd felt at his first glance at the cub who'd invaded his rooms; he'd never before been attracted to any catamite, however pretty. And this creature was a delight for the senses, with chestnut hair, blue eyes, and pouting lips that begged for a man's kiss.

But the moment she'd opened her mouth, revealing herself as a female, he'd wanted to turn her over his knee, strip off that doublet and those outrageous hose, and spank her sweet blind cheeks. This Kate wanted taming. A pity that her Petruchio would have to be someone other than her legal guardian.

Kate sat uneasily on the sofa in Quinn's yellow drawing room, sipping her tea. Her flesh itched in the grubby finery in which she'd slept the previous night, wrapped in her cloak in the taproom of a shabby inn at Staines. Although the costume had served her well, she'd become thoroughly uncomfortable with her garb, and wanted nothing more than a bath and clean clothes.

Moreover, she was rather nervous. When she sought her guardian's help, she'd assumed that her grandfather's crony wouldn't remember her childhood trespasses. Quinn, however, hadn't forgotten any detail. Kate herself hadn't recalled that she'd short-sheeted his bed whilst leaving the frogs. She prayed he'd confine his retribution to teasing, for he had ultimate power over her.

Quinn flung open the doors of the drawing room not thirty minutes after Kate had entered. Kate's mouth dropped open in shock. The untidy young chap in the nightshirt had disappeared. Confronting Kate was a veritable Pink of the *Ton* of commanding mien and immaculate dress, whose midnight-blue jacket appeared to have been made to fit his broad shoulders. Buff pantaloons did nothing to hide muscular, masculine thighs. Shaving had revealed a strong jaw; neatly brushed hair emphasized his expressive eyes. Quinn, Lord Devere, epitomized upper-class hauteur.

Kate lifted her chin. Despite her clammy hands and shaky soul, she was a Scoville, and wouldn't be intimidated.

Eyeing her with the expression a bloodhound might wear while tracking prey, Quinn dragged at the bellpull and bellowed, "Richard!"

Kate jerked at the unexpected noise. She gathered that her guardian was a jovial sort. Well, she could use some good cheer after the travails of the past few weeks. She tried to relax into the stiff-backed brocade sofa.

Quinn regarded her once more and she squirmed self-consciously in her doublet and hose. "So, why on earth are you attired in such a deucedly eccentric manner, my dear?" he asked, advancing into the room, which seemed to shrink as he dominated the chamber.

"I had to escape." Kate kept her voice low and

terse. If her guardian did not treat the threat to her person with the utmost seriousness, she'd be packed off and sent back to Wiltshire, trapped in the same hopeless situation.

"Strange," Quinn remarked, as another gentleman entered. "We received a letter from your uncle, Badham, stating you were well content and wished to marry your cousin Hoskins."

"Osborn."

"So you do wish to marry this Osburt?" He tapped an elegantly shod toe on the carpeted floor.

"Osborn."

"If you wish to marry your cousin, with whom you have been living in apparent happiness, how come you to my bedroom?"

"I wasn't aware that was your bedroom."

"As ungentlemanly as it might be to argue with you, my super-dainty Kate, I was in my nightshirt, in my bedroom."

Kate gave up winning that particular point. "I don't want to marry him. I had to escape because they locked me up! I wrote to you through the solicitor weeks ago—didn't you get my letter?"

"No. And, I take it, you didn't receive mine?"

She shook her head.

"Hmph. In any event, I declined to provide my, er, blessing for the union due to my man of affairs, Richard Carrothers." Quinn inclined his head toward his secretary, a spare, graying man who remained quiet as stone near the door. "Richard has traveled twice to Wiltshire to see you, and both times was denied admittance to Badham Abbey."

"I didn't know that." Surprised, Kate realized that

her uncle had defied her guardian's authority by diverting their letters and excluding Carrothers.

"Be that as it may, that does not explain how you come to be in my rooms at dawn."

"Dawn, my lord? It's past eleven o'clock!" *Mercy. Is he daft?*

"Well, close to it." Quinn waved a hand airily as he sat down in a chair opposite her, folded his arms over his chest, and waited.

"I told you, I had to escape. He locked me in the attic, you see, until I agreed—until you agreed—to marry Osborn."

"There is very little chance I would agree to marry Osgood, and even less chance I would consent to your marriage at this time to anyone at all." Quinn poured himself a cup of tea.

"Anyone at all, my lord?"

"Do you express a desire to marry?" He held his cup poised and eyed her over its rim.

"Not at this time, my lord," Kate answered stiffly. "But I do not see that you should make such a dictatorial declaration when we are not acquainted."

"We are sufficiently acquainted for me to have made that determination." Quinn sipped, then put his china cup onto its saucer with a click. "And, fascinating as this discussion of your marital prospects might be, it does not speak to the immediate questions which occupy me. Ah. Let me think."

Kate waited as he raised his eyes to the ceiling.

"I now recollect. I recall a young girl much addicted to the climbing of trees, and similar pursuits. Please do not tell me you were so improper as to clamber out of the attic dressed in that manner." Quinn's long face assumed an expression of distaste.

Kate wriggled herself further into her cloak. "It was necessary."

"And you found your way from Wiltshire to London. The public stage?"

She nodded.

He winced. "Indomitable Kate! Well, your determination will be rewarded, I am sure. However, mere strength of character will not solve any of our more pressing issues. We must find a place for you to live, with some female to provide you company and countenance."

"Would not the presence of your, er, wife be sufficient?"

"Wife? I have no wife, bonny Kate, to lend propriety to this awkward situation."

Kate gulped. "I need only a maid to attend to me here."

Quinn raised his brows. "Nay, dearest Kate. I would not have your reputation destroyed."

Kate raised *her* brows. "I doubt that would be the case."

Standing, her guardian spoke without a trace of humor as he paced to and fro. "You're not in the country anymore. As yet, no one knows of your escapades, but unless you wish to forever enjoy your fortune in solitary splendor in the wilds of Somerset, you cannot stay here with just a maid. Besides, I also have a reputation to maintain. I would not have it bruited about that I took advantage of my child."

"I'm *not* your child!" Outraged, Kate stood, arms akimbo.

"You are my ward, so you might as well be my child," he told her curtly. "Richard, how about Grillon's for the chit?" Quinn moved to the window.

Carrothers followed. "Doesn't solve the problem of her companionship, my lord."

"We might hire someone." The two males spoke as though Kate were not in the room.

"Can't trust a hireling."

"Open up the house on Bruton Street?"

Kate interrupted. She hated being ignored. "I own a house in London."

The two men paused, looked at her, then resumed their conversation.

"Ring for Harper, find her some clothes," Carrothers murmured.

"P'raps she's the same size as one of the maids." Quinn looked her up and down for what must have been the tenth time.

Kate tried again, keeping her tone polite, firm, and calm, although she felt her back teeth grating. "I'm not sure where my house is. I haven't been to London since before my parents died."

"Can't take her to my mum. Kate would run her ragged. I've got it!" Quinn, excited, thrust a finger up into the air in triumph. "We'll send her to Nan!"

Kate lost her temper and grabbed her guardian's sleeve. "I am not a parcel to be sent off!"

Quinn swatted her hand. "See here, you're crumpling my coat."

"And who is Nan?"

"Anna, Lady Penrose, is my older sister. Has a passel of brats, one of them's about your age, maybe a little older. How old is my niece Louisa, Richard?"

"The Honorable Louisa Penrose is eighteen years of age and is expected to be brought out this Season."

"There you are. You'll be eighteen soon, hmm?

This year it's Louisa's turn, next year will be yours. In the meanwhile, you'll go to Kent until the Season. Hide you in plain sight, as it were."

"Hide me in plain sight?" Kate frowned, mystified.

"Safety in numbers, and all of that. If the wicked uncle comes to call, he won't find you," Quinn explained. "Nan has several daughters and a couple of boys. You can put frogs in their beds, too," he added maliciously.

Kate's mind was elsewhere. "Do you really think he'll try to kidnap me?"

Carrothers cleared his throat. "After we received the letter from Badham, I made some inquiries. Your uncle desperately needs your fortune. Without it, he will have to mortgage Badham Abbey."

"Oh." Kate took a moment to absorb this news.

"You are a considerable heiress, you know." Quinn's tone was unexpectedly gentle. "Must be protected."

Kate hated the thought of being a burden. "I don't want anyone to protect me."

"Then why are you here?"

She bit her lip. "I'm afraid I can't see any alternatives."

"Well, then, you are lucky." Quinn smiled crookedly at her. "Until you're safely leg-shackled, you have me, whether you want me or not. Harper!" His voice rose into a plaintive wail. He yanked on the bellpull.

Kate had the impression nothing happened quickly enough for the earl when he wanted results.

An older woman, attired in plain gray with a white apron, entered the drawing room. "My lord?" She adjusted her mobcap over silvery curls.

"Kate, this is Harper. She runs the house. Harper, this is Lady Katherine Scoville. Bathe her and put her in suitable clothes. I'm taking her to Lady Penrose's today after luncheon. Tell no one." Quinn waved a finger in the air for emphasis. "You know how servants talk. No one but the three of us—no, dash it, Malcolm and Bartram know, but they're trustworthy—no one but the five of us should know Lady Kate has been here, or where she is going."

Two

Scant hours later, Kate found herself with Lord Devere in his curricle, bowling swiftly down a road eastward out of London. She was dressed in the best gown that could be found on such short notice and an old coat belonging to her guardian. The original owner of the dress was shorter than Kate, so her boots protruded from beneath the hem but were temporarily covered by the earl's greatcoat. Rather more of her chest than Kate liked to expose showed at the top of the gown. She pulled the coat's lapels together over her torso.

"Nan lives near Sevenoaks, in the north downs," Quinn shouted over the noise of the curricle's wheels grinding on the road. "Reminds me of your home in Somerset. You'll like it there."

"What if she doesn't want me there?"

"What?" Quinn's grip on the reins shifted and one of his showy, matched blacks shied. He regained control with a quick flick of his whip to the horse's outside. The gelding settled back into a smooth gait, pacing its partner.

"What if she doesn't want me?"

"Pish tosh! What's not to want, sweet Kate?"

"I wish you'd stop calling me that."

Quinn turned his head and beamed at her, surprising Kate with the warmth conveyed by his soulful regard. He really had the most extraordinary eyes.

"Lady Katherine, don't be concerned about your future. I have already spoken to my sister about your come-out. Your unexpected arrival merely advances the schedule."

"Oh." As the day drew to a close, Kate snuggled back into the greatcoat. Although she was a tall woman, Devere's sleeves came down over her hands. His scent, a pungent blend of clove, citrus, and other spicy notes, lingered in the wool. "What about grandfather's will? I'm supposed to be with Herbert."

"Richard thinks we can persuade the Lords to come 'round to our way of thinking."

"What's that?"

He glanced down at her. "The House of Lords passes laws, sweet Kate. They can help. After all, what good are they if they can't do a fellow a favor once in a while?"

"Are you a member?"

"Yes, but I haven't darkened their threshold in a few years, not since my investiture. I say, Herbert should be coming along to London to be presented, as it were."

"He's a ramshackle sort. He may just cut them altogether."

"No, I believe that our Lord Herbert will be along to London soon. He'll go to Parliament and contact the Bow Street Runners to find you." Quinn grew silent for several minutes while Kate sat and worried.

"We'll just have to be quicker and cleverer, shan't we, Kate? I shall return to London tomorrow and begin to see to arrangements. In the meantime, no one knows where you are."

"I'm afraid that I've left some clues," she said. "I visited Forrester, the solicitor, and spoke to a clerk. I used my mother's name, but I said I was your ward in order to find your direction."

He whistled between his teeth. "The clerk would have to be a numbwit not to calculate who you are and to whom you went. And from me it's a short hop to my sister. But be of good cheer, dear Kate. We'll yet contrive."

Kate was comforted by her first view of Penrose House. Although it was situated in meadowlands rather than hills, it did indeed resemble her home. The wide fields were dotted by occasional stands of trees. As the curricle neared the pleasant, Palladian-style residence, Kate could see that the property became formally landscaped. She liked the look of the place, as everything appeared to be properly maintained, and she hoped she'd have the opportunity to explore the manor house and grounds.

As Quinn entered, shouting for Nan and Pen, he bundled Kate unceremoniously into a drawing room to await her host and hostess. He plopped her onto a comfortable sofa upholstered in tufted green brocade. When her astonished hosts appeared, Kate tried to smile, though she felt wretchedly shy and awkward. She wondered what they must have made of her, attired as she was in Devere's cast-off overcoat and a too-small gown.

Attired for a winter afternoon in a blue kerseymere day dress, Lady Anna was as short and round as her brother was tall and thin. She had fair hair and merry eyes. At this moment, those eyes snapped dangerously. "Quinn! How dare you bring one of your fancy pieces to this house!"

Kate sat bolt upright. "Now see here—" she began.

Lady Anna's husband, a stout baronet dressed as an ordinary country squire, agreed with his wife. "I must say, Devere, this is not quite the thing, is it?"

Quinn ignored their discomfiture, and Kate's. "Nan, Pen, we have a bit of a dilemma. This is my ward, Lady Katherine Scoville."

Their lips parted in identical round o's of surprise. Kate restrained a nervous giggle. The Penroses appeared to be a well-matched couple.

"I ask that Kate stay here for the nonce." Pacing back and forth, Quinn outlined Kate's situation. "So, she cannot live with me, for her reputation's sake. And she must be protected from Herbert, Lord Badham."

Lady Anna sniffed. "From what I have heard, all women should be protected from Lord Herbert and his issue. No respectable member of the *ton* gives them entree." She sat down next to Kate, reached out and took her cold hands in her own. "I'm sorry, child, for the way I greeted you. You are most welcome here, for as long as you like."

Kate blinked back sudden hot tears, a sharp contrast to her icy fingers and lonely spirit of the last few weeks. She hadn't told her guardian of the cold hell she'd endured at Badham Abbey, but Lady Anna's kind touch brought her to the realization of the danger of her plight and the narrowness of her escape. "Thank you, ma'am. I'll endeavor to be a thoughtful guest."

"Nonsense! You're Devere's ward, practically one

of the family." Sir Michael Penrose spoke from his cozy wing chair near the fire.

"Pen, we're afraid she'll be traced here by her uncle before we can persuade Parliament to act." Quinn's tone was solemn. "Accordingly, her true identity must be concealed."

His long face was so comically somber that Kate was both jollied out of her tears and irresistibly reminded of the satire, *Northanger Abbey*. She let loose a gurgle of laughter. "Oh, my lord! You are too Gothic!"

"And *you* are too impertinent and careless. Kate, you must tell no one who you are, and we must pass you off as a distant cousin of Pen's." He nodded toward Sir Michael Penrose. "With your permission, sir."

"You have it, of course, if you deem it necessary."

"I do. Consider what has transpired. Badham imprisoned Kate and wrote to me, asking for her hand in marriage to his son and fraudulently claiming her agreement." He wheeled to face Kate. "If, based on his lies, I had written back with my consent, you would not be sitting here now, Kate. You would be Odbert's wife, alone, powerless, and penniless."

Kate sat quite still, shocked into immobility by his directness and understanding. "You are right, certainly, and that is why I left. But I am a Scoville." She lifted her chin. "Despite Uncle Herbert, I am proud of who I am. And a false name seems so . . . so . . . unnecessary. I'm just a girl. Why would anyone go to so much trouble over me?"

"You may not have a clear idea of the extent of your fortune," said the earl. "I do. You have a house in London and an estate in Somerset. You own tin mines in Cornwall and dairy cattle in Devon. In short, sweet Kate, aside from your own, umm, personal attributes, you are a very tempting prize. Men have killed for far less than what you have, and it is my task to take care of you and your estate until you're married, or until you attain the age of majority, whichever happens first."

She stared at him, stunned.

He softened his tone. "So we must have a care, little Kate, and put our heads together and decide who you're to be for the next few months."

A silence fell, broken only by the crackling of the logs in the fireplace.

"If we are to choose a new name," Kate finally said, "it should be similar to my own, so that I'll become accustomed to it quickly."

Quinn smiled at her. "Clever Kate! I knew you'd understand."

Anna spoke up. "But what will happen when we go to London for the Season? You know Louisa is to be presented."

Quinn responded, sounding confident. "Lady Kate will go with you and participate in such minor social gatherings as young girls do in the year before their come-out. She'll hide in plain sight, as I've said, and as *you've* said, Nan, she won't meet up with Herbert and, umm, Osric because no one invites them anywhere."

"But what of those I already know?" asked Kate. "I've met many of my grandfather's friends, and I have schoolmates who will be making their debuts, as well."

Anna said, "We'll have to trust your friends, Lady Katherine. And as for the old earl's companions, I'm afraid many of them are too elderly and frail to move about in society anymore. We're losing the past generation, day by day."

Kate nodded, calmed by Lady Penrose's logic as well as by the confidence of both brother and sister. She was also buoyed by her successes over the past few days. She'd been dreadfully miserable and frightened, but she had now attained a place of safety with people who appeared as anxious about her welfare as any parent could be.

She raised her eyes to her guardian. Quinn stood by the fireplace, leaning on the mantel. His hooded dark gaze raked her yet again. Despite his decorous conduct and proper expressions of concern, she'd never seen a father look at any daughter with quite the expression the earl wore; it more closely resembled that of a hawk eyeing a titmouse. Kate tugged self-consciously at the neck of her gown. She had a feeling that no dress was cut high enough to prevent the earl from divining what lay beneath.

Anna had apparently moved on with her thoughts while Quinn and Kate silently communed. "What about Kendra . . . Caroline . . . Caitlin . . . come on, Pen, help me out with this!" she appealed to her husband.

Pen frowned. "I'd keep it simple. It's an unusual name, but what about Kay? If we choose a second name which begins with a T, no one will give it another thought, even if we slip and call her Kate or K.T."

"Excellent notion!" Quinn waved a forefinger in the air for attention. "We'll call her Tyndale, and she'll be one of our cousins, Nan. There are lots of those. How about if she's one of the old Nabob's younger daughters? No one's heard of any of them since he went off to India thirty years ago."

"That's perfect, Quinn!" Anna exclaimed.

"What?" asked Kate, completely bewildered.

"Righty-o, here it is." Quinn sat down next to her. She ignored his beguiling scent, the same spicy fragrance she had enjoyed on his coat. "You are Kay Tyndale, the, er, fifth daughter of Colin Tyndale. Colin was my father's youngest brother. Having no prospects in England, he settled in Calicut thirty years ago as an employee of the British East India Company."

"My lord, you're amazing," said Kate. "I do believe you should write novels. This is quite the equal of anything from Mrs. Radcliffe's quill."

"Not 'my lord,' " he gently corrected. "Cousin Quinn, Cousin Nan, and Cousin Pen."

"Oh, but I can't," she gasped, embarrassed.

"You can and you must," said Anna. She rose from her chair. "Come!" She held out her hand to Kate. "Let me show you my brood."

Anna led Kate upstairs to the nursery, talking all the while. "I have five, you know. I am very fortunate. You are the only child?"

Kate answered while looking around the comfortable, elegant manse. "Yes. There were two stillborn after me."

Anna's voice was soft. "Yes. That happens. I am the eldest, but my mother lost two babes before Quinn was born. Then she died with the next, poor thing. God grant my own daughters better fortune!" She opened the door to the nursery, where three children in nightwear were eating supper at a small table. A white-haired governess, dressed in sober gray, presided over the trio as they spooned up their warm bread and milk.

"This is Harry, our heir, and Charlie. He's eight. And Margaret, the baby, who is five."

Kate's heart immediately melted. The little girl, who shared the name of Kate's own mother, had enchanting gold ringlets and a sweet smile for Lady Anna as she turned from her supper to stare at the stranger.

"Children, this is our cousin, Kay Tyndale. She's come all the way from India to stay with us. Kay, this is Mrs. Stowe, a very important lady to our family."

As Kate smiled at the governess, Harry, a sturdy ten-year-old, demanded, "India! Can you tell us stories about lions and tigers and wolves?"

Kate turned to Lady Anna, feeling her eyes widen.

"Darlings, Cousin Kay has just arrived, and is very tired. And it's almost bedtime. Perhaps she'll have stories for you on the morrow." Anna intervened with great aplomb, Kate thought.

"Hurrah!" shouted the two boys, while little Margaret dropped her spoon and turned her solemn green gaze on her mother. Anna closed the door, smiling. "They always raise my spirits. I know it isn't fashionable to enjoy one's children, but I vow they are the center of my life, and of Pen's as well." She proceeded down the hall. "We shall put you in this guest room, near Louisa and Pauline. It's a nice cheerful room—"

She broke off as she opened the door. A maid was already dusting the dainty bedroom, which was decorated in pale yellow and green, with lace hangings over the bed. "Bettina, make sure there's a fire, and hot water for Miss Kay when she retires. Is there water now?" Anna checked the pitcher on the dressing table.

Devere poked his head through the open door. "Nan, am I to have my usual place?"

"Yes, Quinn." She turned to Kate. "We keep him away from the nursery wing, else the children would give him no peace. We'll leave you now to refresh yourself. Bettina will bring you anything you need, and can act as lady's maid for you while you are with us."

"There's just one thing, ma'am." Kate spoke quietly, so the servant would not overhear. "I left my maid, Mary Ann, in Wiltshire." She could see Quinn at her side, shaking his head.

"No," he said. "We cannot bring her to you, cousin. But Carrothers can make inquiries and ensure she is safe."

Kate was pacified and, after her guardian and his sister left the room, she began to investigate her new quarters. They were everything she could want, on a par with her bedroom in Somerset.

After Kate washed, Bettina dressed her hair and brushed out the folds of Kate's borrowed gown. Kate fervently wished for more clothes. She had no money, and only the one dress, plus two changes of underclothing borrowed from one of the maids in London, not enough at all. But that problem would have to wait for a solution. For now, it was enough that she was safe.

Kate made the acquaintance of Lady Penrose's two eldest children at dinner. Pauline was a small dark creature; she had fourteen years. Louisa, eighteen and about to make her debut, was the kind of petite, elfin lass who always made tall Kate feel gangling and awkward. Louisa greatly resembled her mother, and Katherine concluded the Honorable Louisa Penrose would contract an extremely advantageous marriage. Who could resist her blond curls and laughing femininity?

Dinner with the six of them was full of lively chatter, and Kate recalled amusing meals with her parents, her grandfather, and his dandyish friends. While the conversation was different, the same happy spirit reigned in the room. Her hostess gracefully controlled the discussion, steering the talk away from Cousin Kay's experiences in India toward the fun they'd have outfitting Kate suitably for her sojourn in England. "For," Lady Anna explained, embroidering freely upon the skeletal tale Quinn had created, "all of Cousin Kay's luggage has been lost, and we must purchase anew!" Anna winked at Kate.

"We have a wonderful seamstress," said Louisa to Kate between spoonfuls of turtle soup. "She comes right to the house for fittings and copies all the newest styles. I want to be all the crack when we go to Town. Mother," she asked, "can Cousin Kay be all the crack, too?"

Kate laughed with the rest.

"Can two ladies at once be all the crack in London?" wondered Pauline. "Uncle Quinn, you're a 'top of the trees.' You must know."

"Pauline, from where did you hear that turn of phrase?" asked her father.

"From Jem, in the stable. He said Uncle Quinn's horses were bang-up prime, too."

"They are," Kate said. "They're a beautiful pair."

"Sweet goers. Cost me a dace or two at Tatt's, but it's no matter. And yes, my little sprite, two ladies at once may be all the crack, and I predict our girls will be top of the trees as well." Quinn lifted his glass and toasted the two of them. "To Cousin Kay and my niece Louisa, a pair destined to take London by storm!"

"Hear, hear!" Sir Pen laughed as he raised his glass.

"When do we travel to London?" asked Kate, as the footman removed the soup plates.

"I go tomorrow," said Quinn. "I must begin to see to a few of my affairs." Raising his brows, he gave her his devilish grin.

"We travel to London for the Season in about two months, when the weather is warmer. That will give you time to rest, and to acquire your wardrobe." Lady Anna smiled at Kate.

Kate was quite willing to rusticate until Louisa's debut. She knew she would benefit from a rest in secure surroundings, as she did not look her best, given the strain of the last few weeks. But she still fretted. "Cousin, er, Quinn, I am concerned about the state of my finances. My, um, ready was lost with my—my other luggage."

"Not to worry, Cousin Kay," said Quinn. "You may draw upon your . . . family accounts at any time. I will arrange it for you. In any event, your expenses are not extraordinary. You shan't need court-dress or anything of that sort. Just day dresses, and perhaps one or two gowns suitable for excursions to the theatre, and the like."

"Oh, Mamma! Can't I go to London also? Surely

it would be unexceptional to attend a play, and I so wish to go!" Pauline appealed to her mother.

Anna frowned. "Your sister did not travel to Town at your age."

"But I'll be all bored here," whined Pauline. "Everyone exciting will be gone."

Her father raised his brows. "Truly, daughter?"

Pauline flushed and stuttered. "No, Father, I mean, I know you will be here, but you will be all involved with Harry and Charlie."

"It is precisely this sort of social gaffe which keeps fourteen-year-olds at home," observed Sir Pen.

"Perhaps she can go for a short while, just to attend the theatre," said Lady Anna thoughtfully. Pauline bounced in her seat with joy. "As long as no jumping up and down occurs," Anna added, eyeing her lively child.

"Do you ride?" Louisa asked Kate.

"Yes, of course," said Kate. "Is there a spare mount in your stable for me to borrow?"

"Yes, and we will have a habit sewn," said Lady Anna.

"You're very kind. I love riding above all things."

"I think a navy or midnight blue, with her eyes," said Louisa. "Oh! I can just see it, with a fine white feather curling over her bonnet."

Pen laughed. "Are clothes all you think of, child?"

"Yes, quite. And why not, sir? In a few months these carefree days will be over, and I shall have to think of getting married." Her small face clouded.

"Why so somber, niece?" asked Quinn. "Like you not the married state?"

"Well, you do not, as you have not wed," answered

Louisa pertly. "But I accept my lot in life. Still, what if there is no one for me in London?"

Kate smiled. "Your mirror must be faulty," she said. Louisa stared, apparently surprised. Kate continued, "I predict you will struggle to choose between your suitors."

"But never you mind," spoke up Quinn. "I'll ensure no rakes or triflers approach. Guard you like a lion!" He curled his fingers into claws.

Everyone laughed, including Kate. The earl, with his large, brown eyes and lean frame, couldn't have looked less leonine.

The Penroses apparently eschewed the custom of separating the genders after dinner when they dined informally in the country. Feeling too tired to linger over the savory, Kate begged leave to retire early from the assembled family.

Weary to her bones, she knew she'd finally achieved the safety she craved. As she lay in her bed, mulling over the events of the day, she basked in a sense of comfort and security she had not experienced since before the final illness and death of her grandfather. A new, happier chapter of her life had begun. She could count herself lucky.

The weeks at Badham Abbey had been a long period of bored discomfort punctuated by moments of startling fear. The news that her Uncle Herbert had written to her guardian to request her hand in marriage to Cousin Osborn had energized Kate. She had penned her own letter to Devere and attempted to send it through the solicitor. She now believed it to have been diverted—most likely stolen—by Herbert or Osborn.

And when she had tried to leave the estate on

horseback to ride to the nearest village, she'd found every gate leading out of the grounds chained and locked. Then Herbert had learned of her aborted departure from a gossipy stablehand. That same night he'd locked her in the attic "Until you are more agreeable, my dear!" His unctuous voice still echoed in her mind and Kate shuddered, moving her legs restlessly in the soft linen sheets of the Penrose's guest bed.

She blessed her hoydenish childhood, which had enabled her to escape from the abbey. Had she been a less athletic girl, she'd have been trapped in that cold tower until the Second Coming.

After her grief, anger, and terror at the cards Fortune had dealt her, help had come from a most unexpected quarter. Quinn Tyndale, the Earl of Devere. She smiled to herself at the memory of his image the first moment she saw him. Such a silly-looking fellow, in his nightdress and cap! But he certainly had accomplished a great deal for her in only one day.

She admired the decisive way he had taken charge; however, she could not think his acts stemmed from pure motives. She had seen the odd, brooding way he looked at her. He had packed her off to the country as soon as he could get her away from his home in London.

She concluded she was yet an unwelcome, unrequested responsibility. Quinn was a bachelor, evidently by choice. He could not desire the obligation of overseeing her until she attained the age of majority. Nor could Lady Anna and Sir Pen, kind though they might be, revel in her unexpected presence in their lives.

Yes, Kate would be pleased to go to London and

be included in appropriate diversions there. She'd marry quickly to relieve her guardian and his family of her charge.

Three

Asleep, Kate dreamed . . .

She walked through the Great Hall of the old abbey, where portraits of her forebears hung. The paintings dated back centuries. Her ancestors seemed to speak to her from the paint and canvas, declaring that her transitory concerns would pass; in due course she would take her place, serenely looking forth at her descendants from her own gilded frame. She found these thoughts immensely calming. Most people felt that the Great Hall was a dusty, cold cavern of a room, but Kate loved it.

Carrying a branch of candles, Kate walked down the hall and stopped in front of a painting of a Tudor courtier. She drew in her breath as she gazed at the portrait of Robert Scoville, the first Earl of Badham. This dissolute gentleman had been a favorite of Henry VIII, who had endowed him with the peerage and the abbey during the Reformation.

A mere stripling, he wore a black doublet, stiffly embroidered in silver thread, over plain dark hose and riding boots. He leaned on a bared sword, its point driven into the ground. His chestnut hair was tied neatly at his nape. Kate cried out in the night as she recognized the pale, ghostly features as her own . . .

Kate sat bolt upright in the bed, gasping as she tried to control the wild beating of her heart. A candle guttered in its wax. Able to take stock of her surroundings, she realized where she was—safe in Penrose House, far away from the chill environs of Badham Abbey.

Leaning back into the pillows, she closed her eyes and sought to fill her dreams with joyous memories: the happy laughter at last evening's meal, the smile on the face of Anna's tiny daughter as she ate her supper. Unbidden, the image of Quinn's broad shoulders and elegant hands crept into her mind. She pushed the fantasy away, as it could only disturb, not soothe, and finally dropped back into sleep.

The next morning, Kate lay peacefully abed, watching sunlight slant through the lacy curtains at the window. Judging by the angle of the rays, she'd slept late.

Piping voices seeped faintly through the door.

"She can't still be asleep, Harry. It's already time for our elevenses."

"Don't be foolish. India is half the world away. It's the middle of the night there. She probably just went to bed."

"If she's still asleep," the first little voice said doggedly, "we should check to see she's feeling all the thing."

After a pause, the second voice said, "If she's sleeping, she'll never know."

The door creaked. Two round heads peered around the opening. Kate peeked at the boys through her eyelashes while they tiptoed in. As they approached her bed, she leaped up and roared like a tiger, flailing her arms in the air. *"Aargh!!"*

The boys shrieked in unison—an extremely satisfying sound—and fled for the door. Smiling, Kate lay back onto her pillows. Her day had begun in a delightful manner.

She reached for the bellpull. When Bettina appeared, Kate beamed at the maid. "Good morning, Bettina. How are you today?"

"Fine, thank you, Miss Kay. You're yet abed?"

"I am about to arise. Where is the rest of the family?"

"The three youngest are at lessons in the schoolroom."

Hah! thought Kate.

Bettina continued, "Miss Penrose is practicing the pianoforte. Miss Pauline is reading her Greek with the master in the library. Lady Anna is conferring with Cook. My lord Devere awakened early and has departed for London."

"Indeed? I was under the impression my cousin Quinn never arose early."

"Quite, ma'am." Bettina, a pleasant-faced woman in her middle thirties, went to a standing wardrobe and removed a dressing gown. She held the robe open for Kate. "It is all the talk belowstairs. My lord Devere has never before arrived without his valet, and has never been known to rise before noon at the very earliest, not even for a day in the field."

"Thank you." Kate tied the belt around her waist. "At what time is luncheon served?"

"One o'clock, ma'am. May I bring you elevenses?"

"Yes, please. A cup of chocolate and a roll will suffice, and hot water for my wash."

"Very good, ma'am." Bettina withdrew.

Kate opened the curtains to look at the pleasant prospect. Below her, a wide balcony hemmed by a low balustrade divided the house from its surrounding gardens. Farther in the distance, she could see rolling fields, perfect for a gallop. The sun glittered off a stream meandering through the meadows. Yes, the day had begun in a remarkably fine manner.

Her serenity was not marred by the absence of her guardian. A less practical girl might desire eligible Quinn to dance attendance upon her, but Kate preferred him at work in her interests in London.

Shivering, she remembered his odd, brooding countenance. What must he think of her, bursting into his room dressed in boy's garb? Yes, it was best that he'd left Penrose House, for she had not the slightest wish to face that curious, penetrating gaze.

To Kate, living with the Penroses felt rather like slipping into a hipbath full of heated water. She conveyed her gratitude to her host and hostess at luncheon, a meal again attended by Lord and Lady Penrose, and the two eldest children.

"Stuff and nonsense!" said Lady Anna briskly. "We're delighted to have you."

"Mamma, shall we go to Sevenoaks after luncheon?" Louisa asked. "I need a few ells of thread-lace to trim my old bonnet. We can visit the seamstress and select fabrics for Cousin Kay while we're there."

Anna considered. "I am not sure Sevenoaks will have all we require. But it will be a start."

So after luncheon, the four females piled into the Penrose coach for the brief drive into nearby Sevenoaks. A charming town, Sevenoaks had an appealing Tudor ambience, boasting numerous half-timbered buildings and cobblestoned streets. The

Penroses, who stood as the local squires, were well known there, and they were greeted with friendliness by the merchants with whom they dealt. Kate was introduced to all and sundry as "Cousin Kay Tyndale, come all the way from India!" The spurious Miss Tyndale was regaled by the most interesting gossip in the teashop and plied with the sweetest cakes.

The draper had a small establishment in the center of town, and while he did not carry the fine silks and satins the women would need for their London social occasions, he showed them plenty of wools and cambrics suitable for everyday wear. Kate hesitated before selecting colors other than black and gray for her ensembles. Despite her disguise, propriety forbade her from indulging in the bright colors which would most flatter her hair and complexion. She comforted herself with the memory that her grandfather had preferred her in vivid plumage.

She chose a deep Prussian blue for her riding habit and several sprigged muslins for morning and day dresses. In the country, she would prefer twilled sarcenet for her dinner gowns, but she knew later, in London, only the sheerest of fabrics would suffice, with only delicate shawls to protect her from the elements. Still, she selected a stout wool for her pelisse, in a lovely warm red.

Louisa was unable to find the fine thread-lace she craved for her bonnet, but prevailed upon her mother to purchase some ribands to refurbish the hat. "For," Louisa told Kate, "it is quite my favorite bonnet for walks at Penrose, and I am loath to replace it."

Anna herself needed no more clothing, but she helped Pauline choose fabrics; the fourteen-year-old grew rapidly and seemed to constantly need new gowns. The visit to the draper was followed by an equally fruitful stop at the seamstress, who measured Kate fore and aft, and from top to bottom. She repeated the same process with Pauline.

The ladies returned to Penrose House near dusk in excellent spirits. They were met at the door by a solemn deputation.

The three youngest children stood in a row. They were neatly dressed, and Charlie blew a small tin horn to get the attention of the adults. Their governess watched from a window embrasure, fondly smiling at her charges.

"Harrumph!" said Harry, who began to read from a scroll.

"Whereas: Cousin Kay Tyndale is visiting Penrose; and secondly, said cousin hales from the faraway and interesting country of India; and thirdly, Cousin Kay took dinner with our parents and sisters; and fourthly, said Cousin Kay took luncheon with the same parents and sisters—"

Here, Harry's voice took on a somewhat indignant note. He continued, "And fifthly: said cousin then went to Sevenoaks—"

Here he was interrupted by little Margaret, who rushed forward impatiently and flung her arms around Kay's legs. "Won't you have supper with us?"

Harry glared at his younger sister. "Mags, get back here. You broke ranks."

"Please? Please? We so want to hear about India!" Charlie tugged at Kate's skirt.

"Now, children!" Anna visibly stifled a laugh.

"It's all right," said Kate, smiling. "I will tell you stories while you are eating your supper, if you will then go properly to bed." She patted Mags on the head. "Now go with Mrs. Stowe and I'll be up directly."

The children retreated up the stairs as Anna laughed into her handkerchief. Louisa said, "Harry takes being Father's heir very seriously."

"I think he's an insufferable little prig." Pauline sniffed.

"You're too harsh," said her mother. "Harry does very well."

"They're lovely children, and you must be very proud," said Kate. In her experience, nothing flattered an assiduous mother more than hearing her children praised.

And so the days passed. Katherine fell into the same pattern of life she had created while at Gillender, and had attempted to resume at Badham Abbey. She rose early and dressed in apparel suitable for outdoor pursuits, then rode or walked for an hour or two. If the weather did not permit those activities, she read, worked embroidery, or practiced piano. She occasionally borrowed Louisa's watercolors or charcoals. While Kate was but an indifferent artist, she was loath to lose whatever skills she had acquired at Miss Elizabeth's School in Bath.

After luncheon, Kate and Louisa would amuse themselves by dancing while Pauline played the piano. Miss Elizabeth employed a caper merchant to teach her charges, including Kate, the latest steps. Louisa had learned from her parents. Kate, the taller of the two, partnered Louisa through country dances and quadrilles with glee. She even led Pauline through the rudiments of the waltz.

"How odd it would be to be held by a man so!" Pauline laughed as Kate expertly twirled her around the drawing room floor. The carpets had been kicked aside, and Louisa played a waltz on the upright. "Dashed unpleasant, in fact!"

"Only unpleasant if you didn't like the cove," Kate said.

"Kay and Paul! You know what Mamma will say if she hears you using cant!" Louisa lifted her hands from the keys. "Cousin, from where did you learn such language? Do people speak so in Calicut?"

"The officers do," said Kate recklessly. "Bup bup-bup, pa pa-pa," she hummed in three-four time, continuing to whirl Pauline around. She felt she had fielded the question rather well. The cant and slang Kate spoke came from her friend, Bryan St. Wills, as well as from the brothers of her schoolmates, who were permitted to visit Miss Elizabeth's between the hours of three and five on Saturdays. The young people would sit, drink tea, and engage in such social intercourse as was deemed appropriate. Even the close supervision of Miss Elizabeth did not, however, prevent some improprieties. Thus came Katherine's considerable vocabulary.

"Will you dance the waltz in London, Louisa?" Pauline asked as the dance came to an end.

"Only if the patronesses of Almack's say I might," she answered, beginning her scales.

Pauline sniffed. "I think it's silly, a crowd of stuffy old ladies telling us what we should and shouldn't do."

"I daresay you are right," said Kate. "But that is

the way of our world, if we want to marry well. What other choices have we?"

"I could become a governess," argued Pauline. "And Papa says my Latin and Greek are very good. I could teach in a school."

The two older girls looked at her with astonishment writ large upon their faces. "Whyever would you want to do such a silly thing?" Louisa wanted to know, her hands temporarily still. "If you marry rightly, you would never have to work for your keep."

Pauline protested, "It doesn't seem fair. Other women have to work. Just because our father is a baronet and our grandfather was an earl, it means we marry and have babies, and that's all."

"But that's very important," said Kate. "Your Uncle Devere is a member of the House of Lords. They make laws and help run the country. Who would lead if gentlewomen ceased to have children?"

"Cromwell wasn't a gentleman."

The two young ladies shuddered.

"You have a bit of an independent streak, I vow," Kate said.

"Best not let Mamma and Papa hear these sentiments. Your trip to London would be in grave doubt." Louisa resumed her practice.

Pauline began to look alarmed. Kate squeezed her hand. "Don't worry," she whispered. "We won't tell."

Kate settled into life with the Penroses with ease and contentment. She formed the habit of taking her afternoon tea with the three younger children in the nursery. She invented tales of India which were drawn from her generous imagination as well as from her education. Sir Pen's library helped. After a week, she declared she had no more India stories, saying, "I'm only seventeen, you know! Not much has happened to me." She told them fairy stories and tales from history instead.

As spring warmed the earth, Kate's activities moved out of doors. She found willing companions in Harry and Charlie, showing them that she could match any adventurous boy at riding, climbing, or archery. She loved the spring weather, and would often take a book to read in the boughs of her favorite old oak.

Absorbed in *The Odyssey,* his ward appeared unaware of Quinn's scrutiny from beneath the tree. Leaning against the trunk, Kate sat at her ease with her legs astride one large limb, presenting a picture which would fill any man's mind with the most lustful thoughts. Her frilled petticoats peeped from underneath her too-short gown, exposing her ankles and calves. As Quinn watched her, an image of her legs clad in revealing hose popped into his thoughts. With difficulty, he dragged his mind away from the memory, recalling instead the frogs she'd put in his bed on the occasion of their first meeting.

He swallowed, then called to her. "Good morrow, Kate, for that is your name, I hear!"

He'd startled her, for she grabbed the limb with her free hand as her legs clenched around the branch. The flesh at Quinn's groin tightened, and he swore softly under his breath. He had promised himself he wouldn't even think of swiving the chit. *Most improper! Can't take advantage of my own ward!* And yet, he couldn't stop himself from envisioning her mounted on his body instead of the bough.

Kate interrupted his fantasy. "Where did you study all this goodly speech?"

"It is extempore, from my mother-wit." Laughing, Quinn caught the book she tossed down to him.

Kate swung one leg over the limb, climbed down to the next convenient branch, and dropped out of the tree.

"The Odyssey, dainty Kate?" He smiled, gently mocking. Her occupation was anything but dainty.

She reddened. "I but seek to improve myself, sir."

"What portion do you read?" he asked. As he opened the book at the purple ribbon marking her place, she tried to grab it out of his hand. Despite her height, he was a head taller. With limbs to match, he easily evaded her grasp, flipping the volume open.

"Ahem! My Greek is weak, as it has been a few years since I left Oxford, but I can translate: 'I mounted the glorious bed of Circe!' "

"It's Pauline's. Give it back!" She made another unsuccessful snatch at the book. Her face flushed in a most becoming manner.

"I am not sure if either my ward or my niece should be reading about Odysseus and Circe." Lifting the volume far above her head, Quinn danced away from her darting hand.

"Perhaps the tale of the lotus-eaters is more to your taste?"

He staggered back, one long hand clutching his chest. "Thou hast hit it! Do I strike you as such a lazy fellow, then? I assure you I have been most prudent and prompt in regard to your affairs."

"Oh?" Kate stopped grabbing for the book.

"I have introduced a bill into the House of Lords to remove you from Badham's care. Carrothers is away, inspecting your various holdings. The solicitor and his clerk have been warned off from blundering into this matter in any way. Herbert and Oswald are not in London. They are in Bath, I fear."

"His name is Osborn."

Quinn waved a languid hand as they walked toward Penrose House. "I give your detestable cousin's name all the attention it deserves."

"Did they go to my old school?"

"I believe they did." Quinn tucked her arm into his. "I have received a letter from a Miss Elizabeth Telmont. She has been contacted by the current Earl of Badham, and expresses concern in your regard."

"She was my schoolmistress, and dear to me. I wish I could tell her I'm safe."

"Can she be trusted?" Quinn handed Kate the book and opened the gate to the kitchen garden. He escorted her past the orderly rows of late winter vegetables.

"I'm sure of it. But one never knows into whose hands a letter may fall." Her hand tightened on his arm—a pleasant feeling, he realized.

"You are correct. On to more amusing topics. Sweet Kate, I had thought you had purchased more appropriate clothing, but I see you are still in the gown borrowed from my tweeny."

Kate looked down at her mussed skirts. "Oh, I use this dress for tree-climbing and games with the children, sir. We have made several excursions into Sevenoaks and I have close to a full wardrobe. You, of course, are as fine as fivepence." Her voice sounded oddly choked.

He laughed. Quinn wore a fitted coat of blue superfine, with a waistcoat and unmentionables of primrose twill. He'd tied his cravat in his usual exacting manner. He walked with her through the kitchen garden, then entered Penrose House through the buttery, evading the cooks in the kitchen, where preparations for luncheon were in full force.

"I'd best change," Kate said.

Kate slipped her arm from his and ran lightly up the stairs, clutching her book. She slammed the door in her haste and, once safely inside her room, threw the volume on her bed. Leaning against the door, she pressed her hands to her burning cheeks.

Why, oh why, did her guardian have to catch her reading that particular passage of *The Odyssey?* And what was it about the man which overset her so? His conduct toward her was everything proper, and his attention to her affairs diligent. *He still looks like a setter dog,* Kate told her tumultuous heart. But his shoulders, in the handsomely cut coat, appeared wide and masculine. He moved with unusual grace and power for someone so long-limbed.

She remembered the strength in Quinn's arm as he escorted her through the gardens. *He's surprisingly muscular for a dandy,* she thought. She imagined his beautiful brown eyes held his entire soul as he looked at her. But he saw her as his child, and finding her perched in a tree doubtless confirmed rather than changed his perception.

Kate poured water from the pitcher into the bowl on her dresser and splashed her face. She grabbed the bellpull, and told herself to stop refining upon such a tedious matter. She hoped he would not tease her at luncheon in regard to her choice of reading materials.

Bettina entered to assist Kate out of her dress and boots. Kate stripped off her damp shift. She wondered why the garment felt moist, as the day was not so warm as to cause unnecessary heat. She rubbed a cloth soaked in cool water over her sticky body, then put on fresh underclothing.

"The primrose muslin?"

"The blue, I think." For no reason Kate could define, she wanted to look her best at luncheon. The celestial shade flattered her eyes and complexion more than did the yellow.

"You did not wear a hat this morning, Miss Kay," remarked Bettina, as she braided Kate's hair. "You will freckle and turn brown as a berry if you are not more careful, and all the town bucks will call you a bran-faced miss."

Kate, teased out of her megrims, laughed. "Well, there are worse fates!"

"Your parents sent you to England to marry well. They will not be pleased unless you return to India with any less than a baronet, I'm sure." Bettina coiled the braid on top of Kate's head, pinning it. She left a few curls to frame Kate's face.

"I wonder if they have considered I may not return at all. It is possible that any husband I marry won't wish to travel or live in India."

"Do you miss your home, ma'am?"

Kate paused, unsure of her answer as an image of the frigid, moonlit attic of Badham Abbey at midnight flashed through her mind. She pushed the unwelcome memory away and thought instead of her parents. "Yes and no. I'm lonely for my family, of course, but the Penroses have made me feel so welcome that I am scarcely ever homesick. I miss the weather," she said, recollecting the contents of one of the books she'd perused regarding India's climate and geography. "It is much warmer, and here I find I am often chilled, though not, of course, on such a fine day as this." She donned her hat of chip-straw and tied its blue grosgrain ribbons beneath her chin.

The weather permitted luncheon to be served on the sunny balcony outside the dining room. The day would have been too warm but for a slight breeze; Kate gratefully felt the air soothe her hot nape.

Quinn watched the soft wind lift a chestnut curl touching his ward's cheek. He wanted to be that tender breeze. Staring at Kate from across the table, he imagined caressing her hair. Dressed in a gown which flattered her eyes, she was entirely captivating.

She had been so delightfully flustered when caught reading the salacious passage from *The Odyssey;* he had wanted to press her down into the tall grass, and show her exactly what Homer had meant. She barely looked at him at lunch, sweet torturer. Did she know how much one look from her fine blue eyes affected him?

His Kate. *His* Kate. Dear God, he was already thinking of her as his own possession. He ground his teeth, frustrated. A young woman as independent as Katherine Scoville, who climbed out of attic windows and traveled alone over half the country, would surely object to such an approach. And what of his own honor?

Quinn avoided temptation by leaving after luncheon. Despite his hasty departure, he spared some time for a private *tête-à-tête* with his sister. They sat in the drawing room and hatched their plans while Pen dozed in his wing chair after the heavy meal. The open French doors allowed Quinn to hear the shouts of the children at croquet. Bees hummed in the fragrant rose-vine just outside.

"I'll open the house on Bruton Street whenever you give the word, Nan," Quinn said.

"Next week, I think. But we will not be going about for a fortnight after. I must take Louisa and Kay to Madame Mirielle's first."

"Bring back memories?"

Anna smiled. "Yes. It was not so long ago that I prepared for my debut. 'Tis a monstrous exciting time for the girls."

"And how does my ward go on?"

"Very well. She is a most pleasant girl. She is quite the favorite with everyone, especially the boys. She can run and climb with the best of them, but she knows her way around society. You need have no fears on her behalf. She and Louisa will have their pick of suitors, I think."

"Hmph." Quinn did not know quite how he felt about the prospect of Kate having suitors for her hand in marriage.

"Once we have Louisa launched, we'll introduce Kay. Mind you, she has the occasional nightmare, but I believe there is no lasting damage because of her experiences."

"Nightmares?"

"The first week, Louisa told me she heard her cry out in the night."

"Damn and blast!"

"There's nothing we can do, Quinn! For all her cheerful smiles, she is a very private child. She denies any sorrows and, I must say, her demeanor has improved as time has gone by. What of her other problems?"

"As well in hand as can be," he said. "The Lords are a most ponderous crew, I fear. They are at present involved with questions concerning the prospective queen. We may have to file in Chancery."

Anna winced. "We could wait until the twelfth of never for a decision from Chancery. Any word of Badham?"

"He's not in London yet, but he will be, I am sure." Quinn flicked lint from his lapel. "We should keep Kate quiet until the Lords have acted."

"That should not be difficult. Pauline will be coming to town also, and the two of them can amuse themselves at the theatre and Vauxhall while I escort Louisa."

"Mind, there should be a chaperone with her at all times. If need be, send 'round a message and I'll watch her, er, them."

Anna looked at him a bit strangely, he thought, before she smiled and rose, saying, "I'll see you out. You're determined to leave so soon? We had hoped to keep you here longer, Quinn."

He shrugged, affecting a careless mien. "I'm for Surrey, and then back to London. Don't worry about the house. Harper will make sure everything is right and tight for you."

Four

Quinn rested that night in his Surrey estate, and attended races at Ascot the next day. Stalking through the peers' enclosure toward the track, he was intent upon observing the progress of his well-bred nags. Based on the attention he received, he gathered others had different goals.

A flock of females, dressed in their fashionable best, surrounded the lords like so many fluttering butterflies. The mating season had begun.

"Lord Devere, allow me to present my daughter, The Honorable Gillian Calmont-Trent," twittered one matron. Quinn raised his lorgnon, casting the older lady a sweeping glance meant to depress pretension. The tiny child hidden by her skirts merited no attention whatsoever; Quinn especially disliked the custom in some families, widespread in the prior century, to dump fourteen-year-olds into Polite Society. This chit, cheeks still rounded by baby fat, belonged in the schoolroom, not in the *ton*. Nevertheless, he'd do his duty. 'Twouldn't be fair to cut the girl. He stretched his mouth into a smile.

"Miss, er, Calmont-Trent." He made a courteous bow before he was diverted by yet another eager mamma. This large lady, dressed in unflattering puce, sought to bring her little chick to his notice.

Fortunately, one of his friends grabbed his arm to haul him over to a group of owners before Quinn became mired in the swamp of fortune-hunting females.

Quinn turned his regard to his companions and their horses.

"I say, Devere, you're devilishly cool with the ladies today," said the man who grasped his arm. Quinn recognized Viscount Byland from Northumbria.

"I tire of the dance."

" 'Tis your fate. Wealth and title engender feminine attention."

"Is it so foolish to want to be desired for oneself, rather than the contents of one's pocketbook?"

Byland laughed. "Not at all, Devere. But look at us!" The florid-faced, overweight lord patted his own belly. "I, for one, am grateful to have been born a wealthy peer. Otherwise, I'd never swive a single maid!"

Quinn joined his friend's laughter. "And I, the bran-faced, ginger-pated Duke of Limbs, would awaken alone forevermore!"

" 'Tis not so bad for you. The ladies enjoy your amiable personality." Byland poked Quinn in the ribs and waggled his brows. "Especially that little opera dancer, oh, what is her name?"

"My lips are sealed," Quinn said. In fact, he had dropped the lovely Mistress Granatt as soon as she had spread her favors beyond one bedmate. Quinn did not share.

"Sealed with her ardent kisses, I vow! But which of your devil's spawn are you racing today?"

Quinn chuckled. "Your favorite rival, Tyndale's Treat, runs in the second heat against your Bylander." The big black stallion, Quinn's pride and joy, was descended from the Darley Arabian. At age five, Treat was unbeaten.

Treat ran well, winning his race. Quinn collected his winnings, plus several offers for the purchase of the flamboyant, swift-footed black. Smiling, he refused all of them.

He returned to London to give orders concerning the Tyndale town house on Bruton Street. Although he had once lived in the early-Georgian home, which had belonged to his parents, Quinn preferred his smaller residence on Berkeley Square. However, Bruton Street, boasting a spacious ballroom as well as numerous bedrooms, saloons, and drawing rooms, suited the presentation of the young women to London society.

Quinn stared moodily out his window onto Berkeley Square, watching late afternoon fade to dusk. It being late March, the square was free of frost and snow. A light mist gathered to shroud the harsh contours of the buildings which lined the Mayfair streets. Unaccountably restless, but with no engagements that night, he determined he'd visit his club in St. James.

Dressed in evening wear, Quinn crossed Piccadilly, keeping an eye out for the odd mishandled equipage. Though early in the evening for the *ton* to be hurrying to engagements, numerous carriages clotted the busy thoroughfare.

His mood lifted as he spotted Sir Willoughby Hawkes. Game to a fault, Hawkes could be counted on to take Quinn out of Crab Street. But Hawkes wore a frowning brow. What could be bothering him?

"You know, old chap, I'm thinking of becoming

leg-shackled. Must protect the lineage and the estate, and all that. Any prime articles coming out this year?"

Quinn eyed Sir Willoughby warily. A fine fellow, Hawkes, but one had to be canny about encouraging Sir Willoughby. Quinn didn't know if he wanted a closer familial relationship with his crony. Although a landed baronet, Hawkes, a notorious rake, could not be considered the best possible catch for his niece Louisa. As for Katherine, that was not even a question.

"Can't rightly think of anyone who might suit you, old man," Quinn said, keeping his voice casual. "Off to White's for a spot of supper?"

"Oh, it's early yet. I thought I might call at the Nymphos Hotel to examine the new talent."

Quinn found his friend's inclination odd, but remained mum. If Hawkes wished to form a lasting connection with a suitable miss, the Nymphos, a notorious buttocking shop, was not the place to frequent. Quinn himself had no interest in the place anymore. The bachelors parted at the corner of King Street, one to proceed east to Leicester Square and the aforementioned Nymphos, the other to turn to St. James and dinner.

After dining at his club, Quinn amused himself gambling. White's, a haunt of the older generation, was a trifle dull for his taste, but Quinn made it his business to be seen there. He kept half an ear open for political gossip, believing at this juncture awareness of the inner workings of the House of Lords could be greatly to his ward's benefit. While he heard nothing of direct assistance to his cause, he hoped that his presence in the company of political animals would help.

Quinn rose from the table two hours later, several hundred pounds richer, caring nothing about the game or his companions. He wandered back home feeling hollow. What was missing from his life? Normally he would have accompanied Hawkes to the Nymphos, and released himself in the body or mouth of some street princess. Why had he hesitated?

Kate. His Kate was the reason. No other woman held a shred of interest for him. Everything about her, from her shining chestnut hair down to her lovely little ankles, entranced, enthralled, and enchanted.

"Damn," he said aloud, whacking his cane against an iron fence at Berkeley Street. His heart ached when he thought of her distress due to the losses she'd suffered, as well as the effects of the brutality of Herbert and Osborn. For all he knew, Kate had never talked of the experiences to anyone, keeping all her pain inside. He wanted to ease her, but did not know how without sacrificing his honor, and hers.

The Penroses removed their household to London shortly thereafter; except for the three youngest children, the entire family moved to Bruton Street in a parade of carriages, landaus, barouches, coaches, and traps.

"What exactly is a Season?"

Kate broke off her conversation with Louisa to listen to Anna's response to Pauline's question.

"And why do we have to have one? What's so important?" Pauline, who had revealed herself to Kate in the past weeks as inquisitive, even curious, pursued the issue.

"La, child!" Anna threw her head back and laughed. "The questions you ask!"

"Seriously, Mamma. I have heard talk of seasons all my life, but no one has explained to me what 'the Season' is." Kate knew that Pauline would chase her answers as tenaciously as any foxhound tracked its prey.

Pauline's mother answered, "Well! The London social season is very important, to be sure. It is most significant to a young woman of birth and breeding."

"To catch a husband, you mean?"

Anna frowned. " 'Catch' is truly not the proper term. It would be best to say that for quite a few years now, well-born persons gather in London after the worst of winter has passed. The gentlemen have hunted every fox and pheasant to extinction, and everyone has grown heartily bored of their country properties."

"I thought the Season began with the first race at Ascot, in March," said Kate.

Anna's brow creased. "There is no official event which begins the London social season. It merely seems as if the weather clears sufficiently in spring to allow easy travel from the country to London."

At that moment, the horses pulling the landau splashed through a mud puddle. Kate suppressed a smirk.

"So in the spring," Anna continued, "we go to London to socialize with our friends and relations after the winter has passed. That is all."

"There is more awaiting me, though, Mamma, isn't there?" demanded Louisa.

Anna smiled. "For a young woman of marriageable age, the parties and social events are an opportunity to see and be seen by young men."

"The mating dance, so to speak," Kate said.

"But no one knows Lou, Mamma, and you don't go to London except to buy clothes. How will Louisa be invited to any parties?" asked Pauline.

"As soon as we get to Town we shall give a ball for Louisa after she is presented at court. We'll invite all our old friends and our relations. They'll reciprocate with invitations for Louisa," Anna explained. "Unless, of course, they have eligible daughters. They will not invite Louisa because our Lou is sure to cast everyone else into the shade!"

Kate laughed with the others. "How long will we be in London, ma'am?"

"No longer than two months, perhaps three. London becomes quite stifling in the summer, so we'll go back to Kent." Anna glanced at Louisa. "By that time, I hope you will have made some new acquaintances, both male and female. We'll get up a little house party in Kent with your special friends."

Pauline frowned. "Special friends, as in eligible *partis?*"

"Well, yes, I hope so. But Lou mustn't be rushed. She's only eighteen and has plenty of time to form a connection. Marriage is an extremely important decision. Remember that, girls. When you select a husband you will make the most significant choice of your life. But we will be by your side to help you always." Anna smiled at Kate, who had been listening. "After Louisa it will be Kay's turn."

Kate felt her stomach flutter. *A home. A husband. A family. Safety and security.* All within her reach, so soon.

She lifted her chin. "I look forward to forming an eligible connection quickly. I have no wish to impose upon you for an indefinite period of time."

"Pish-tosh!" Anna slapped Kate's knee. "You are no trouble at all, *cousin.*" Her blue eyes snapped a warning. "We will all enjoy the social whirl. You will be accounted quite a treat, Cousin Kay. Curiosity is rife concerning all manner of things Oriental, whether they be Chinese, Indian, or purely imaginary." Anna winked at Kate.

They arrived at Bruton Street in midafternoon after lunching at an inn near Bromley. Kate could see that the elegantly appointed town house had been made ready for the family's occupation. Carrothers or Harper, she supposed. The covers had all been removed from the furniture, draped in watered green silk, in the drawing room. Dusted and polished to perfection, the house gleamed. Kate's own room, in the front of the manse, was decorated in green and blue, the bed made up with freshly laundered linens.

While Anna went through the entire edifice in the company of the recently engaged housekeeper, Kate, with Pauline and Louisa, explored the small back garden, pleased by what she found. The shrubbery had been recently trimmed and the fountain, while still dry, had been cleaned of winter's dead leaves and twigs. The herbaceous borders had been weeded and the graceful plot made ready for the enjoyment of the family and their guests.

"No large trees to climb," Kate said critically.

"Surely, cousin, you did not expect to indulge yourself with such pastimes here in London!" Louisa stared.

"I suppose not."

"Why on earth not?" asked Pauline. "Whatever harm could climbing a tree cause, in London or anywhere else?"

Rolling her eyes, Louisa retreated into the house.

"Reputation," said Kate gloomily. "The older one becomes, the more one's conduct is restricted. No tree-climbing, no running, nothing fun or you're labeled a hoyden. Enjoy your youth, Pauline!"

Quinn appeared at the door dividing house from garden, and Kate's heart gave a hop as she spied him. Immaculately hatted and gloved, he filled the narrow passage. He carried a short whip, apparently having forgotten to leave it with his equipage. His chocolate-brown driving coat suited his coloring remarkably, Kate thought.

Unlike Kate, who felt a certain restraint trapping her voice in her throat, Pauline capered to greet her uncle, giggling with delight. "Uncle Quinn!"

"Hullo, Paul!" Quinn greeted his niece with equal warmth.

Kate tried to repress a twinge of envy. Quinn had the affectionate family she wanted. She admired the genuine connection he maintained with them, surely his most endearing quality.

After hugging Pauline to his side, Quinn fixed his gaze on Kate. His scrutiny, as palpable to Kate as though he'd touched her face with his hand, made her flesh tingle with an unaccustomed warmth. He pressed Pauline's shoulder, saying, "Pauline, run and find your mother, if you will. I wish to speak with her."

Pauline scurried inside to do his bidding.

"My ward." Quinn spoke softly.

Kate raised her gaze to meet his.

He bowed over her extended hand. "Would you be so kind as to accompany me to the park? There are matters I wish to discuss."

"Very well, my lord." Why on earth would Quinn need to speak with her privately? She hoped that Uncle Herbert had not located her or made himself a nuisance. Kate quite enjoyed living with the Penroses and did not wish her situation to change. "I'll get a hat."

"I'll meet you out front. The horses are fresh and require walking." Quinn gestured her through the door into the house. Without ringing for Bettina as she entered her dressing room, Kate reflected. Did Quinn have an actual interest in speaking with Lady Anna, or had he sent Pauline off on a pretext in order to talk with her alone? But a drive with his "cousin" would be unexceptional, even at the fashionable hour of five o'clock.

Her mind whirled and twirled through the possibilities like a spinning top. For the umpteenth time she reminded herself to stop her ruminations in regard to her guardian, his acts, and his motives. He continued to be a mystery and would remain so. As she tied the yellow grosgrain ribbons of her chip-straw hat beneath her chin, she told herself to cease her inappropriate interest in the Earl of Devere.

She looked out her window to see Quinn's tiger walking the black horses harnessed to the earl's curricle. Kate decided to wear a spencer. Driving in the open equipage, even in the sunny spring day, could bring a chill.

Despite the clement weather, a haze hung in the air from the thousands of fires lit for cooking and heating in the metropolis. Unaccustomed to the sight of garbage in the street, to say nothing of the human pollutants, Kate tried not to wrinkle her nose or cover her ears. London overwhelmed her. She closed the window before leaving the room for the drive with Quinn. Whatever must he want?

As she approached the marble-floored foyer, she heard her guardian and her hostess in conversation.

"I declare, Quinn, this house has never shone so brightly."

"Harper," Quinn said, with a complacent tone to his voice. "A jewel, is she not?"

"You must thank her for me. If you could give her this vail—" Entering, Kate saw Anna press a coin into Quinn's hand.

"I shall. And, no, you may not have her under any circumstances."

Anna stepped back, a look of mock surprise on her face. "My dear brother, I am shocked—shocked!— that you would think that I am so treacherous as to attempt to steal your servant."

Kate tried not to laugh. She knew full well that Anna would like nothing better than to hire Quinn's paragon of a housekeeper. Indeed, Anna had expressed such a sentiment more than once.

Quinn raised his brows. "I am all in favor of reasonable vails, sister mine, but a gold sovereign? This would not be in the nature of a bribe, would it?"

"Certainly not." Anna affected a demeanor which reflected both good humor and mild huffiness.

A neat trick, thought Kate. She made her arrival

known by clattering her heels on the marble a bit more loudly than necessary.

"But here is Kate," Anna said. "It is most unseemly to quarrel about servants in her presence." She smiled at Kate. "So you drive with my brother in Hyde Park at five? You will indeed be quite the thing!"

"If I am all the thing it is because I shine in the light of Devere's reflected glory," Kate said, laughing.

"Indeed not," Quinn said. "I am graced by your presence."

"Is it wise to take Kate to so public a place?" Anna asked.

"Town is yet thin of company. There's no danger, Nan." He offered Kate his arm to lead her from the residence. He guided her up into the curricle, then sat beside her. He took the reins from his tiger. The horses plunged forward, restive. Quinn controlled them as his tiger hopped onto the back of the curricle.

"I must say, it is a relief to be addressed by my own name," Kate said. "The constant pretense has become a strain."

"I am sorry, Kate, but we will have to continue the charade a while longer. And you must stay close to home." He drove through Berkeley Square to Mount Street.

Kate swallowed. "What has happened?"

"Carrothers has traveled to Somerset to, er, dispossess your uncle and his spawn of your property."

"Gillender House? They went to Gillender?" Anger infected Kate's soul. She could not bear to think of Herbert and Osborn in her home.

"Indeed they did. We received a missive from one

Tompkins in that regard." The curricle crossed Park Lane, evading the cross-traffic.

"Tompkins has been our butler for an age, since my father's day."

"He seems to be quite a responsible fellow, but not Badham's equal. He was unable to eject the earl even after an appeal to the local magistrate."

"That's an outrage!" Kate's fists clenched, gripping her reticule.

"Yes." Upon entering the park, Quinn slowed the pair. Taking the reins into one hand, he awkwardly patted Kate's fists with the other. "But not to worry, sweet Kate. I've sent Carrothers off with all the proper documents. We'll have them sent off in a trice."

"Will they come here?"

The horses set off while Quinn answered, appearing to consider his words well. "I don't know. That would be logical. But then again, I thought they'd come directly to London and enlist the help of the Bow Street Runners. Badham has not yet come to Town, so we're still several steps ahead of him."

"In what way?"

He smiled at Kate. Although concerned about her future, she could not help but be cheered.

"We have applied to the House of Lords for help and he has not. We have hired the Bow Street Runners and he has not." Quinn, slowing his pair, bowed to a passerby.

"We have?"

"Yes, Lady Kate. Don't refine upon the matter, I beg of you. Everything that could possibly be done for your safety has taken place." Quinn guided the curricle past a stylish coach complete with postilions uniformed in pale blue and cream, apparently to match the equipage before which they rode. An elderly lady, in an old-fashioned, powdered wig, waved her fan from the carriage at Quinn, who bowed in response as the woman stared at Kate.

Kate lowered her eyelids demurely while restraining a giggle. The lady apparently set great stock in complementary colors, since she was bedecked in cream and blue like her coach. She looked as though she were about to fly away on a cloud. The manes and tails of her creamy-hued horses, braided with blue ribbons, seemed absurd and affected to country-bred Kate. She sighed inwardly. Would there ever come a time when she would feel comfortable in the whirling throngs of London?

Quinn, having reached the Serpentine, slowed the horses to a stop. He handed the reins to his tiger. Alighting, he reached for Kate. "Come, let us walk."

She allowed him to assist her from the curricle, but lost her balance on the small step and fell straight into his arms. Quick as a flash, he clasped her about the waist. Her feet dangled above the ground, but she'd never felt so safe . . . or so threatened. Quinn's scent, spicy and compelling, enveloped her. He held her so closely that she feared her ribs might not survive the experience intact.

"Kate," he said, looking down into her face. He sounded curiously breathless.

She couldn't tear her gaze away from the heat in his chocolate-brown eyes. Loosening his grip, he let her body slide down his. From top to toe, Kate tingled with heat and desire. She grasped his shoulders. She didn't want to let him go.

A shout from Quinn's tiger tore the moment apart.

Kate stumbled back, away from Quinn, regaining her balance as he steadied her. Looking about, Kate realized that the intimate moment had gone unnoticed by the fashionables parading through the park. Fortunately, no one seemed to be watching. Even Quinn's tiger was busy with the horses. Good. Kate had no desire to be labeled "fast" months before she planned to make her debut.

"My dear Kate. Are you feeling quite all right?" Quinn's voice had again returned to the bantering drawl he customarily affected.

"I think not, my lord. I am touched by a strange dizziness."

"P'raps the fresh air will help." He offered her his arm.

She took it at the elbow, feeling like a fool. How did he have such an effect upon her usually calm state of mind? *This must stop,* she told herself. Kate took a deep breath. A close call, that. What would she have done if he'd tried to kiss her?

As they walked, she became thunderstruck by the realization that she wouldn't have minded at all. Looking at Quinn's mobile mouth, she wondered what he would have done if she'd kissed him.

Kate distracted herself by examining the park. Although spring had come early this year, Hyde Park's flower borders had not yet come into their own. The odd daisy and crocus flowered underfoot. Kate stepped around the flowers. She had already seen that natural beauty rarely showed its face in London.

Another fashionable equipage, this time a landaulet, pulled up alongside Kate and Quinn. Its red-haired occupant leaned out to blatantly scrutinize Kate, who stiffened. *I will never become accustomed to*

Town manners. Kate thought the woman rude, but both the redhead and Quinn behaved as though nothing were amiss.

"Devere." The woman inclined her head and extended a hand, as majestic as a queen.

She cut Kate. Quinn raised a brow.

"Good afternoon, Lady Staveley," he said politely. "May I introduce to you my, er, cousin, Kay Tyndale, lately come to visit us from India?" He sketched a bow at the woman's outstretched hand without releasing his hold on Kate. "Kay, this is Bertha, Lady Staveley."

"Lady Staveley," Kate said, loosening her grip on Quinn's arm. She had not realized that she clutched him tightly, a most improper action.

Quinn failed to take the hint, and Kate was powerless to free herself. She would not engage in a tussle.

"A pleasure, Miss Tyndale," said the lady. "Do come call upon me while you are in Town. Devere knows the direction, of course." She cast a languishing gaze upon Quinn.

Kate glanced at her guardian. Quinn's cheeks had flushed. She bit the inside of her mouth to keep from chuckling at his embarrassment.

"Good day, Lady Staveley." Quinn stepped away from the landaulet.

The carriage drove away, but not before its occupant winked at Quinn.

"Perhaps it would be best if we returned to Bruton Street," Quinn said.

"As you wish, Cousin Quinn." Kate, though jealous, was determined not to show that ugly emotion. She winked at Quinn.

"Stop it, Kate." He handed her back up into the curricle.

She laughed.

"Wretched child." Climbing in after her, he took the reins.

"I am sorry, my lord. I realize that my presence was, um, a bit *de trop.*" Kate fluttered her eyelashes at him, imitating Lady Staveley, though inwardly hurt because he called her a child. Nothing had changed between them. She must have been mad to imagine that he'd nearly kissed her.

"You are not *de trop.* Lady Staveley delights in shocking others. Please do not emulate her by winking at unattached males, or in any other manner."

"Yes, my lord." Kate's heart felt bruised. She had thought that playing the coquette would bring her into her guardian's good graces. She knew not what to do to make it easy between them again.

"Oh, the devil!" Quinn stopped the curricle and looped the reins, turning to take her hands in both of his. "Kate."

She avoided his gaze. "Yes, my lord?"

"Look at me, my ward."

She looked.

His mouth made a firm, uncompromising line. "You need not change for me or anyone, do you understand?"

She blinked, utterly confused. "I believe so, my lord."

"Very well, then." He released his hold on her hands.

Kate spent the rest of the drive wondering what on earth had happened between them. Quinn blew hot and cold by turns. *And Shakespeare thought women were flighty and frail,* Kate thought. Old Billy had it all wrong. Men were the inconstant, flighty gender.

Quinn had a fit of the dismals, an increasingly frequent occurrence since he'd met Kate Scoville. He glanced over at her as he reined his horses in at the Bruton Street house. The brim of that blasted hat concealed her expression.

Running into Bertha Staveley was a piece of bad luck. He'd shared Staveley's bed on a couple of occasions and the lively young widow made it clear that she'd welcome him back. But since he'd met Kate, he'd lost interest, without making an effort to smooth the fiery redhead's ruffled temper. He supposed he'd best call upon Lady Staveley. Yes, that was the ticket. Or p'raps he'd send 'round some flowers.

And why had he taken Kate to Hyde Park at five in the afternoon? What had he been thinking? Nan had been right. They'd drawn more attention than a Bedlamite at Almack's.

Damn and blast. He'd taken Kate for a drive because he'd wanted to share her company, and for no other reason. He'd wanted to court her, like any other man . . . like any man other than her guardian.

He ground his teeth. It couldn't happen again.

Five

The next day was marked by a visit to Anna's fashionable modiste, Madame Mirielle. Louisa was measured for court-dress as well as for any number of ball gowns and evening dresses. Kate ordered two gowns in the lightest Georgette crepe for her few evening excursions, as well as day dresses in a more fashionable cut than her purchases made in Sevenoaks. She did not know for what precise events she would wear the frothy creations, gathered under the breasts and festooned with lace flounces and velvet trim, but Anna assured Kate she would rarely be at home alone.

The first several evenings were spent with the entire family writing and addressing hundreds of invitations to the formal ball which would present Louisa to Polite Society. Kate threw herself into the preparations with vigor, finding her training from Miss Elizabeth's School most useful.

But Pauline grumbled and groused. "The Honorable Louisa Anna Michaela Penrose! Lou, why do you have to have so many names?" She stretched her fingers.

"You have as many names as I do," Louisa said. "You're the Honorable Paulina Tyndale Devere Penrose. What a mouthful!"

"This isn't fair," whined Pauline. "Cousin Kay and I shouldn't have to help Louisa with her come-out. She won't be around to help with ours."

"Why, where am I going?" Louisa appeared genuinely astonished.

"Hopefully, daughter, you will be married and in your husband's home, having his babies, when your sister is presented," said her father.

"Gracious! You make it sound as though I'm to be transported. Any husband *I* have will be a part of this family, just as I will be a part of his. I'm not going anywhere, Pauline," Louisa admonished her sister, poking her on the shoulder with the stem of her pen. "Besides, I thought you did not care for the thought of a Season and marriage."

Kate saw Pauline wince as her parents raised their eyebrows simultaneously.

"Whatever could you be thinking, Pauline?" inquired her mother. "Pauline?"

Pauline laid down her pen. "It simply sounds so fearfully inevitable. I feel like Penelope waiting for Odysseus. Except I don't know who Odysseus *is.*"

"That's the excitement," said Louisa. She glanced at Kate. "For myself, I can scarce wait until I fall in love!"

Kate flushed. She had an odd feeling Louisa knew more than she said aloud. "Just make sure you don't fall for the wrong person!" she retorted.

"I don't see how that can happen," Louisa said. She winked slyly at her father. "I know my parents take very great care that I never meet 'wrong persons'!"

"That is no exaggeration," said Pen. "I prefer that

you do not even speak to the stableboys, advice I wish Pauline would take."

Pauline grinned. "You know I have an interest in languages. How else would I learn cant, if I did not talk to coachmen and stableboys?"

Anna shuddered. "Please do not talk cant in London. That is the most sure way to obtain a reputation as fast."

"I want to be a prime article. Why not begin practicing now?"

Her parents sighed, and Kate divined their thoughts with ease. Pauline would have to be carefully watched while in proximity to the manifold perils of the city.

The butler opened the door of the library and announced the advent of the Earl of Devere. Excitement fluttered in Kate's stomach like a butterfly escaping from its chrysalis. She hadn't seen Quinn since that ill-fated drive in the park. Drat the man, she'd even had trouble keeping him out of her dreams.

Dressed casually for the visit, her guardian wore a fitted coat of fawn worsted over trousers of cream pin-striped twill. His Hobys gleamed in the mellow candlelight.

"Uncle Devere!" Pauline squealed. Kate watched as Pauline seized upon her uncle as a diversion from the undesirable occupation, leaping up from her place at the large library table. Pauline hugged Quinn around the waist.

Kate said a shy hello and went back to her labors, observing him covertly.

Anna rose. "Quinn," she said, and gave him her

hand to kiss. After he bent over her hand, she added, "Pauline, that's enough. Get back to work."

Pauline swung Quinn's hand back and forth. "Not with Uncle here," she said cleverly. "That would be rude."

Her mother glared at her. Kate suppressed a smile.

"Shall I ring for tea, Mother?" Pauline asked.

"Oh, no, no, no, no. No need to make a pother," said Quinn, waving his free hand in the air.

Letting him go, Pauline yanked the bellpull. "It's not a bother, really, Uncle Devere. We were just going to have tea. We need a bit of extra nourishment, since we've been working so!"

"And what is this?" Quinn advanced to the library table and lifted his lorgnon to view the scattered sheets. "A ball—for the Honorable Louisa Anna Michaela Penrose! And all these hundreds of invitations to be written out in one's finest hand. Oh, how well do I remember." He cocked his head toward his niece. "And you, dear Pauline, are not submitting to torture with good grace."

"No, I'm not," said Pauline. "I'm dreadfully bored."

"Well, it may be that there is a special treat in store for a good little girl who helps her sister prepare for her Season," said Quinn. "And perhaps for her cousin, too," he added, smiling at Kate.

His smile both warmed her and tied her tongue into knots. How on earth did he manage that trick?

Pauline didn't seem to notice anything amiss. "Why, whatever do you mean, Uncle?"

"Astley's," he said.

"*Astley's!*" All three girls screamed at once.

"Astley's Amphitheatre. The evening after these invitations are completed and sent out, we shall all go to the circus. With your permission." Quinn bowed in the direction of his sister and her husband.

A footman entered with the tea tray as Pauline dashed back to her place at the table. "Jenks! What are you doing here!" she snapped at him. "We don't want your catlap! Can't you see we're busy?"

"Look at that woman." Kate nudged Quinn with an elbow and pointed with her fan to the other side of the sawdust ring. During the interval between acts at Astley's, the family amused themselves by watching the passing throngs and commenting upon their appearance and manner of dress. "Her hat looks exactly like the cockade on the dancing horse!"

Quinn pretended he needed a better angle to see the woman, creating an opportunity to edge closer to Kate. He liked her subtle lilac scent. "You're right. Those feathers are the same appalling shade of puce." He raised his lorgnon to get a better look. "All of London comes to Astley's, Cousin Kay. You may expect to see many wonderful sights, but not all of them are part of the circus."

Laughing, Kate leaned past Quinn to address Louisa. "Don't stare, but you're the focus of some very intent male attention."

Quinn turned, recognizing the tall, dark nobleman. "Oh, good Lord! We're in for it now." Leaping to his feet, Quinn stood in front of the two girls and turned his back on the stranger.

"Do move aside, Uncle Quinn. I can't see." Louisa tried to peek past Quinn.

"Devere!" The man addressed Quinn, despite

Quinn's best efforts to cut him. "Please make me known to the ladies in your box." Hawkes had no eyes for his ward, Quinn realized with a tiny shred of relief, but kept his pewter gaze fixed on Louisa, who stared back. *Damn. Louisa's a beauty, all right.* Unfortunately, his niece looked particularly pretty this evening in an ice-blue gown with a silver shawl.

Quinn winced as his family looked over Sir Willoughby Hawkes. His friend was a devilishly attractive gentleman, with a classically tall, dark, and handsome appearance. Tonight, Hawkes wore impeccable evening gear. *Rakes are successful with the ladies because they are good-looking,* Devere growled to himself. That was all right, he supposed, as long as the rake's prey was not one's own niece. Quinn himself had shared more than one night drinking and wenching with Hawkes, and didn't like the attention the fellow gave Louisa.

"Hmph," Quinn said. "May I make known to you Sir Willoughby Hawkes." Anna drew in her breath. Quinn continued glumly, "Sir Willoughby, m'sister, Lady Anna Penrose."

Sir Willoughby bowed over Anna's outstretched hand. Quinn noticed her reluctance, but his sister was too canny to give the cut direct to one of society's most popular baronets just prior to her eldest daughter's introduction.

"Sir Michael Penrose." The gentlemen bowed. Pen showed no unusual reaction; Quinn knew his brother-in-law took no interest in the gossip that was the daily bread and tea of the *ton*.

"My nieces, Louisa and Pauline Penrose, and my cousin, Kay Tyndale." Quinn performed these introductions hurriedly, with the sincere hope that Sir Willoughby would be unable to separate one damsel from the other.

The ladies made small, formal curtsies to the stranger as he made his bow. Visibly transfixed by Louisa, Sir Willoughby asked, "May I call upon you tomorrow, Miss Tyndale?"

Kate gurgled with laughter. "You surely may, sir, but I do not believe that you truly wish to do so!"

Sir Willoughby flushed a dull red. "I beg your pardon. I would be pleased to call upon all the ladies if allowed."

"Certainly," said Anna stiffly. "Devere knows the direction."

Quinn watched as Hawkes bowed again, taking his leave with as much dignity as he could muster while Louisa favored him with her brightest smile. Sir Willoughby looked as though he'd been hit upside the head; Quinn hoped he did not exhibit the same idiotic expression when Kate turned her gaze his way.

After he had gone, Louisa exploded. "How could you! Kay! That poor man!" She fanned herself vigorously.

Both Kate and Pauline rocked with laughter. Kate wiped her streaming eyes with a lace handkerchief hastily pulled from her reticule. "Lou, I'm sorry. I'll apologize to him tomorrow when he calls—if he calls."

"I'm afraid he will." Anna glared at Quinn.

"Whatever is the matter, Mamma? I thought Louisa is to encourage eligible connections. Sir Willoughby appeared most eligible, if a bit old," said Pauline.

"He's not old," flashed Louisa. "Can't you see, he's everything that is gentlemanly?"

Quinn exchanged a concerned glance with his sister.

Pen said, "I know it's exciting to have made a conquest so early in the race, my dear. But you might wish to place bets on more than one horse."

"Especially when one of those stallions is Hawkes," murmured Quinn. Louisa glowered at him. A stormy outburst was averted by the timely interruption of the orchestra, which struck up a lively tune to herald the resumption of the show.

After the farce, they watched the fireworks. Their acrid scent battled with the combined smells of horses, sawdust, and unwashed crowds as the Penroses left the circus; the performance was not over, but Pauline complained of fatigue.

Sir Willoughby Hawkes watched their departure. He had conceived the most astonishing interest in the personal affairs of his old school friend, Quinn Tyndale. He had no previous notion of Devere's involvement with his sister's family, but as he watched the earl usher Pauline from the box, handling the tired, cranky girl with a deftness clearly born from experience, he realized that his friend's attachment to his relations was long, deep, and sincere.

Startled, Hawkes noticed a rough-looking duo watching Devere and his niece. He edged closer to eavesdrop.

"Is that 'er?"

" 'e said a dark-haired tib, but I ken she were older and bigger."

"Blast him for havin' so many young female relations!" said the first fellow bitterly.

"Shut yer gob! Just twig the cull, that's what we're paid for." The pair fell silent as Hawkes passed by, swinging his hawkheaded walking stick. Sir Willoughby made a point of glaring at the two Captain Sharps, who were dressed in cast-off finery which looked for all the world as though they had been rejected by footmen in a bawdyhouse. The tarnished frogging on the lapels of one rogue could not have done him credit even when new, and combined with the cauliflower ear and broken nose of its wearer, it created the image of a very tough customer. The other character was dressed more plainly, in dusty black with an old-fashioned beaver drawn over his forehead.

Sir Willoughby hesitated. He had no reason to accost the rascally pair, even if he thought they might have designs on the contents of his pockets or the property of his friends. He contented himself with warning them off with another glare. He whacked the ebony stick suggestively into the nearest pillar; it sank deeply into the soft wood. He jerked it out with a powerful twist of his wrist, and gave the toughs another frown.

" 'e's a lively one, isn't 'e?"

The other hesitated. " 'e be awake to us. That's bad, 'e twigs our lay, and 'e's a friend of th' earl. All them gentry coves know each other."

"Aye," agreed his companion, sounding impressed by his cohort's knowledge of the doings of the Quality. "But we'd best not tell the old man. Might lose this job."

Sir Willoughby Hawkes was the undisputed holder of the title of the Most Notorious Rake in London.

He exhibited all the outward tokens of appearance

which any aspirant to rakedom must: the height, the handsome face with lowering brow, the fine figure which would strip to advantage. He regularly traded blows with Gentleman Jackson, clipped wafers at Manton with his unerring shot, and purchased his nags at Tattersall's. He was a dandy without any of the affectations of that accursed breed. His collars were high without absurdity, his coat cut by Weston, and his cravat impeccable. His fine Hessian boots gleamed with a blacking made from champagne.

Eighteen hundred and twenty heralded a fresh new era in England. The nation stood on the brink of empire. The mad old king had died, leaving the Prince Regent the undisputed claimant to the monarchy. The Industrial Revolution promised riches for those peasants who would show the imagination to seize the historical moment and courageously uproot themselves from their rural antecedents to relocate to England's booming industrial heartland. London teemed with excitement as it filled with lords and ladies eager to resume the mating game as a new Season began.

The thrills of the time evaded Sir Willoughby. For Wicked Willy, as he was known to the London wags and Covent Garden abbesses, the accomplishments required of the Most Notorious Rake had palled; the seduction of virgins held no more mystery; the prospect of a duel bored him to tears, so much so that he could not be bothered to ravish his friends' wives. He felt disinclined to set new fashions or to depress the pretensions of upstart mushrooms of society. Whereas his exploits had previously been attended to with a certain lust for experience, he approached his thirtieth year with uncharacteristic ennui.

Then, all had changed, like a sudden thunderclap on the afternoon of a sultry summer day. He had beheld Purity and Love in the form of the Honorable Louisa Penrose, and he would never be the same man.

The day after his epiphany, Sir Willoughby presented himself at the front door of the Penrose home on Bruton Street. Discreet inquiries through servants led him to believe that an early visit would favor his suit. Hawkes had become aware that the mistress of the house would be occupied with housekeeping details, such as conferences with cook and butler, and that the master would be tutoring the younger children.

Hawkes knew his planning had borne fruit when he was escorted into the drawing room by an inexperienced footman. For a treasured moment, the object of his affections was both alone and completely unaware of his presence as she practiced the pianoforte. *Mozart,* thought Sir Willoughby. *The Sonata in C Major. And rather well done,* he decided, listening to the rippling scales and cascades which flowed from Louisa's clever fingers like a waterfall.

He saw that his nymph was one of those fortunate ladies who are flattered by the clear, harsh light of morning. The sunlight streaming through the window lit her aureole of blond hair, turning it into a halo. She wore pink, and that very feminine color awakened mad thoughts of marriage in the breast of a gentleman who had previously referred to wedlock as "a damnable state, fit only for weak-livered clerics and timorous virgins."

As the footman announced Sir Willoughby, she looked considerably jolted. For the first time, Hawkes experienced a flash of regret over his misspent youth, and wondered if any breath of scandal had come to his fair darling's ears.

Probably not, he thought with relief, for after the young lady had recovered her composure, she calmly ordered the footman to tell Lady Anna there was a visitor, and to bring tea. That task completed, Louisa was alone with the Most Notorious Rake in London.

Hawkes saw that she was as nervous as a filly confronted by the bridle for the first time, but he couldn't fault any aspect of her manner. She dealt with him with a degree of equanimity unusual in such a young lady.

"Good morning, sir." She remained formal as she curtsied slightly.

"Good morning." He bowed. "I ask your forgiveness."

"Pardon me?"

"I fear to address you incorrectly. Devere introduced three lovely ladies in rather quick succession. I am sure you are not Miss Tyndale," he added with a sarcastic edge to his voice. "May I assume you are Miss Penrose?"

"Yes, I'm Louisa Penrose."

"Your mother has been hiding you in the country, I daresay," he remarked. "I could not fail to notice you had we previously met."

"Yes, I'm to be fired off this Season," she stated, with a trace of humor in her voice.

Though miffed, Sir Willoughby concealed his reaction. Fancy Devere keeping this diamond out of reach! Hawkes remembered he'd asked Devere if there were any eligibles making their debuts, and Devere had denied the existence of anyone who might suit the baronet. Hawkes's brows drew together as he deduced that his friend had concluded Sir Willoughby was not a worthy match for Devere's niece. *But I've no one to blame if my reputation is, perhaps, a bit tarnished.*

The door flew open and Lady Anna entered the room, followed by a footman with the tea tray. "Sir Willoughby, a pleasure," she said through gritted teeth. She allowed him to make his bow over her hand, which he grazed with his lips before she snatched her hand away. "Tea?"

They had barely sat before another young chit rushed into the room, followed by the snappish Miss Tyndale, who curtsied and sat down.

"Are there apple tarts?" the child demanded.

"Pauline!" her mother reproved. "Mind your manners and make your curtsey to Sir Willoughby. Sir Willoughby, you have met my second daughter."

"Good morning, I'm Pauline Penrose." Pauline reached for the pastries. "Would you like a tart? They're very nice."

With a grin, Sir Willoughby accepted a pastry and a cup of tea, which the footman placed on a small ormolu table near his seat on a Windsor chair. He liked the girl's easy, unaffected behavior; despite Lady Anna's obvious misgivings, he felt this was a family he would enjoy. Sir Willoughby was also the scion of a large clan, his parents being the fortunate progenitors of six children. Being the eldest, Sir Willoughby was accustomed to the happy disorder several siblings could create.

"The tarts *are* very good," he remarked to Lady Anna. "My compliments to your cook." He stared at

Louisa, feeling like a complete fool as he uttered the commonplace sentiment.

"Did you receive an invitation to my come-out party?" Louisa asked. "It should have reached you today."

Sir Willoughby frowned and thought. "I cannot recall seeing it, but I will certainly instruct my secretary to bring it to my attention."

"You need not, sir." Louisa went to a buhl writing table and opened a drawer. She withdrew an extra invitation and presented it to Sir Willoughby.

"A ball, on Tuesday next!" He reviewed the solicitation, neatly written on a half sheet of heavy, hot-pressed paper. "Well, I shall certainly attend, and I thank you for this honor." Hawkes stood and bowed to her as Pauline and Kay giggled into their teacups. He grinned as his nymph glared at her younger relations.

"Thank you for coming, sir." Anna stood as he finished his cup of tea.

Louisa accompanied Hawkes to the door of the drawing room.

"There is one more matter." Hawkes smiled at her, deliberately probing her eyes with his, noting with pleasure that she flushed slightly, but held his gaze without a waver. "May I be permitted to lead you out in a dance, perhaps your first waltz?"

"Ahem! I believe that honor will probably go to her father, sir!" Lady Anna interrupted the pair. "And only after she has been permitted to waltz at Almack's."

"Yes, of course," murmured Sir Willoughby. "Pardon me, I did not mean to presume."

"Perhaps one of the quadrilles," Lady Anna said.

Chuckling, he realized that he'd been ruthlessly consigned to a dance during which little physical contact between himself and the object of his interest would take place.

Lady Anna opened the door to the drawing room and gestured for him to exit. A footman handed Sir Willoughby his hat and cane; Hawkes was ushered out onto the doorstep almost before he knew exactly what had transpired.

Hawkes turned and regarded the door, which the butler closed with a snap. He knew he should be insulted by the cavalier treatment meted out by Lady Anna. Despite his reputation, his address and fortune were respectable enough that he'd been a target of the matrimonial intentions of numerous scheming mamas and minxes since his own debut a decade ago. He had never been unceremoniously tossed out onto the Bruton Street pavement by a domineering matron who made clear his ineligibility for her precious daughter's hand. But he didn't care, because he'd see Louisa again within a very few days.

Laughing aloud, Hawkes twirled his walking stick deftly as he strode to his home on Half Moon Street. He knew he had no one to blame but himself if a cautious parent looked at him askance, and he resented Lady Anna not a whit. He actually would enjoy his clashes with her; he liked the lady, who seemed awake on all suits. He would not approve of indulgent, casual breeding in any marital candidate.

The apple never falls far from the tree, he murmured to himself. He had more than once been frightened away from an otherwise charming damsel because her mother was a dragon of a female. While Lady Anna Penrose tried to act the stern matriarch, she

was not convincing; she still stood on the near side
of forty and was handsome withal. Should he select
the Honorable Louisa as his bride, her mother was
proof Louisa would not fade like a spring flower. He
could look forward to viewing Louisa's fairylike
beauty for many years of married life. Moreover, he
could see by the behavior of the young dark sprite
Pauline that the household was firmly but fairly run.

Six

The members of the Penrose household and their "cousin" continued preparations for Louisa's debut. Ball gowns were duly completed and delivered from Madame Mirielle, and Anna finished decorating the ballroom of the Bruton Street manse.

"You've outdone yourself, Nan!" Dressed in his evening best for the occasion of Louisa's ball, Quinn lifted his lorgnon and regarded the ballroom. Over two stories high, it ran the entire length of the back of the mansion and now contained a lavish display of flowers. Filled with the scent and freshness of springtime, the house gleamed.

"It's early in the social season, but we'll set the standard tonight," she said. "I want this ball to be forever in Lou's memory."

"Well, she'll be a hit," Quinn predicted.

By eleven o'clock, he knew he'd been right. Although the throng overcrowded the ballroom and the drawing rooms, flowing outside onto the balustrade, guests still drove up to the double doors of the house, and were greeted as they entered by the Honorable Louisa Anna Michaela Penrose, and her parents, the baronet Sir Michael Penrose and his Lady, Anna. Quinn thought his sister might burst with pride as Louisa greeted the scores of lords and ladies with admirable aplomb and, truth to tell, he was also delighted with the chit.

His niece, a fairylike vision in white satin and silver gauze, had a crown of white rosebuds in her coiffure. Few girls could carry off the starkness of the color, but it perfectly highlighted her golden hair, blue eyes, and rosy mouth. Anna, with similar coloring, wore clothing more suited to a matron: rose-pink and gold. Sir Pen was in impeccable evening dress.

Far from arriving late and leaving early, his ordinary practice, Quinn had entered the ballroom punctually and led out his niece for her first dance, as Sir Pen still greeted late arrivals. At the behest of his sister, Quinn also made a point of cutting out Willoughby Hawkes from most of Louisa's dances. Quinn felt Anna held up well throughout all the bustle, but there was no reason to test Nan's good nature by allowing one of London's most notorious to monopolize the attention of her child.

Quinn left Louisa in the center of a circle of male admirers, all of whom were about her own age, and who appeared to have suffered from the excessive attentions of tasteless valets. Quinn winced at the sight they presented. The young gentlemen who surrounded Louisa all sported padded shoulders, unnaturally nipped waists, and collars up to their cheekbones.

One of them, a stocky dark fellow whose thick hair had been crimped into a bad imitation of a cherub style, detached himself from the group and hesitantly approached Quinn. He twitched the lapels of his bottle-green coat as he neared.

The fellow bowed. "Sir, may I renew our acquaintance? I am Bryan St. Wills, and have come as the guest of Ambrose Blakeney." He nodded in the direction of another young blade who formed part of Louisa's court. Quinn recognized Blakeney as one of the Penrose cousins. St. Wills continued, "I believe we have previously met, many years ago, in Somerset."

Quinn's mind was bereft of any memory of the cub, but he bowed nevertheless. "Your servant, sir."

"Thank you, my lord." St. Wills inclined his head. "I wonder if I may have a private word with you."

Quinn raised a brow. "I do not know about what subject we would need to be private, sir."

"Your ward, Lady Katherine Scoville. As you must recall, our family and hers were close, our estates bordering."

Quinn's mind cleared. "Ah. Yes. St. Wills. Next-door neighbors." He smiled while his thoughts raced. He did vaguely recall from his childhood visit with the Scovilles, many years previous, a callow dark lad who appeared to have been attached to little Katie as though he were her shadow. Quinn decided to dissemble until he could decide what, if anything, to do about St. Wills. "And have you news of my ward?"

"That is my concern," St. Wills said. "I have written to her at Badham Abbey more than once, with no response. Kate—I mean Lady Katherine—would not be so discourteous. I am concerned."

"Hmph."

"How does Lady Katherine tarry?"

"I, er, believe the Lady Katherine tarries, er, quite well."

"Why would she not answer my letters?"

"Perhaps you have displeased the lady," Quinn evaded.

St. Wills frowned. "I doubt it. I have been sent down from Oxford, but I do not think she would have heard of it."

"Sent down?"

The young man's face reddened. "Just an unfortunate matter of a dancing bear in the, er, dean's study. A trifle."

"A dancing bear. Yes, I quite understand. If it were not a dancing bear 'twould be a dancing barmaid, would it not?" Quinn smiled reminiscently. "Do you intend to stay in London long?"

"A few weeks, 'til the end of term." St. Wills paused.

Quinn came to an abrupt decision. If Bryan St. Wills stayed in London for any length of time, he would come across Kate. Young people tended to flock together. *'Tis better they meet privately with no to-do,* Devere thought. "You are correct," he said aloud, "this is a matter to be discussed quietly. Follow me."

The young man looked mystified but obeyed. Devere exited the ballroom and turned up the staircase leading to the private portion of the house. A light burned in the library where Kate, no doubt unable to sleep due to the excitement and noise, read.

His ward made a lovely picture. She sat alone in the dim library, with the light of several candles glowing on her chestnut hair and green brocade dress. Her head was bent studiously over a volume. She looked up to greet her guardian with a smile.

Advancing into the room, Quinn plucked the book from her hand. *"Lysistrata,* my dear?"

She was distracted from making a response by the sight of the figure following Quinn. *"Bryan!"*

A shard of jealousy, unexpected and violent,

stabbed through Quinn's body as Kate impetuously threw her arms around her old friend. St. Wills pulled away from her hug, exclaiming, "Kate! You hoyden! It took me an hour to tie this cravat and get into this coat!"

"Coats, cravats, who can care about such paltry matters at a moment like this one?"

Quinn silently agreed with his ward. He'd give away his fortune for a joyous greeting like the one Kate gave her childhood playfellow. St. Wills merely brushed at his lapels, the fool.

"Bryan, it's so fine to see you." Her gaze searched her friend's demeanor. "But what happened to your hair?"

"It's the latest style, but a child like you wouldn't recognize it," he responded. His smile took the sting out of his words as Quinn raised his eyebrows.

Child? Is he blind? Kate's no child!

"My lord, you are the most complete hand," St. Wills continued. "I had no notion you had any idea where Kate was!"

Quinn calmed when it became obvious that these two were not loverlike at all. "Wasn't going to tell you, either. And, see here, St. Wills, you mustn't tell anyone Lady Kate is in London. She is here under a false name."

"What!" exclaimed St. Wills. "Why? I'll warrant that Lord Herbert had something to do with it."

"He did," said Kate. "But it's all right, Quinn is taking care of me. And I'm ever so happy with the Penroses. But you're not to call me Lady Kate. My name is Kay Tyndale now, and I'm from India."

St. Wills stared. "India?"

"It's a bit of a tale," began Kate.

By the time she had finished, Quinn had con-sumed a brandy as he moodily watched the young people chatter without inhibition. Would he ever have the same easy relationship with Kate as Bryan St. Wills did? Perhaps not, but Quinn liked the light in his ward's eyes he had seen when he had entered the room, and the way she occasionally sought out his gaze as she conversed with her friend.

"It seems to me, Kate, you are not now so per-turbed regarding Devere as when you met ten years ago!" Wills apparently couldn't resist twitting Kate about her changed attitude.

She blushed. "That is true, and I am ashamed to recall my conduct on that occasion. My lord Devere has been all that is kind."

"My lord Devere, indeed! I thought we were be-yond the 'my lord' and 'my lady' stage, sweet Kate." Quinn ignored St. Wills's glare of disapproval. *She's my ward and I'll call her whatever name I choose!*

"Quinn, then."

"Thank you. And now, St. Wills, we must return to the ball, before our absence is noted." Quinn arose, with Kate's book still in hand.

"My Aristophanes, sir?"

He regarded her down his long nose. *"Lysistrata* is as inappropriate as Circe, my ward. Read Plato, in-stead. *Not* 'Symposium,' " he added hastily. And with that shot, he departed with Bryan St. Wills in tow.

Less than one week later, Kate encountered her old friend at Lady Ursula Damaris's *alfresco* luncheon.

Twirling her parasol, Kate strolled along the shore of a lovely artificial pond located on the extensive grounds of Lady Ursula's Palladian residence, which was nigh to the edge of Hampstead Heath.

Kate recognized the pond's unnatural genesis, but enjoyed it nevertheless. She knew she'd be more comfortable treading a carefully flagged footpath in her soft cloth slippers than struggling over a muddy track in her boots; she delighted in the reeds swaying from the slight breeze, more than she would in the thorns which doubtless would flourish by the margin of a genuine tarn. Bees buzzed in the foliage.

She looked across the pond and observed Bryan St. Wills and several other young bucks engrossed in conversation with Louisa Penrose. *How nice it would be*, she mused, *if Bryan and Louisa were to fall in love!* Kate sighed. She knew there was no chance of Louisa looking any further than the dark countenance of Sir Willoughby Hawkes. She failed to understand the attraction, finding the baronet stern and forbidding. Having had a life marked by sorrows, Kate sought joy.

Kate did not enjoy Sir Willoughby. She preferred the company of a gaggle of girls or even that of her guardian, who invariably was jolly. She still found Quinn's smile charming, at least when his gaze didn't take on that hint of devilry which overset her so. Her mood dimmed a bit when she realized that Lady Ursula had not invited Quinn to the picnic. No one over the age of twenty-one was in attendance, including their hostess, the young wife of an absent diplomat. Quite a few of the guests were still in the schoolroom.

Kate stared again at her old friend. Today, Bryan was attired in another green coat, but with a startling striped waistcoat and trousers. His Hessians gleamed in the sunlight, and his cravat was tied in a bizarre approximation of the Mathematical style. Kate giggled. She'd always looked up to Bryan, rarely finding fault with him. However, contact with more polished gentlemen had refined Kate's taste. She was sure neither Devere nor Hawkes owned a green striped waistcoat. She remembered Quinn's attire at Louisa's ball. No color had relieved his sober, elegant evening ensemble but for a single ruby in his cravat. The contrast between the severe black and white and the one jewel made him all the more striking.

The rustling of taffeta broke Kate's reverie. Searching for the source of the sound, she was perturbed to see a familiar figure, dressed in fashionable primrose yellow, dashing along the flagstoned path toward her.

"I say, Katherine!"

Kate clapped her hand over the mouth of the smaller woman. "Shh! Sybilla!"

Lady Sybilla Farland struggled against Kate's hand. Lady Sybilla, although she was three years Kate's senior at Miss Elizabeth's School, was six inches shorter than her old schoolfellow, and no match for her physically. "Mmmph! Mmph!"

"I'll let you go, if you promise not to say anything until you've heard me out!" begged Kate.

Sybilla, her eyes round over Kate's gagging hand, nodded. "You always were a bully!" she sputtered as Kate released her. "I say, Kate, I believe I'm owed an explanation!"

"I'm not Kate Scoville anymore."

"What!"

"Call me Kay Tyndale."

"Why?" Sybilla attempted to straighten her bonnet, which was askew due to Kate's attack.

"Well, it's a long sad story," said Kate. "Let's just

say that the name of Scoville became dangerous after my grandfather died and left me with the money."

Sybilla knit her thick, dark brows. "A fortune is generally said to be a blessing rather than a curse, Kate."

"It's a curse if money leads your relations to lock you in the attic."

"Locked in the attic! Ah, so that's the way of it! Small wonder everyone cuts the new earl. Where are you living now?" Sybilla retied the yellow grosgrain bow beneath her chin.

"With my guardian's sister, Lady Anna Penrose." Kate nodded across the water. "That's her daughter, Louisa."

"The one they all call the Fairy?" Sybilla gave up on the bonnet.

"Is that what they're saying about her?" Kate threw back her head and laughed. "Well, they should see her lording it over her little sister! Nothing fairylike about her then!"

"Who's the dandy kissing her hem?"

"That's Bryan St. Wills, a friend from Somerset."

"Is he party to the secret of Katie Scoville?"

"Of course, there was no helping that. He's known me forever."

"Good-looking man, if he knew how to dress. What's he done to his hair?" Both girls laughed. Sybilla continued, "Speaking of good-looking men, if you're staying with Anna Penrose, your guardian has to be the Earl of Devere, eh?"

"Yes, Quinn is my guardian. But no one knows I'm here. Everyone thinks I'm a cousin of the Penroses. Otherwise, Herbert might come after me again and force me into marriage to get my money," Kate explained. "If I marry his son, Herbert controls my inheritances, even my mother's fortune. So I have to stay out of sight for the while." She tugged on Sybilla's elbow, urging her farther down the path.

"Out of sight in London during the Season?" Sybilla trilled with laughter. "Whoever thought of that plan must have been touched in the nob!"

Kate flushed. "We didn't have too many choices. Quinn felt that I would go unnoticed in the crowds of young people in Town."

"More likely he wanted to keep you around."

"Why, what do you mean?"

"Your guardian has a bit of a reputation with the ladies, Kate." The diminutive brunette continued around the pond.

"Quinn? He looks like a setter dog," said Kate. She hoped she was not blushing. But why did she feel the need to mislead Sybilla?

Sybilla raised her thick brows. "Not everyone shares your opinion. I'll wager he kisses as enthusiastically as any dog. He's known to be quite the Corinthian. Rumor is he's hunting Staveley."

Kate's attention was piqued. "Who's Staveley?"

"Bertha, the Countess of Staveley. Wealthy widow, two brats."

"Oh, yes, I met her in the park. But Devere wouldn't chase someone else's leavings!" Shocked, Kate realized she again felt jealous. Jealous because of Quinn? Mercy!

"Why not? She's a proven breeder, still young and beautiful, and rich to boot. What's not to love, or even just to bed?"

"Sybilla!" Kate found her friend's cynicism new and startling.

"Don't be such a prude, Kate. He isn't married. Do you think he's untouched?"

"Well, he hasn't touched *me,*" Kate said, concealing her disappointment. "He thinks of me as his child."

"I didn't mean to imply either of you had behaved improperly." Sybilla hastened to assure her friend that she had no reason to doubt Kate's honor. "You must have observed things are different for men than they are for us."

"You sound bitter."

Sybilla's wide, expressive mouth tightened. "It's hard not to be bitter, with my father continually reminding me of my faults, the chiefest of which appears to be that I was not born male."

"That is most unfair and unreasonable. You are not responsible for your gender."

"All Father ever seems to say to me is that he will not have a son to follow in his illustrious footsteps." Sybilla rolled her eyes. "It is all too tiresome."

"He is very prominent in the government, is he not?"

"Yes, he prides himself on being one of Prinny's—excuse me, His Majesty's—inner circle." The two young women had reached the fringes of the crowd surrounding Lady Ursula's buffet tables.

Kate snorted. "For all the good that may do for him!" Like most of England, Kate had great contempt for the licentious, lazy Prince Regent, now George IV.

"I quite agree. But the royal blunders do not prevent Father from bemoaning his sonless state." Sybilla picked up a plate and began to load it with delicacies. "Have you eaten yet?"

"Yes. I'll have some lemonade while you eat. It's good to see you, Sibby, but we only just met, remember?" Kate murmured as Bryan and Louisa approached.

Louisa wore an expression Kate had labeled her "Sunday Go to Church" look: a bland smile that went nowhere near her blank, bored eyes. Bryan, stuck to Lou's side like a burr in a spaniel's tail, continued to chatter into her ear until the pair arrived at the buffet table. Louisa detached herself from Bryan in favor of the food. Bryan, ever the gentleman, came to make his bow to Kate, who introduced him to her friend.

Kate held her breath as Sybilla Farland smiled up at Bryan through her thick, dark lashes. Unlike Louisa, who Kate noticed had already become spoiled with the attentions of Town beaux, Sybilla was a bit out of the ordinary in looks. Small and dark, she had a tendency toward gruffness and plain speaking which Kate imagined would not stand her in good stead at stylish parties, where hypocrisy held sway.

As Bryan bowed over her friend's hand, Kate could see that he was immediately struck by Sybilla's large, dark eyes, which always held a glint of intelligence and humor. Her pale primrose taffeta set off her peachy skin and dark coloring. While Sybilla had no interest in fashion, she was nevertheless dressed in high style. Kate presumed that Sybilla had an excellent dresser; Sybilla herself wouldn't notice if she were dressed in sackcloth as long as the apparel was comfortable.

Kate grinned as Bryan's eyes shifted to Sybilla's welcoming smile, then down to her bodice, cut low in the fashion of the day. After clearing his throat, Bryan asked if he might call upon Lady Sybilla. Visiting cards were exchanged as Pauline trotted up, in the company of their hostess, fresh from croquet and ready for luncheon.

"Lady Ursula, this is marvelous. All the desserts you could possibly want!" Pauline made a dive for the buffet table.

"Paul! Stop acting the hoyden or Mamma will hear about your want of conduct!" reproved Louisa. Pauline stopped in her headlong flight and hid behind Kate, red-faced with embarrassment.

Kate exchanged a speaking glance with Sybilla, who dabbed her mouth with her napkin, concealing her smile. "Pauline," Kate said softly. "Let me make you known to Lady Sybilla Farland."

Pauline removed herself from behind Kate's flowing skirt and hesitantly came forward.

Kate continued, "Lady Sybilla lately attended Miss Elizabeth's School near Bath, a select seminary for young ladies of learning." Kate turned to Sybilla. "Pauline has an interest in languages."

"Indeed." Sybilla bent her intent gaze upon Pauline. "Have you yet read Latin?"

Pauline nodded. "Yes, and Greek also."

"Latin and Greek!" Ursula Damaris was visibly astonished. "When did young ladies of breeding take up the study of ancient languages?"

"Many young ladies of breeding have always been educated," said Kate.

"Whatever for?" Louisa asked. "I have never understood this passion for book learning you and Pauline exhibit. We are destined to marry and produce children. Of what earthly use is Greek?"

"You are one to talk," her sister said. "Of what use is your skill upon the pianoforte?"

"To entertain my husband and guests, of course."

"Nonsense! You do not practice Mozart and Bach for three, four hours every day to amuse prospective cicisbeos," Kate said. "You study music because it pleases you to do so, and because you have true talent."

Louisa blushed.

Pauline agreed. "Don't deny it, Lou, anyone who has heard your performance knows it to be altogether out of the ordinary."

"If that is indeed the case, Miss Penrose, we would be enchanted to hear you play after luncheon, if you would be so kind." Lady Ursula sounded delighted to have hooked the latest favorite of the *ton* into performing.

Louisa appeared to regain her composure. "My sister exaggerates. My skill is no more than commonplace."

Kate knew Louisa was modest but not truthful. After lunch, the sky clouded. Lady Ursula called the group into her drawing room to again urge Louisa to play upon the pianoforte. Kate had seen her "cousin" at the instrument many times, but she never ceased to be struck by the change in Louisa's demeanor which took place whenever she played the pianoforte. Gone was the Fairy; here was a pure spirit attempting to wrest something real and true from the inanimate ivory, wire, and wood of her instrument.

Kate listened with pleasure as Louisa played a Bach fugue with both precision and fire. When she finished, there was a short silence, then the room erupted in applause.

"I told you," said Pauline. "She looks like her garret is empty, but there is substance underneath all that fluffy hair."

"It's your turn, Paul." Louisa beckoned to her sister.

"Mine?" Pauline gasped. "You can't be serious!"

"Absolutely." Louisa gave Pauline her most wicked grin. "Since you and Kay have seen fit to puff my talents, the least I can do is return the compliment." She turned to their hostess. "Ma'am, you must hear my sister and my cousin sing."

Kate's stomach hit bottom. She felt it unwise to draw attention to herself, given her situation, but she had no choice. She knew that a becoming modesty was unexceptional, but it wouldn't fadge to refuse. "Very well. Perhaps one short tune."

" 'The Oak and the Ash'?" Pauline suggested.

Louisa nodded, then struck the opening bars of the famous old English folk song. As was their habit, Kate took the melody and Pauline, who had a pleasing contralto, sang the harmony. By the time they reached the second verse, everyone joined in on the chorus.

One song followed another, and the hours sped by until the scheduled end of the luncheon at three o'clock. Lady Ursula made her good-byes to the flock of young guests as a parade of barouches and landaus left along her graveled drive, heading back to Town.

"We shall have to invite her to some entertainment of ours," remarked Pauline to Kate. "She is really very charming."

Kate buttoned her pelisse. Although it was not raining, their open landau was chilly in the cloudy afternoon. "Yes, I enjoyed myself thoroughly. Oh, do get up quickly, sir," she called to Bryan, who had abandoned the crowd of males with whom he had traveled to Hampstead in favor of accompanying the Penrose party back to Town.

"It's dashed cold," complained Louisa, wrapped in a cloak. "Can we close the top of the landau?"

Bryan checked the hinges. "I believe the mechanisms to be stuck. No use trying to pull it out, that'll just make it worse. Spring 'em!" he shouted to the coachman as he swung up into his seat.

As they headed back to London, the coach was forced to travel more slowly when they entered Edgware; a small fair crowded its High Street. Since carts displaying produce of farmers and wares of local craftsmen blocked any direct route, the coach threaded cautiously through rickety booths set up only for the day. Kate saw colorfully dressed locals mingled with pickpockets and cutpurses come from London to pluck the country pigeons at the fair. Suckling pigs oinked and chickens clucked while their owners bartered with purchasers.

"Look, Louisa!" Kate noticed a dark blue tent, set off to the side of the fair, spangled with myriad golden stars and silver moons. A dark lady clad in colorful shawls and veils stood outside the tent.

The lady's eyes met Kate's as Louisa cried out, "Oh! A fortuneteller! Do stop, coachman!"

The coachman pulled back on the reins. The team came to a rumbling halt on the gravelly road.

"What foolishness is this?" inquired Bryan. "Miss Penrose, you cannot mean to tell me you put any credence in the cupshot mumblings of some grubby, dishclouted Gypsy!"

She turned to him, her face red. "I'll thank you

not to criticize what you don't understand, sir! Set me down at once!"

Bryan rolled his eyes, the picture of masculine exasperation, as the landau stopped. At that moment, the sun came out, and he said, "I suppose you will now say that the sunshine is a good omen!"

Ignoring him, Louisa grabbed Kate's hand. "Come with me, Cousin Kay. You must want to know something of your fate, so far away from home!"

"I know of my fate," said Kate, who nevertheless clambered down from the landau after Louisa. She did not want Louisa going into the dark tent alone. "I will marry some eligible here in London, or I will travel back to India and wed! There is no mystery."

The fortuneteller glanced at her, her dark eyes sparkling. "Oh, but there is indeed a mystery, my lady. You are not what you appear to be, and you will never see India."

Louisa emitted a tiny shriek of delight. "See! See, Kate, she already reveals all manner of important things to us."

The Gypsy smiled. She had large, glittering eyes and a flashing smile. Her gravid body was hidden by flowing, exotic robes in all shades of pink and purple. "You, first." She nodded to Louisa. "Then you," she said to Kate. "And what of you, my little elf?" she called up to Pauline, still seated in the landau.

"I don't think so, ma'am," responded Pauline politely. "It would be rude for us all to abandon Mr. St. Wills."

The Gypsy laughed. "You do not believe, young skeptic. That is all right. You will grow up and become a woman, and then you will understand there are more things in the world than that which you see with your eyes.'' She brushed aside a filmy cloth panel and gestured for Louisa to enter the tent.

Seven

Kate waited outside as the coachman walked the horses up and back, up and back. Finally, Louisa exited the tent, her blue eyes sparkling with mischief. Despite her misgivings, Kate asked, "What did she say?"

Louisa refused to speak of any predictions, saying only, "Her words are a secret. But see if she doesn't tell you of your heart's desire!" She pushed Kate into the tent.

The interior was dark, lit only by short chubby candles. Incense smoked in a burner in one corner, filling the air with the exotic fragrance of sandalwood. The Gypsy sat at her ease upon large pillows with a large bowl of water set before her. As she stirred it with one hand, Kate saw her fingers were long and shapely, with well-kept nails.

"I surprise you," the Gypsy said, in a lightly accented voice. She smiled up at Kate, who still stood. "I was once a lady's maid to the Duchess of Avon, but I earn more here. Please, sit."

Kate sat on another floor pillow, unbuttoning her pelisse. She bent her head to look into the bowl, which appeared to contain ordinary water.

"What is this about India? You have nothing to do with India!" said the Gypsy. "But have a care, young lady, for you are pursued. But the danger is transitory." She swished her hand through the water. "Those near you love you and will protect you from harm." *Swish, swish.*

Intrigued, Kate realized that the Gypsy did seem to have some strange ability. "Is there more?" she asked. "Louisa told me you could tell me my heart's desire."

The Gypsy smiled at Kate, then looked at her reticule. Removing a coin, Kate handed it to the woman, who looked directly into Kate's eyes.

"You already know your heart's desire. But the one you want will never ask you for your heart, though he would take it. You must willingly give yourself to him should you wish to attain happiness in this life."

"Oh." An image of Devere flashed through her mind while an unaccustomed languor pervaded her limbs. She breathed deeply, and the dizzying scent of sandalwood filled her head. "Is there more?"

"There is a great deal more. One near you will be in danger." She spoke casually, as though predicting sunshine on the morrow.

"Bother. Who?"

"That I cannot see. But I see triumph, and many—no—two journeys, or more. An ocean voyage, mayhap."

"I thought you said I wasn't going back to India!"

The Gypsy hooted. "You have never been to India and you never will! You mock me. Now, go!"

Kate stumbled forth from the tent, having been given a great deal to think about. She clung to the landau for a moment, recapturing her balance and her serenity. Bryan helped her climb into her seat.

She was in a contemplative mood. Both the fortuneteller and Sybilla had provided more information about her guardian than Kate wanted to consider. Nevertheless, the words spoken to her nibbled at her thoughts, like mice in the larder. *Your guardian has a bit of a reputation with the ladies . . . he's known to be quite the Corinthian. . . . The one you desire will never ask you for your heart, though he would take it.*

The thought that she, Kate, would have to act firmly to take her own marital happiness was a new one. Perhaps she'd been naïve, but she'd always dreamed she would be courted by some Prince Charming (or at least a viscount) and, when the time came, she would easily enter a joyous and untroubled marriage. Precisely what that marriage would entail was vague to Kate, but she feared it not. Her parents had been happy together, and she had never seen any reason to consider that an equally delightful union would evade her.

Now she had cause for concern. How was she to "give herself" to attain her heart's desire, while maintaining the standards of conduct which had been drilled into her from earliest memory?

And if Quinn would take her heart, with what would he leave her? A gentleman who had a reputation as a Corinthian and a rake might never change his habits. A loveless marriage was not within Kate's plans. She knew she had pride enough to require loyalty, and she was prepared to give the same. Was this what the Gypsy meant when she said Kate would have to "give herself?"

They drove out of the crowded fair toward London. There was little conversation. Louisa and Kate were particularly quiet. After Bryan and Pauline had stopped teasing them about their experiences in the fortuneteller's tent, the journey was silent except for the crunch of the wheels on the road, and the occasional shouts of the coachman to the team.

As they passed through the new park which the Prince Regent had built, Kate saw a flurry of movement along the edge of the shrubbery just before a shot rang out. Louisa screamed, a high, panicked sound. Clutching Pauline, she dropped, trembling, into the Kate's lap, who threw herself over both girls.

"Are you all right? Are you all right?" Kate released Louisa and Pauline, then grabbed Louisa again when she saw that Lou trembled with fear.

"Yes! Yes! Only I am sure I felt the shot brush by my cheek!" Louisa turned to Bryan. "St. Wills?"

"I am not injured, Miss Penrose. May I see your bonnet?"

Louisa's fingers shook as she untied the hat.

Bryan examined it. "I am sure you imagined the shot coming so close to your person. If you had felt the bullet on your face, it would have left a hole in your bonnet. See, it is intact. Drive on, coachman," he called to their driver, his voice calm.

"P'raps the shot merely seemed close because this district is excessively quiet," Pauline said, a hopeful note in her voice. "It has nothing to do with us. Cousin Kay! Whatever is wrong? You're white as a sheet!"

Kate's thoughts were in agitation. The fortuneteller had seemed so truthful when she stated danger was transitory. She had made it seem as though there was nothing to fear. However, Kate knew that if she were killed, her funds would go to her last remaining relatives: Herbert and Osborn. As much as she loved them, the Penroses were not her family, despite the deception they practiced upon the whole of London society.

"Let's get back home as soon as possible," Kate said. "Driver! Spring 'em!"

Upon their return to the Penrose residence, Kate retired alone to the library to compose a letter to Quinn, entreating him to call upon her at his earliest convenience.

Anna entered as Kate struggled over her missive. "Kay, whatever is the matter?"

Kate raised teary eyes from her task. Balls of crumpled stationery littered the desk. "Ma'am, this is my fault. I must leave your house at once."

"Stuff and nonsense!"

" 'Tis true! Whyever else would anyone shoot at us were it not for me?" Kate snuffled into her handkerchief.

"No one shot at you. I spoke to St. Wills about the matter. The shot was far away, and had nothing to do with you at all." Anna shook Kate firmly by the shoulders. "Now, I want you to take a bath, have some tea, and go to sleep early tonight. And there will be no more talk of leaving!"

Nevertheless, Kate's message went out to Quinn, who was not in London. He had traveled to his Surrey home, and attended races for several days. After he had the pleasure of watching his horses win and place, he returned to London to yet another pleasure. His lovely ward desired his presence.

His heart beat faster as he read her note.

Bruton Street

My Lord Devere,

    I pray you shall attend me at your earliest convenience.

Sincerely, K.G.S.

He frowned. Katherine had never before written him a note to ask him for anything, least of all his company. He had an uncomfortable inkling that all was not right in his ward's world, despite his efforts to cocoon her with the Penroses. Something had happened to overset her serenity.

After washing off the dust from the road, he walked the short distance from Berkeley Square to Bruton Street. It was three o'clock in the afternoon, and he did not know if he would find Kate at home. Nevertheless, he felt in need of the walk.

He found the household quiet. An inquiry made of the butler revealed that the Penrose ladies were out; Lady Anna had promised to show Misses Louisa and Pauline the delights of the Burlington Arcade. Sir Pen was at Whites'. Kate was alone in the house, but for the servants.

Quinn found her in the small back garden.

Bees buzzed in the perennial border of herbs and flowers. The fountain ran, with the cupid statue spitting water in a never-ending stream from the center of the fountain into the bowl. The tinkle of water was greatly calming. In contrast to the frantic tone of the note she'd sent, Kate's face looked serene as she napped in a chaise longue beneath a vine-covered arbor, which partially shaded her from the afternoon sun.

Quinn stood over his ward, watching her rest. Her chestnut hair, piled on top of her head, reflected reddish lights in the dappled sun admitted by the arbor. One curl had escaped and lay on her neck. She did not wear a tucker for modesty on this warm spring day, and the bodice of her thin, pink muslin dress was cut fashionably low. He could see gentle curves inside the fabric puffed over her chest. Her bosom rose and fell with her breath. Her creamy skin glistened with a slight sheen of moisture. Although her face was shadowed, her mobile lips, parted slightly, were eminently kissable.

It would be such a simple thing to steal a kiss, just one kiss, from her rosy, open lips, slipping his tongue inside her mouth to meet secretly with hers, just one tender, sweet, lover's kiss. And it would be just as simple and easy to free one of her lush breasts from its flimsy confinement, to weigh its heavy roundness in his hand; to taste the delicate peak, feel it harden and pucker beneath his lips—would it be sweet, like the strawberry it resembled, or would it be salty with her summer sweat?

She'd be hopelessly compromised.

They'd have to marry.

Quinn smiled. She'd be his, then, to explore, to touch, to probe, to feel and caress, to tease her legs apart and taste the very depths of her, and then to take her—

To take her.

All without a word or gesture of assent on the part of his ward.

His *ward*.

Quinn shook his head, then sat on the edge of the chaise longue.

Asleep, Kate dreamed.

She stared at the fine double portrait of her parents which dominated the hall at Gillender House. Her mother had been a graceful blond lady and the memory of her painful death did not surface in Katherine's contemplations as she gazed at the picture, which had been painted shortly after Bennett married Margaret. Dressed in a blush-pink morning gown, Margaret sat addressing the viewer with a steady blue scrutiny. Her husband stood at her side with his hand resting on her shoulder. Pictured in profile, Bennett looked down at his wife fondly.

By some strange magic, the portraits seemed to transform. Was it Kate who sat in the chair? Did the hand on her shoulder belong to the first earl, Robert? The faces and clothing of the individuals shifted and coalesced.

A redheaded man looked down at Kate as she sat in the wing chair. He had a familiar visage with soulful brown eyes. She scented a spicy fragrance, cloves with a touch of citrus.

Her body, starting with her hand, tingled in an unfamiliar but pleasant fashion. A shadow seemed to cross her vision . . .

Kate awoke with a start to find Quinn perched beside her on the edge of the chaise longue, watching her as she slept. He had possessed himself of her hand, tickling her palm with his fingertips. The flesh at the apex of her thighs stirred with a liquid, coiling heat. She jerked her hand out of Quinn's. The slight smile on his face did not disappear, but broadened into his familiar devilish grin as the book she had been reading slipped from her lap and fell to the ground with a bang. Quinn picked it up.

"Petronius Arbiter? I am surprised, sweet Kate, that Petronius put you to sleep."

Kate, irritated, frowned at Devere and snatched at the book. There was something immensely annoying about being watched as one slept. Did she drool, or twitch, or even (heaven forbid) snore?

"You seem to be unusually interested in my choice of reading material, my lord. Be advised I merely refresh my knowledge of Latin."

Quinn glanced at her. His expression was unreadable. "Be advised that your choice of reading material tends to border upon the salacious, my ward. It is not unnatural for you to have an interest in, um, such matters. Perhaps it is time for you to marry, and for some strong male to teach you what you wish to know."

Kate gasped. *"Ma-marry,* my lord? I'm only seventeen!"

"You are six months away from your eighteenth birthday." He cocked his head. His eyes mocked, or did they flirt? "Bryan St. Wills seems to be an eligible *parti,* and a good friend."

"Bryan? He's the merest child!"

"He must be at least twenty, sweet Kate. I assume from his deportment his birth and breeding are appropriate."

She pressed her lips together and sought to disguise her discomfiture in idle chatter. "The St. Willses are originally French nobility, I believe. Bryan's father sold off the family properties just before the Revolution, and they came to England to settle."

"Their true name?"

"Saint-Guillaume. My lord, I have no desire or intention to marry Bryan St. Wills. Recently he seems to have developed a *tendre* for Louisa." Kate stretched, fumbling with her hair.

"Is that so?"

"It'll amount to nothing. Louisa seems intent upon her boring baronet." Kate sniffed.

"Willoughby Hawkes?"

"Yes. I fail to understand the attraction." Kate jabbed a hairpin into her topknot, securing a stray ringlet. She realized, to her embarrassment, that the pose lifted her breasts inside the flimsy muslin. Moreover, her guardian watched her as closely as a gentleman at a track observing the finish of a hotly contested race on which he'd wagered his entire fortune.

"I confess, I have never before heard Wicked Willy called dull."

Quinn said nothing about her appearance. Had her imagination run riot? "Is that how he's known, as Wicked Willy? Why so, my lord?"

"Er, nothing you need to worry about," Quinn said hastily. "It's just that, when a cove's been on the loose for a time, he develops a reputation, so to speak."

"And you, my lord? Have you not been, as you say, loose for a time?" Prompted by Sybilla's gossip, Kate probed.

Quinn squirmed. "I am, I assure you, quite unexceptional."

Kate raised her brows.

"But you, sweet Kate . . . what manner of man catches your eye?"

"Certainly not a frowny old man like your friend

Wicked Willy. What care you, my lord?" Kate pushed some more.

"Quinn," he corrected. "You are my ward and my charge and it is my obligation to see you are, er, disposed of properly."

"Disposed of properly!" The rein on Kate's temper loosed. She stood up, shaking out her skirts. "My lord, I am not an item of yours to dispose of. I am a person who has a life. Good day to you, Lord Devere." She turned to go into the house. Her back was to Quinn, so he could not see her angry tears.

"I beg your pardon!"

"What?" she snapped.

"You requested my presence. I do not believe it was to discuss your marital prospects."

She kept her back turned. "I'll join you in the drawing room in ten minutes, if you please." She stalked into the house.

Kate was livid, not only at her guardian for his patronizing treatment, but also at herself. She'd become convinced through the Gypsy's maunderings that Quinn was her heart's desire and could be her own for a snap of her fingers. She was infuriated to find Devere still perceived her as a precocious child, one who needed instruction from a cub like Bryan St. Wills.

She stamped upstairs to her room, and, after ringing for Bettina, stared out the window at Bruton Street with sightless eyes. Perhaps Devere was right. Perhaps the solution to all her problems was a quick marriage. Married, she would cease to be a target for Herbert or a drain on the Penroses' generosity. Marriage would also provide the stability Kate had lacked since her grandfather's death.

Kate wanted very much to marry for love, and had convinced herself that Quinn was her desire and her fate. It did not seem so. What manner of man would suggest marriage to another if he was sincerely attached? Even if she married Devere, there was no certainty he would change his rakish habits. Kate would be miserable in a loveless marriage. She loved, but she needed love, craved love's return as much as she required air to breathe and food to eat.

Kate knew persons of her class rarely wed for love. The custom was for young noblewomen to marry suitable noblemen early and produce children. She had heard rumors that, later in life, a woman might take a lover who would be more to her preference than her husband. There were many second sons and third daughters who did not resemble their fathers.

Kate hated the idea of such a sham. It clashed with her innate honesty and loyalty, and she refused to accept this future for herself. She resolved to wait, to look beyond Devere. She would be introduced to the *ton* in just a few months, and would have ample suitors from whom she could choose. She hoped she would have forgotten her *tendre* for the earl by that time. *Puppy love, nothing more!* she told herself.

After having brushed her hair, washed her face, and arranged a tucker in her bodice, she entered the drawing room to face her guardian with a calm demeanor. Quinn surveyed her modest apparel and frowned. She reminded herself that she didn't care. His moods could be his own.

"My lord," she said, seating herself in the wing chair, "there is the possibility that Lord Herbert's designs on me have become something more than conjecture."

Devere listened to her tale with a solemn mien as Jenks came in with the tea tray. Kate poured as she talked, then offered Quinn the cook's prized apple tarts. She knew Quinn liked them as much as Pauline did.

When she finished her tale, he rubbed one side of his Roman nose and fiddled with his lorgnon. She stared at his long, restless fingers, and, despite her resolve, envisioned those elegant hands caressing her body the way they had stroked her palm. She bit her lip to destroy the distracting, useless, unaccustomed sensations, pleasurable feelings she had no words to describe. She only knew they threatened to devastate her fragile composure.

When he finally spoke, breaking the silence which had arisen, she was startled by the unusual timbre in his voice, a dark, serious note. Her good-natured guardian, however irritating, was rarely anything but jolly.

"Well, Kate, 'tis a pretty problem you've brought to me. It is true that Lord Herbert is to be invested into his title this week, so he is in London."

"Truly, sir? No one has mentioned it to me."

Quinn shrugged. "The information is available for all to read, in the *Times* and the *Morning Post*. But worry not, we'll get to the bottom of this coil, you'll see!" He had an odd brooding glint in his eyes as he stood up hurriedly.

Kate was surprised anew. "You'll not finish your tea?"

"Ah, er, no. No, thank you, my lady. I have recollected an errand which must take place before the day is out." Devere gripped the bellpull and shouted for his curricle before he remembered he had walked from Berkeley Square.

He had asked her forgiveness before he stalked out, all long limbs and flashing, polished Hobys, but she was dismayed by the entire encounter. She still sipped her tea when the Penrose ladies came back from Burlington Arcade, full of tales and stories of their happy day. They were to attend *Macbeth* at Drury Lane two evenings hence, wasn't it exciting? asked Pauline. Louisa had found several ells of the loveliest silver-blue sarcenet, did Cousin Kay not want some to trim her blue bonnet?

She heard them all as if they were very far away, or as if they were speaking another tongue, and she were a visitor to their strange land. She shook herself loose of her mood and reentered their world, feeling as though she'd been insufferably rude.

Lady Anna watched her with a thoughtful expression. "Did my brother visit, Cousin Kay?"

Kate lifted her teacup, pleased to see that her hand did not shake. "Yes, we discussed the events of yesterday."

"And?"

"And nothing. He said nothing, merely recalled an engagement elsewhere." Kate did not want to mention the presence of her uncle in London while Louisa and Pauline were in the room. She continued, "He seemed to be in a peculiar mood."

"No more so than some, I vow." Anna eyed Kate. "Do you accompany us tonight to the Lambs? Lady Caroline is expected to read from her new novel."

"May it be as scandalous as her first!" exclaimed Louisa. They all laughed. Lady Caroline Lamb's outrageous conduct concerning the poet George Gordon, Lord Byron, had not been forgotten. Her doings never ceased to amuse the *ton*. Society had been greatly titillated by the publication of *Glenarvon,* the melodramatic satire which slashed Lady Caroline's own family to shreds. All hoped her new book would be equally shocking.

"No, I do not believe I shall be abroad tonight," said Kate. She did not feel she could tolerate shallow social intercourse in her current emotional state. "But what is this excursion to Drury Lane?"

"It's for Pauline, mostly. Kean in *Macbeth,*" Louisa said.

"As though you won't enjoy it," grumbled Pauline.

"It's for all of us." Anna sought to pour oil on the troubled waters.

"Mother, we had such a fine time at Lady Ursula's, p'raps we should invite her to share our box?"

"Why, what a thoughtful idea, Pauline. Yes, you may write to Lady Ursula today and invite her, with my compliments. Shall we also invite Bryan St. Wills?" Anna tipped her head to one side to regard both Kate and Louisa.

Louisa winced while Kate agreed. "And, ma'am, I saw the nicest girl at the luncheon. Her name's Lady Sybilla Farland. If there's room in the box, might we invite her also?"

"That would make a party of seven, all females but for St. Wills and your father."

"Poor Bryan!" mocked Louisa.

Her mother ignored her. "We shall also invite

Quinn. Kay, I am afraid your new friend will have to wait for another occasion."

"We could ask Sir Willoughby," suggested Pauline pertly.

Louisa blushed and held her tongue while Anna considered. "Well, the dessert denied is the tasty morsel most sought. Correct, Louisa? Yes, that would be fine."

Louisa bounced in her seat.

Her mother fixed her with a quelling stare. "I'll write to him myself. Shall we serve a light dinner for the party before we set out? Perhaps Quinn or St. Wills knows of an escort for Lady Ursula, to round out the party." Anna speculated aloud. "You do understand, Lou, that you will not in any case be partnered with Sir Willoughby."

Kate could see, glancing at Louisa's excited, flushed face, that Louisa had not thought about the details of the evening.

"Why, what do you mean, Mother?" Louisa asked.

"It is unlikely Lady Ursula will attend. I've certainly never seen her at the theatre. So, as ranking peer, your uncle will escort me and you will be partnered by your father," Anna stated calmly. "To do anything else would be quite inappropriate."

"Who cares about propriety!" snapped Louisa.

"We do. If your *tendre* for Sir Willoughby does not turn out as you hope, you will be glad of my caution," her mother said. "Don't scorn my advice. Restraint, Louisa! Men are hunters. They love the chase, and will treasure the object of their desire all the more if it has led them in a merry dance."

Louisa's brow furrowed as Pauline asked, "Who will escort me?"

Anna thought. "St. Wills, if he attends. 'Twill give you a touch of adulthood, child." Anna ruffled Pauline's hair. "And you, Kate, will accompany Sir Willoughby."

"Stuck with the boring baronet!" Kate looked at Louisa as Pauline and Anna laughed. "I'd trade with you, Lou, but I'm afraid Lady Anna has laid down the law!"

Eight

Bryan St. Wills lost no time in pursuing his new love interest. Though he had been sent down from Oxford, he was resolved not to neglect his education in any way; he merely set himself to acquiring different skills. Gambling and wenching, cocking and racing were the chief pleasures of young males of his social class. Bryan was determined to experience all.

The very day after Lady Ursula's luncheon, Bryan presented himself at the door of the Farland mansion at Cavendish Gardens.

Again dressed in green, he attempted to make himself exceptional among his dandyish peers by wearing only the one distinctive color. His waistcoat and unmentionables were lemon yellow. His groom walked his horses, tethered to his curricle, around Cavendish Square. Bryan hoped to take Sybilla driving in Hyde Park at the fashionable hour of five o'clock.

The door was opened by a footman who informed him that Lord James and his wife were both absent from the household. Bryan presented his card, and begged to be honored by the company of Lady Sybilla. The drawing room in which he waited was decorated in the first stare of fashion. Evidently Lady Farland spent much time selecting furniture and wallpaper.

Sybilla dashed in, stripping a pair of heavy rough gloves off her hands. Bryan stared. He'd never met any lady, other than his friend Kate, who felt sufficiently secure in her person to meet a gentleman dressed in anything other than her finest. Lady Sybilla wore a drab stuff gown and appeared to have dirt on her boots.

"Good afternoon, sir," she said, extending a very white, very soft hand in Bryan's direction. As he bent over it, he noticed the well-kept member belied her grubby state. "If you would care to give me a few minutes to make myself presentable . . ." She trailed out of the room. As she left, he could hear her ordering the footman to bring tea, "And whiskey, if the gentleman desires it!"

Not fifteen minutes later Sybilla was back, perfectly attired. Though Sybilla might not care about her appearance, her lady's maid evidently knew her business. Today Lady Sybilla was dressed in pale jade silk.

Bryan dropped his teacup back into his saucer with a clatter. The cool elegance of the ensemble did not disguise Sybilla's pleasure in his visit, revealed by her sparkling eyes and sweet smile.

"My curricle is outside," he said. "Perhaps a drive?"

"After tea, yes. I'm parched." She poured for herself, then freshened his cup.

He hesitated fractionally, then asked, "You are a particular friend of Lady Kate Scoville?"

"Yes, she told me that we two are among the few who are in on her charade."

"If you are good friends, perhaps you will not mind me asking. Umm, in what pursuit were you engaged when I interrupted?"

"Oh, that!" Her rich laughter trilled. "Please do not reveal my pastime. It shames my parents greatly. I am a peasant, you see."

"I beg your pardon!"

"So my father says," murmured Sybilla demurely. "I have a passion for gardening—flowers in particular. May I show you?"

The back garden of the mansion was surprisingly large for a London house, large enough for her to express herself in flowers, explained Sybilla.

"You have a particular fondness for sweet peas, I observe."

"Yes." She buried her face in a pot of bright pink blooms, humming as she inhaled their spicy scent. "I am engaged in breeding true colors, particularly blue."

"Blue?"

She turned an excited countenance to Bryan. "Have you never wondered why there are few purely blue flowers, sir?"

Bryan blinked. "Can't say I have."

"Well, I have. It is very difficult," she informed him. "Most sweet peas are pink or white. Reds tend to be orangey—a horrible shade—and the blues are purplish, really. I am growing pure blue and red flowers. Each succeeding generation I come closer to my goal."

Despite his complete disinterest in the subject matter, Bryan found himself warming to the conversation, and to the lady. Sybilla's fascination with her flowers was infectious. Her movements, as she walked through her orderly flower garden, were swift and deft, and Bryan was struck by her resemblance to an inquisitive, restless hummingbird as she went from flower to flower. She even hummed as she fluttered around the garden.

"How, precisely, do you breed the flowers?"

"Oh, it is very complicated. Most flowers breed due to the motion of bees among them, drifting from blossom to blossom. I must protect the buds I wish to propagate." She gestured at several stalks, which sported papers tied over their tips. "I transfer the pollen from one flower to another, using a paint-brush. I don't know exactly why, but I suspect if I breed the bluest flowers together, the color will eventually come true. Also with the reds." She waved at a different corner of the yard, where riotous red sweet peas dominated the landscape.

Impressed, Bryan concluded that there was a thinking mind behind those fine dark eyes. "I gather your parents do not approve of your hobby, Lady Sybilla."

"No, but they do find it useful. I have taken to filling my father's study and my mother's boudoir with flowers. I have found sweet peas result in sweet tempers."

He laughed and offered her his arm.

The evening of the theatre party, Kate stood in her bedroom adjusting her ensemble. She had not seen or heard from her guardian since that dreadful scene in the garden, after which he had walked out of the drawing room and, apparently, out of any meaningful part in her life. Try as she might, she could not banish him from her thoughts. Her brow puckered as she considered the situation.

He had sent a gift to his niece Pauline to celebrate her first visit to the theatre, but nothing for Kate, not even a message to assuage her concerns. Kate would have been jealous but for her own fondness for the spritely dark creature. Kate admired Louisa, but Kate and Pauline were birds of a feather. They shared the same impish sense of humor and love of languages, especially street cant.

She could not understand what act or word had led to the peculiarity of mood which had swept over him. Had she somehow displeased Quinn? It would be a very uncomfortable evening unless he'd recovered his usual sunny demeanor.

Her maid tossed the white crinkled silk gown over Kate's head and adjusted its blue velvet bodice. The ruche of silk set off Kate's figure while the blue trim drew attention to her eyes. Kate wore matching blue slippers and would don gloves later. She sat still while Bettina arranged her hair into an artful chignon. Short crops were more fashionable, but Kate preferred her hair long. Bettina pinned blue velvet flowers into the chignon. The flowers matched those which trimmed the double flounce edging the dress at Kate's ankles.

Dinner was elaborate, far beyond the light meal Anna had blithely proposed. A tasty lobster bisque was followed by plaice, delicately bathed in lemon cream sauce. The fish course preceded squabs roasted with blackcurrant glaze, and the savory was accompanied by an assortment of tarts and syllabubs. Numerous removes, including a ham and a roast beef, sat on the buffet.

As delicious as dinner was, Kate found the emotional undercurrents present at the table more interesting than the food. While his heart might be engaged to another, Sir Willoughby's manners left nothing to be desired. Kate was, for the first time, favorably impressed by Wicked Willy. That she now knew his sobriquet infused their conversation with rather more sparkle than the gentleman expected or desired. But he covered any discomfiture admirably, and even flirted a little. Kate was cheerfully diverted from her preoccupation with Quinn.

Because Kate had no designs on the baronet, she didn't understand why Louisa glowered at them from down the table. During a lull in her conversation with Hawkes, Kate looked down the table at her hostess. Lady Anna chatted with Quinn about the latest gossip. Next to her uncle, Pauline visibly reveled in her first adult party. Dressed in pink muslin with cream lace trim, she took unabashed pleasure in the occasion. Although he could not be diverted by a fourteen-year-old, Kate knew that Bryan St. Wills possessed sufficient address to engage his young dinner partner in such conversation as would put her at ease.

Later, on the way to the theatre, Pauline amused Kate by flirting with her fan. The elegant trifle of silver sticks and pink silk had been sent to her by her Uncle Devere for this occasion, her first trip to the theatre.

She hid her eyes behind the widespread fan, then batted them at her uncle, who sat opposite. He smiled, recognizing the silent message: *I love you.* His grin broadened as she closed her fan, and touched it to her left ear: *Do not betray our secret.* Watching them, Kate's lips twitched. Pauline's eyes darted quickly from one to the other, and she tapped her fan to her lips. *Be quiet, we are overheard!* Both Quinn and Kate burst out laughing as the carriage drew up in front of the Drury Lane Theatre.

The great Kean, still popular, had drawn a crowd. The pit was jammed with dandies and bucks of all description, many of whom turned their opera glasses on the ladies in the boxes, rather than on the stage.

The Tyndale family maintained a large box and Pauline sat at the front, since this was her special treat. Bryan St. Wills, her escort, sat in the chair next to her. Anna placed Kate and Louisa in the front also, the better to keep her eye on her eldest daughter. Anna kept Sir Willoughby close by her and entertained him with the latest *on dits* which she'd learned from Quinn at dinner.

The play began, entrancing Kate. While she was well educated, she'd never had the opportunity to attend the theatre in London. As she watched the witches on the heath, Katherine wondered if she could cast a spell to ensorcle Quinn. She sighed as she remembered that the predictions of the Gypsy, who had seemed so enlightened, were only fake and flummery. No. If she wanted something, she'd best reach out and take it.

She examined Quinn, seated on the other side of the box, under cover of the darkness of the theatre. Dressed in his usual immaculate evening clothes, he'd cut his hair short. She'd heard Roman styles for males were back in vogue; was his crop a Caesar, or a Trojan? She didn't know, but the mode emphasized his expressive eyes and generous mouth. She licked her lips as she wondered if his kisses were as fiery sweet as she imagined. Her glance traveled to his long, elegant hands. Her breath quickened as she remembered how those fingers had felt caressing her palm. She couldn't believe she'd thought he looked like a setter dog when they'd met. She bit down on her lower lip. There was no profit to this line of thought.

During the interval she again glanced at Quinn. Leaning in his chair, he balanced precariously on its two back legs. "Hi-ho," he said casually. "I say, Willy, who's that dandy in the pit ogling Louisa?"

Two heads turned as both Anna and Sir Willoughby sat up straighter. Hawkes moved to peer over the rail of the box.

"That's no dandy, that's Cousin Ambrose Blakeney." Louisa sniffed.

"Cousin Ambrose? I haven't seen him in forever and a day," said Pauline.

"Yes, you have," contradicted her sister. "He was at Lady Ursula's party, don't you remember?"

"No. In any event, why would he be staring at you?"

Kate watched Louisa blush. Ambrose was one of the Fairy's admirers. Kate stifled a laugh as Sir Willoughby glowered down into the pit.

"He's probably not ogling Miss Penrose," said Bryan. "He's a friend of mine, also."

Quinn raised his brows. "Please do not say he is ogling you."

"What's that creature near to him?" asked Hawkes.

"Which one?" Kate wanted to know.

"That tough, in the black."

Kate scrutinized the crowd carefully, as did they all. "I'm afraid I don't know who you mean, Sir Willoughby. Would you like a better view? I'm quite willing to change places," she added, giving her "cousin" a sly look. Kate had noted Louisa's blue mood, and, with a view to her own self-interest, hoped to improve Louisa's temper. A happy Louisa was easy to live with; moody Louisa cast a pall over the entire house.

"Yes, thank you," he said, as he slid into Kate's seat. To her surprise, Hawkes did not use the new proximity to Louisa's person to flirt. He seemed intent upon the scene below.

"Who's that lady staring at us, Uncle Quinn?" demanded Louisa. She nodded across the pit to a box, where a petite redhead dressed in apple-green held court, surrounded by a group of bucks and fops of varying age. Kate saw the flame-haired lady raise her head to rake their box with a long, cool glare. Kate knew that arrogant redhead perched on her chair as though it were a throne—Staveley.

Lifting her nose, Kate turned away. She'd never imitate Lady Staveley's shabby manners.

Both Quinn and Hawkes looked over. Quinn turned away from the sight, looking comically embarrassed. "Er—old friend! Didn't expect to see her here!" He looked at Hawkes and grimaced.

"Better go over and do the pretty, Devere, or there'll be the devil to pay!" Hawkes advised.

"The devil to pay! Why, what could you mean, Sir Willoughby?" cried Louisa.

He didn't answer, but Quinn abruptly left. Kate noticed that he emerged a few minutes later in the box opposite. While Kate continued her conversation with Anna and Pen, she kept an eye on Quinn, who made his bow over Lady Staveley's hand, sipped from a glass of champagne, then returned. For all of her stares, the lady paid little or no attention to Quinn once he was within her orbit. Kate thought the entire scene a bit odd.

A footman came 'round with glasses of champagne on a tray. Pauline politely refused the champagne, asking the footman, "Could you please bring me a glass of lemonade? Thank you so much." She smiled up at the lad, flirting with her dark eyes. As the bedazzled young footman turned to leave the box, he stumbled over his feet and smacked his head against the door post.

Pauline's parents winced.

"Paul, you're a caution, and no mistake," said her father. "We'd best get you back to Kent before you land in serious trouble."

"Oh, Papa, no!" begged Pauline. "I have still not been to Vauxhall Gardens."

Pen frowned. "Vauxhall? Everyone knows young ladies could get into all sorts of scrapes at Vauxhall at night."

"And Hampton Court Palace," said Pauline. "It is historical, is it not? I should not miss Hampton Court. I'm sure Uncle Devere can get us entree."

"One week, Pauline, one week only," said Pen. "Don't you miss your brothers and sister?"

Pauline looked mutinous. She appealed to her uncle. "Uncle Quinn, you'll take me to Hampton Court? And to Vauxhall?"

Kate noticed that Quinn kept his expression blank, but said, "Ah, er, I am not sure we should be discussing this in front of our guests."

"Well, I am sure they would like to come," said Pauline. "We'll have loads of fun. There's a maze and everything." She glanced at Kate. "Cousin Kay can ask her new friend, what was her name? Sylvia?"

"Sybilla Farland. That's a very generous idea, Pauline," Kate continued gently, "but you must first ask your parents if your scheme meets with their approval."

Anna sighed. "Very well, Pauline, but you must understand your presence in Town is but temporary. Hampton Court and Vauxhall Gardens only, then back to Kent with your father. No protests or whining, do you understand?"

The crowd leaving the theatre was even thicker than at their arrival. Members of the *ton* cared little for culture but they certainly cultivated their reputations. As a result, many members of the audience sauntered in just before the first interval in order to be seen. However, everyone wanted to leave at the same time.

Having been put on guard by the sight of oglers in the pit, Hawkes was mindful of the toughs he had observed at Astley's Amphitheatre watching the Penroses, and looked about alertly as the party waited for their carriage to arrive to pick them up. He knew the crowds of swells jamming the sidewalk were fair game for the assorted pickpockets, canters, and buzmen that populated London, and that the busnappers, however worthy the constables might be, were no match for the spawn of St. Giles which plagued the honest Londoner.

He noticed St. Wills had the lively Miss Pauline well in hand, while Pen and Anna surrounded the Fairy; Louisa pointedly ignored the bucks who jostled to see her as she stood in the portal of the theatre. Sir

Willoughby kept Kate's arm tucked in his as Quinn went for their coach.

As he made inconsequential conversation with Kate, Hawkes scrutinized the throngs which flooded the sidewalk like a flock of many-colored birds. Most were unimportant hangers-on and minor members of Society; he knew many of them, and introduced Kate to such notables as came their way. She acknowledged Lord Fribble and Lady Snuggle; yes, Countess Whozits was positively charming! The carriage arrived, and Sir Willoughby handed the Penrose ladies up into it with a rush of relief. He had felt unaccountably tense since he had espied that odd personage in the crowd in the pit at the theatre.

He lingered with Devere on the sidewalk as Pen climbed up into the carriage. "Walk, Devere?" Hawkes invited. It sounded more like a command.

"You won't come back to Bruton Street for late supper?" asked Lady Anna, poking her head out of the barouche.

"We think not, but thank you," said Sir Willoughby, jabbing Quinn with his hawkheaded cane. Hawkes resolved to send Lady Anna, who had been unfailingly gracious, a gift of some sort as thanks for a delightful evening. He knew he was taking himself off in a manner which bordered on discourtesy, but felt an urgent need to engage in a serious discussion with the Earl of Devere.

As the gentlemen set forth westward, a light drizzle began to fall, and Quinn shrugged himself more closely into his evening cloak. He examined his friend. Hawkes's pewter eyes glinted coldly as he glowered at Quinn.

"Well, Devere, are you going to tell me what this is all about?"

Quinn kept his voice light and noncommittal. "Can't say what you mean, old man."

"I'll show you precisely what I mean." Hawkes grasped Devere's arm and swung him around. Quinn would have taken offense, but Hawkes pointed with his cane at the toughest customer Devere had yet seen. Sturdily built, he wore a battered greatcoat, and a tricorne concealed his face but exposed a cauliflower ear. Altogether, he looked like a refugee from the ring. He stared down the street at the back of the Penrose barouche.

"A boxer? Good God!" Devere started toward the personage, who immediately ran down an alley. Devere whistled, and a fellow with a red vest concealed beneath his overcoat trotted up out of a side street.

"A Bow Street Runner?" Hawkes gaped.

"Milord?" The man saluted with two fingers touched to his hat.

"Did you see a large person, greatcoat, tricorne?" Devere demanded.

"Yes, milord."

"Follow him."

"Yes, milord." The man turned and headed in the direction of Macklin Street.

"Wait! Where is the current location of Badham and his spawn?" Devere asked.

"Still stayin' at Limmer's, milord, talkin' of an evening in the vicinity of Covent Garden."

Devere winced and watched Hawkes roll his eyes.

The worst hells and whorehouses were located there. Even if Quinn's affections had not been bestowed elsewhere, he'd never endanger his health with a Covent Garden Miss. He knew Hawkes to be equally fastidious.

"Very well. You may be off." Quinn gestured. "Full report tomorrow afternoon."

Alone, the males eyed each other. Hawkes broke the silence. "Devere, how long have you known me?"

"Since Brasenose College, Oxford," responded Quinn promptly. "M'first year. Caught you in the buttery with that maid, what was her name?"

"Alice, or was it Angelique? Either way, she was an angel to me!"

"To you and anyone else with a Yellow Boy or two!" Quinn laughed and started down the lane.

"Have I ever given you cause to distrust me?"

Devere's brow wrinkled. " 'Course not. You're a gentleman, Hawkes, for all of your rackety ways."

"I'm rackety? I beg your pardon! I could take lessons from you, Devere!" Hawkes's cane tapped on the pavement as he walked.

"Nonsense! I learned my games at your knee, Will."

"I suppose we could concede we egged each other on. But back to my point. Devere, there's something devilish strange going on with your family, and I want to know what it is."

"With all respect, old man, how might it affect you?"

Hawkes paused.

Quinn stopped and looked at his friend, who wore an extremely serious expression.

"I have been given hope," Hawkes said.

"Aha!"

"I was pleased to be one of the party tonight. Surprised and pleased."

"Given the way you left, such a signal honor may not be repeated." Quinn continued down the street.

"Rest assured, Lady Anna's sensibilities will be soothed."

"Hmph. M'sister ain't easily gulled, Hawkes."

"I won't even try. The lady is clearly awake on all suits. Devere, between ourselves, I mean to offer for Miss Penrose when the time is right—when I feel she's ready."

Quinn didn't hesitate. "Hawkes, between ourselves, are you truly ready to marry? My niece deserves a loyal husband, not Wicked Willy."

The older man flushed. "I am quite aware of the romantic notions which fill the hearts of young girls. I must admit that, until I met your niece, I had never desired to become leg-shackled to anyone with such illusions. But Louisa—Louisa has changed everything."

"Hmph."

"But you understand my interest when I observe strange personages loitering about your family."

"Hmph."

"I have noted persons of a lower order lingering on not one, but two occasions."

"Hmph?"

"Two rather unattractive characters at Astley's, and again tonight."

"What of these rascals at the circus?" This was new news to Quinn.

Hawkes shrugged and tapped his stick against the curb of Great Queen Street. They crossed, walking at a brisk pace. "Two scurvy-looking rogues, talking thieves' cant about a 'dark-haired tib' accompanying a certain lord."

"Damn and blast!"

"I am glad you have engaged the Bow Street Runners. But what has any of this to do with the new Earl of Badham?"

"Hmph. Well, you seem to be more than halfway to discovering this business for yourself. I am well aware that a few guineas in the right quarter would reveal all to you in any event. You have become acquainted with my ward, Lady Katherine Scoville."

"No, I don't believe I've had the pleasure."

"Yes, you have. She was your dinner partner tonight, using the name of Kay Tyndale."

"Good Lord. I suppose she has a reason for such an outrageous imposture?"

Hawkes and Quinn crossed Russell Street.

"It was my idea," said Quinn, somewhat affronted.

"She is the granddaughter of old Badham, is she not? And she is going about in society using a false name? Scandalous, Devere!"

"Scandalous is better than dead, Hawkes, and I'll thank you for keeping my trust."

"Oh, no problem with that, milord." Hawkes waved his stick in the air. "What do you mean, *better than dead?*"

Quinn told him the whole story, ending with the shot which had been fired at the landau in Regent's Park.

"Good Lord," said Hawkes again. "Well, old boy, you can count on me to help keep the young lady safe. Though she won't ever be safe until she marries, will she? Until she is twenty-one and can make a valid will, her heir is Earl of Badham. Unless she marries, in which case her husband becomes her heir, who will also control her funds and properties."

"Yes, but until then, I am handling her affairs. Or, rather, my secretary is doing so."

"You have quite a task. Haven't you thought of marrying her yourself, Devere? She's a pretty little chit, nice manners, and wealthy besides."

Quinn found his teeth grating. "Marrying my own ward would hardly do me credit, Hawkes."

"Now, don't climb onto your high horse, milord Quinn." Hawkes chuckled. "It's just a suggestion, since that's the way the wind—er—blows."

"The role of father-protector comes uncertainly to me, Hawkes." Quinn grimaced.

The older man laughed. "Glad I'm not in your Hobys, Devere. Playing Papa to a lively child on the verge of her first Season!"

"Hmph."

"You'll be fighting suitors off, unless this imposture offends the *ton*."

"Hmph."

"People do not like to play the fool, y'know," advised Sir Willoughby. "Has she gone about much?"

"No, just a few family parties and select soirees. Nothing to speak of. The devil of it is, Willy, she's the only woman I've ever really thought of marrying."

"Don't see a problem with it, Devere."

"Unbecoming. People will think I've taken advantage of her."

Hawkes laughed. "Only if they've never met her! She's got a mind of her own, she does!"

"Very much so." They had arrived at the vicinity of Covent Garden, and Quinn cocked his head at Sir

Willoughby. "Hi-ho, sir," he said gaily, "I believe I'm off to a house or two to find Lord Herbert. Want to come along?"

Sir Willoughby smiled. "Wouldn't miss it for a sackful of Yellow Boys, old man!"

The Satin Covey was home to an assortment of street princesses who, while past their prime, were still sufficiently attractive as to command reasonable prices from such country squires and green cubs foolish enough to enter the premises. After passing through several hells and brothels, it was long past midnight when Quinn and Hawkes arrived at this particular one. An orgy was in full swing in the lavish formal drawing room of the mansion.

Stripped down to a singlet and stockings, a blindfolded female sprawled prone on a dais in the middle of the room. Two Corinthians, half-undressed, had paid for the privilege of making sport with her, impaling her fore and aft as she bucked. Couples lounged on sofas and chairs arranged in a circle around the show. Several elderly dandies had their trousers open as they fondled their cods, and one was serviced by the mouth of an older whore who knelt before him as he stood watching the trio on the dais.

"Can't see either of them," said Quinn. "Can you?"

"As I said, I'm not quite sure what the new earl looks like. I saw him only distantly at his investiture. You!" Hawkes gestured at an overpainted woman in a red dress trimmed with cheap black lace. He gave her a coin, which she bit. "There's more if you bring me the Earl of Badham."

She simpered. "It'll cost you more, sir, for that kind of sport. H'earls don't come cheap."

Quinn laughed out loud.

Hawkes looked gravely offended. "I don't want to rut with the man, merely to find him! We have business with him."

She stared at them, her painted eyes suddenly hard. "We all be doing business here, sir!"

She obliged him, nevertheless. It was but a few minutes until both Herbert and Osborn were brought by the abbess to the front hall, where Devere and Hawkes waited.

Herbert complained drunkenly at being disturbed at his pleasures, but stopped short and fell silent as he encountered the tall, frowning strangers in the front hall of the Satin Covey. Osborn was still tucking his shirt back into his trousers as he entered. Staring at him, Quinn felt physically ill. The thought of his Kate making love with—no, being raped by—that pimply, grubby queernabs was enough to turn his stomach. Small wonder she climbed out the attic window!

Burying his distaste, Quinn advanced. "Well met, Lord Badham."

"Don't believe we've met, sirrah!" Herbert blustered.

"We have had correspondence, I believe. I am Devere." Having assumed his most top-lofty manner, Quinn stared down his Roman nose at Herbert. He adjusted the cuffs of his black evening coat, which fit him as though it had been painted on. A fine fall of lace partially covered his elegant, gloved hands, and a ruby twinkled in his cravat. "We have a mutual interest. My ward, Katherine Scoville. Have you news of her?"

Herbert's eyes fell before the earl's bright, ironical gaze. "Lady Katherine is well and happy at Badham Abbey. My son and I have business to transact in the city at which her presence would not be appropriate."

"Business?" Lifting a brow, Quinn looked around the entry of the brothel.

"I was invested into my title just yesterday."

"An appropriate occasion for a visit by a young woman to the capital, I should think."

"What happens to Kate is not for you to say!"

Devere bent his brilliant eyes upon Herbert. "I beg your pardon, sir. I believe we were speaking of my ward."

"She is a most stubborn puss. She—er—declined to leave Wiltshire, professing her most complete happiness there."

"Truly?"

"Truly."

Devere invented hastily, "My correspondence has gone unanswered, Badham. Why is that?"

"Nothing to say to you, Devere."

Devere stiffened at the thinly veiled insult. "When Carrothers went to visit my ward, my secretary was denied admittance to Badham Abbey. Twice. Every gate was locked."

"A thousand pardons." Herbert bowed mockingly. "We have been plagued by, er, footpads. Should your secretary write to us in advance of his visit, we will be sure to make him most welcome."

"Thank you." Devere drew on his gloves. A footman jumped to open the door. Quinn tossed him a coin.

Herbert emitted a sigh which sounded suspiciously relieved.

Devere smiled. "One more item, Badham."

Herbert, on his way back to his doxy, stopped with a jerk.

"Should I ever find Lady Kate has been harmed, I will hold you personally responsible." Devere looked at a point about a foot over Herbert's head, then shifted his cold, dark gaze to Osborn; he then stared directly into the tubby peer's eyes. "Personally responsible. Do you understand?"

Herbert's jaw slid open.

A girl entered the room and giggled playfully at Herbert. "Come on, milord, let's 'ave a bit o' sport!" She trotted over and put her tongue into Herbert's open mouth.

The door closed with a click behind Devere and Hawkes as they stepped into the black London night.

Nine

The attic of the abbey was dusty, unlighted, and unheated. It was filled with myriad shadows. The moon rose, shedding its silvery, pale light into the attic through a narrow window. It shed weak but adequate illumination, outlining the contents: some of the more interesting detritus of deceased Scovilles, randomly scattered. The room was crowded with all kinds of furniture, from ancient commodes to the nude marble sculptures which had been the passion of the fourth earl; trunks there were a'many, filled with costumes and clothes of all styles and sizes.

Shivering with cold, Kate secured the rope she'd found to one of the upright bars of the window. She could see the flat gray slates of the second-story roof, three floors beneath her, glistening and slippery with frost in the moonlight.

Kate crawled through the window, and broke out into a light sweat despite the wintry weather. Though her palms were damp, her leather gloves retained their grip on the rope.

She pushed her boots against the abbey wall, then let out a small span of rope. Her boots slipped. She dangled helplessly, flailing at the end of the line, desperate to find purchase on the wall with the toes of her boots.

Kate awoke, her scream stopped in her throat as she remembered not to make a sound, lest she awaken the household. Her racing pulse steadied as she gulped deep breaths and recollected her location. She felt the featherbed enveloping her and swung her legs to the side of the bed. Her nightdress clung to her sticky body.

Hands shaking ever so slightly, she lit a candle; gas lighting, though it had been installed on nearby Pall Mall a few years before, still had not been introduced into this older mansion. She made her way to the window, then opened it. It had to be three or four in the morning, and the air of the early morn cooled Kate pleasantly.

A slight fog drifted over the street, touched by moonlight. It lay gently against the houses and trees without obscuring the view. Off down the street, Kate believed she could perceive the dim outline of two gentlemen staggering slightly as they made their way down the avenue.

Kate squinted, then remembered Bettina's many admonitions on the subject. She deliberately smoothed her brow as she strained to see the two roisterers, who sang an off-key, bawdy ditty as they wandered. They seemed familiar.

Kate suddenly realized she was surreptitiously watching her guardian and his friend as they made their way home after an evening of batching it. Grinning, she settled herself into a chair by the window to watch the show.

Their gestures were exaggerated by the effects of drink, and Kate could perceive the exact moment their attention was attracted by her candle gleaming through the open window. Two well-groomed heads turned as one. Hawkes pointed with his ever-present cane at her as they weaved toward the front gate.

"Good morrow, Kate, for that is your name, I

hear!" Both men burst into uproarious laughter as if the quip were original. Kate wished Quinn would quit teasing her with that silly, embarrassing play. Was she really such a shrew?

"Lady Katherine, your pardon for the appa—app—appalling conduct of my friend." Hawkes gestured with his stick, whacking it into the iron fencing.

Kate stared at Quinn. "You told him, my lord."

"C-couldn't help it, m'dear. He was halfway to guessing shomething shmoky was up."

"I was not halfway to guessing," Hawkes said. His deep baritone contrasted pleasantly with Quinn's lighter tenor voice. Sir Willoughby's intonation was more deliberate than usual. He visibly struggled to keep his dignity, although he was drunk as, well, as a lord—at least as drunk as the lord staggering down the street by his side. Kate restrained a giggle, knowing Hawkes loathed to be the object of female laughter.

He continued, "It was very smoky already, young lady. You are going to have to watch thy step!"

"Mind thy manners, or, ra-rather, thy Herberts!" Quinn chimed in.

"Walk carefully!" Hawkes thought he outdid his friend.

"Step on a crack, break your mama's back!" The gentlemen collapsed against the fence, roaring with laughter. Kate's brow crinkled. What was so bloody funny?

Quinn recovered himself. "Not—not to worry, sweet Kate. We bearded the old fellow in his lair. Foxed him perfectly, even if I do say so meself!"

"You appear to be the one who's foxed, my lord," said Kate.

Hawkes chuckled, poking Devere with his cane. "She's got you there, old boy!"

Quinn shoved the cane away. "Not jesting. Tricked Herbert finely, we did. Nothing to worry about, Katie. He told me you're still in Wiltshire."

"He must know I've left. It's been months!"

The gentlemen chortled as though she'd been very clever. "Told you she was a clever chit," said Hawkes to Quinn. "Alive on all suits, she is!"

"You see, he didn't want to admit he'd lost track of you," Quinn explained disjointedly. "And I surely di-didn't tell him I had you, so he had to pretend he knew what he was about. It was really rather funny, wasn't it, Hawkes?"

"He didn't think it was funny. I thought his eyes would fall out of his head when you threatened to kill him if anything happened to Lady Kate."

Kate raised her brows.

"I didn't say I'd kill him, precisely," Quinn protested.

"You made it clear enough when you said you'd hold him responsible for Kate's well-being."

"Yes, well, quite." Quinn waved his hand in the air. "So, Katie, there's nothing to worry your liddle head about anymore. Hawkes, I'm to bed! Nighty-night, sweet Kate!" He turned toward Berkeley Square.

Hawkes saluted Kate with his stick. Waving it in the air, he narrowly missed Quinn, instead striking himself on the head. He recovered quickly. Kate smothered her chuckle behind her hand as Hawkes rubbed his temple. "Lady Kate, we vow to porteck—protect you. I'll call tomorrow!"

Kate watched as Hawkes, swaying gently, followed Quinn down the lane. Blinking, she reviewed the conversation with her cupshot saviors. So, Sir Willoughby knew, did he? And they had tracked Uncle Herbert down and warned him off her?

Well, none of that was bad. The only bad part of it all was that Quinn remained firmly entrenched in his role as protector, not lover, despite his talk of "sweet Kate."

Kate returned to bed. As she blew out her candle, she reflected that all was not lost, could not be lost. Quinn and his friend had gone to a great deal of trouble for her. That meant something, didn't it?

The afternoon warmth heated Kate's skin where her bonnet did not shade her. The thin, low-cut muslin dress did little to protect her shoulders from the brilliant spring sunshine. She dashed through the maze at Hampton Court, laughing and breathless as she eluded the rest of the party. Quinn had promised a special prize for whomever of the young people reached the center of the maze first. *Whatever you want*, he had said, winking at Pauline when she wanted to know what the surprise would be. Kate was determined to be the recipient of the treat.

She wondered if she would dare to demand a kiss from Quinn.

Extending her left hand, she kept touching the side of the hedge. She had read that if the searcher kept to the left, always to the left, she or he would inevitably reach the center of the maze.

* * *

Accompanied by her second cousin, Ambrose Blakeney, Pauline trod sedately through the maze. Surprised by Pauline's slow pace, Louisa eyed her sister.

"Paul, are you feeling quite the thing?" she demanded.

After Uncle Quinn's generous offer, Louisa expected Pauline to race through the tall hedges. Pauline's unusually staid behavior concerned her older sister.

"I may have eaten too much or too quickly," Pauline said. "But, oh! What a lovely picnic!"

"Lord Devere did go all out." Bryan St. Wills followed them with Sybilla Farland. Her hand was tucked into his arm as they strolled, enjoying the lovely afternoon and the company.

"Ahem!" Sir Willoughby Hawkes coughed.

"Yes, quite." Louisa turned to regard her admirer. As the days had passed, she had become more comfortable and more familiar with the formerly somber baronet. He visited Bruton Street daily, turned the pages of her music as she played, drove with her in the park. Her parents seemed well content to permit the relationship to take its natural course. "You went to a great deal of trouble to have us admitted to some of the more private precincts of Hampton Court. Sir, we thank you most sincerely."

Hawkes bowed as the rest of the party courteously echoed her sentiments. But his mind must have been elsewhere. "Perhaps, Miss Pauline, you would feel better sitting in the landau for a while?"

"Oh no, no. I will be fine," Pauline assured him. "I just am not in the mood to rush around."

"Cousin Kate seems very eager to reach the center of the maze first, in any event. I wonder what she will demand of Uncle Quinn as reward." Louisa met Sir Willoughby's gaze and winked.

Hawkes's lips quivered. Sharp-eyed Louisa had no doubt seen what he also had noticed: Quinn and Kate were interested, very interested, in each other. Lou, however, did not yet know Katherine Scoville's secret. Hawkes wondered how Louisa would react to the deception.

They came to a branch in the path, and disagreed on the proper course. Louisa and Sybilla were convinced the correct way was to the left, while Ambrose and Pauline believed the route to the center was straight on. Hawkes, a veteran of several romantic interludes in the location, favored the right, but not because he wished to reach the center of the maze. He did not particularly wish to be accompanied by Bryan and Sybilla. Devere was nowhere to be found.

Quinn, armed in advance with a plan of the maze, now waited in the center for his quarry. Having seen the determined glint in his Kate's eyes, he knew she would find her way to the heart of the maze first.

He sat on a stone bench and wondered what she'd ask of him. He counted himself fortunate that Fashion now favored loose trousers rather than skin-tight, knitted pantaloons. The clear evidence of his emotions at the picnic had been disguised by his pants.

Kate had been subtly yet clearly flirtatious the entire day. Her pink sprigged muslin appeared to be worn over dampened petticoats. She met his eyes constantly, then let her dusky lashes sweep her flushed cheeks. She had even brushed against him once or twice as they toured Hampton Court Palace.

How on earth had she learned such wiles? And from whence? Quinn frowned. He'd have a great deal to say to this Elizabeth Telmont, of Miss Elizabeth's School in Bath, if they ever met. Whatever was she teaching her young ladies?

But he had to credit Katherine with discretion as well as coquetry. She had frequently taken the arm of her friend Sybilla Farland to giggle with her over some joke. Kate had sat next to Bryan St. Wills at the picnic, choosing to use her eyes and her smile rather than proximity to tempt her guardian. Quinn doubted anyone else knew the little witch was torturing his feelings, except perhaps for Willoughby Hawkes. The sharp-eyed rogue wouldn't miss the byplay, since he already knew Kate's identity as well as Quinn's desire for the girl. And if Hawkes knew, there was a fair chance Louisa knew also. Quinn didn't understand why Anna tolerated the growing intimacy between Hawkes and Louisa but, as it wasn't his business, he kept his nose out of the affair.

Affair. That was the word, wasn't it? He wanted to have an affair with his ward . . . or more.

His breath caught in his throat as Kate appeared at the gap in the hedge, then entered the center of the maze.

They were alone. A butterfly fluttered 'round the silk flowers on Kate's bonnet. She untied the ribbon beneath her chin, then sat down next to him on the narrow bench.

* * *

Bryan and Sybilla had broken off from the rest of the group at the next junction in the maze, but found themselves at a dead end. "Oh dear," remarked Sybilla placidly. "I fear we are lost." She turned to Bryan and smiled.

Louisa swallowed hard as Sir Willoughby Hawkes took her hand and led her into an isolated corner of the maze. Though greatly attracted by the rake, she now felt she had perhaps overstepped herself.

Pauline and Ambrose quarreled cheerfully about the route to the middle of the maze until they had actually made a complete circle of its rim and found themselves at the entrance.

"That's it," Pauline said. "My feet hurt in these wretched slippers, and I'm thirsty. Let's go back to the landau and see if there's any tea or lemonade."

Kate smiled at Quinn. "I believe I've won your prize, my lord."

"So what shall you demand of me, sweet Kate?"

She tipped her head to one side and regarded him, still flirting with her eyes, her smile. He could tell she was nervous, yet expectant. He did not know if he should encourage her.

"I'm not quite sure yet." She touched the tip of her tongue to her upper lip. "What do you have to give me, my lord?"

His voice rasped in his throat. "Quinn. Please, call me Quinn."

"My lord Quinn," she said, with just a trace of mocking good humor in her tone.

"Kate," he said, taking her chin gently between his long, strong fingers. She flinched slightly but did not pull away as he stroked her cheek. Her response rippled through her body as he drew her into his arms.

Yes. The first kiss was as sweet as he had known it would be. For a few moments, he forgot why he had denied his desire, and hers, for so long.

As he touched his lips to hers, it was as though a spark flashed between them, igniting their emotions. Their mouths caressed and danced. When his tongue sought admission, she did not refuse him entry. He groaned as his embrace tightened, pulling her onto his lap. She reached up, touching his shoulders, tentatively at first, then with more confidence as their kiss deepened. Her arms wound around his neck as he held her close. He could feel her breasts, barely confined by the flimsy muslin, pressing against his chest. Her heartbeat was quick as a rabbit's, and knowing she was excited aroused him all the more.

When they finally parted he regarded her with amazement. "My darling Kate. Where *did* you learn to kiss like that?"

She chuckled as she wriggled on his lap. He moaned as she unwittingly rubbed her backside against his erection. Good God, how he wanted her.

"Are you all right, Quinn?"

"I'm fine, sweetling, but let's move you back onto the bench for now." She shifted her weight, then let him entwine her fingers with his. He raised her hand to his lips and kissed each fingertip, then the back of her hand, appreciating the delicate interplay of bone and muscle. "That was not a rhetorical question. I am sure neither Aristophanes nor Homer discuss kissing in such detail."

"I am not entirely book-learned, sir. I have had some small contact with boys."

" 'Some small contact with boys'?" he repeated. "Need I be outraged, my ward?"

She laughed again. "I trust not, my guardian. The brothers of my schoolmates would occasionally visit Miss Elizabeth's, and I did steal a kiss or two."

"And how do I compare?"

"Ummm . . . very well, I must say. You exhibit natural talent as well as considerable experience, my lord."

"Oof!" Slapping his chest, Quinn affected a shot to the heart. "I suppose I deserved that."

"Completely. I felt for a moment you were questioning my virtue."

"Absolutely not. But you do exhibit natural talent as well as, um, some experience, my ward." He looked down at her and smiled.

She met his gaze without a flinch, lifting her mouth to his again. "Only *some* experience, I assure you." She broke off as they both heard shouts in the distance, followed by a rustle in the shrubbery.

Bryan and Sybilla dashed into the clearing, panting. "We're being followed! It's the oddest thing—" Bryan began to explain.

Both Kate and Quinn stood up as a shot rang out. Quinn grabbed Kate to force her down onto the ground beneath his body. Bryan protected Sybilla, whose aqua silk would never be the same after a tumble onto the damp grass.

Sir Willoughby Hawkes ran into the clearing. He brandished his unsheathed sword-cane in one hand.

His other arm was wrapped defensively around Louisa. Lou's hair was disheveled, and her mouth slightly swollen. Quinn was distracted by the thought that each couple appeared as though they'd had a delightful afternoon of dalliance, except for unexpected gunshots.

"What on earth is going on!" burst out Louisa. "Where are Pauline and Ambrose?"

"I don't know!" Quinn was deeply dismayed. "Let's get to the landau. Hopefully we'll find them on the way out."

"We should separate to search every corner," argued Bryan.

"No! We're stronger as a group," Hawkes said.

"Better listen to him," advised Quinn. "He did fight at Waterloo."

The rest of the party turned admiring eyes upon Sir Willoughby.

"You fought Napoleon?" Louisa sounded breathless.

Hawkes's lips thinned. "Yes, but this is not the time to discuss my past. Come, let's away."

Dragging her by the hand, he left the clearing. The others followed at a quick pace. They dashed out of the maze, encountering no one. Whoever had been responsible for the gunshot was gone.

As they left the maze, Quinn was astonished to see Ambrose and Pauline seated upon a blanket drinking tea as though nothing were amiss. Quinn's landau was close by. A footman dozed on the grass while the groom walked the horses.

"Oh, there you are," said Pauline. "Apple tart, anyone?"

The group rushed her en masse. "Did you see any-one leave the maze, Paul?" asked Quinn.

"No, Uncle Quinn, no one except that cully over there," said Pauline.

Ambrose gestured with his teacup at a shabby fig-ure in a greatcoat mounting a horse a distance away. The rider took off his tricorne and waved it at them with a flourish as he cantered down the lane toward Richmond.

When they returned to Bruton Street, Kate hauled Quinn into the library and rang for a footman. "Please request Sir Pen and Lady Anna to join us."

Quinn watched as she paced back and forth, back and forth. *What on earth does she have in mind?* When her host and hostess entered, she was blunt. "It's hap-pened again, and I must leave."

"What?" The Penroses stared at her, mystified.

Kate somehow managed to calm her breath. "There was another attack." Quinn began to demur, and she raised her hand and her voice. "No! Don't argue with the evidence of mine own eyes and ears, Lord Devere. I know what happened."

"Kate, be reasonable!"

"It's more important for my friends to be safe than it is for me to be reasonable."

"Where are you going to go? Where? Katherine, I am your guardian, and you shall do as I say!"

"How dare you put your family in danger!"

He brought down his fist onto the table, which jumped from the force of his anger. "No one is in danger and I demand you hear me out!" He calmed his voice. "Katherine, I have hired the Bow Street

Runners. Herbert and his cub are in Cornwall and what happened this afternoon has nothing to do with you! Stop believing you are the center of the world!"

She stared at him. Her eyes filled. "That's mean, Quinn."

"Will someone please explain what has happened today?" requested Pen. "Kay, I gather another untoward event has taken place."

She nodded, visibly miserable. Anna sat and pulled Kate down beside her, putting her arm around Kate's shoulders. Katherine lost her composure completely and began to sob in Anna's arms.

Anna looked up, glaring at Quinn. "Get out."

"But—but—" Quinn began.

"Quinn, get out. You've done enough."

Quinn turned. "I didn't do anything wrong," he muttered to Pen as they left the room.

His brother-in-law raised his brows as he led Quinn into the drawing room, and closed the doors. Pen poured a brandy, and handed it to Quinn. "When the ladies turn on the faucets, my boy, it's best to leave them to their own devices. What steps have you taken to safeguard your ward?"

"I warned Badham off her, while convincing him I didn't know where she is."

"A fancy trick. How do you know they were persuaded?" Pen poured for himself.

"I put the Runners onto them. They have been followed to Cornwall, to Lady Kate's holdings there. Apparently the Gillender tin mines in Cornwall are the only properties they have not checked for her presence."

"When did they leave?"

"Wednesday, late."

"Four days ago. It isn't likely that they'd be back in London for two or three more days," mused Pen. "You are right, this attack must be from another quarter. But who?"

Kate cried for awhile, feeling guilty and wretched. When she finally emerged from Anna's embrace, she looked at the older woman's face. Kate was surprised to see a tender, maternal smile.

"Don't you blame me for putting everyone in danger?"

"My dear Kate, this is absolutely not your fault. Quinn is right in this instance," Anna said tranquilly. "He is your guardian and you must do as he says. Go to your room and wash your face, and you and Quinn will discuss what should be done."

Kate faced Quinn with no pretense of equanimity. Her fingers plucked the fabric of her skirt as she paced across the room. "My lord, it appears we are at an impasse."

Quinn leaned against the mantel above the library fireplace and moodily kicked at the carved marble trim decorating the hearth.

"I would not have you so angry with me, Katherine," he said at length. "Please accept my most sincere apology."

"No, it was I who was at fault, my lord. You are my guardian and it is my obligation to do as you deem fit."

He raised his head. "Such meekness is not characteristic of you, sweet Kate. What have you in store for me?"

She eyed him and frowned. "You are very suspicious. I am merely trying to make amends for my lack of appropriate gratitude and courtesy."

"You are capable of anything. I hope your surprise will be pleasant, like your kiss, rather than like the frogs in my bed."

"The least you could do is accept my apology."

He smiled. "Let us say, then, we treated each other cruelly, and resolve to be more kind in the future."

"As you wish." She inclined her head. "However, I remain concerned for my safety and that of your family."

He waved his hand in the air. As usual, she was charmed by the useless, silly gesture. "All is being done that can be done, Lady Kate."

"And yet, we are endangered." She paced. "I have a solution."

He frowned. "Here it comes."

She glared at him, then plunged forward. "The other afternoon, you suggested I marry. My lord, you are right. Married, my property and my person belong to my husband, and he would become my heir. I would cease to be a target for Herbert or Osborn."

"I thought you had determined not to marry as yet." His voice was cold.

She touched her tongue to her upper lip. *I had no idea this would be so difficult,* she thought. *Small wonder men talk to a woman's parents first!*

"Marry me, Quinn."

"What!"

"It's the perfect answer," she argued hurriedly. "You already have control over my person and my fortune, and you've proven yourself trustworthy with both."

"Kate, you've got bats in your belfry! I'm not going to let you throw yourself away—"

"That's a nice way to think of yourself!"

"Well, you've got a nice way of thinking of marriage!"

"I'm trying to take a practical approach."

"Practically speaking, Kate, you're not even out yet. 'Twould never work!"

She gulped. "Is there someone else?" She managed to ask.

Innocent and unsophisticated, perhaps her kiss had disappointed experienced Quinn. She remembered again the gossip passed along by Sybilla Farland: *Your guardian has a bit of a reputation with the ladies . . . he's known to be quite the Corinthian . . .* And wasn't he interested in that redhead, Staveley?

"Of course there's no one else! What kind of man do you think I am? Would I have kissed you this afternoon if there were someone else?"

"I don't know, Quinn, would you?"

"Kate, stop it, just stop it!" Quinn raked at his hair with both hands.

Her voice weakened as she realized he wouldn't say yes, would never say yes. "Don't you want me?"

"Not want you?" He stared at her with disbelief writ large on his lean countenance. "Not want you?" He uttered a shaky laugh. "What place does simple desire have in the practical arrangement you propose? Good God, Kate, can't you see how impossible this is?"

"No, I don't."

"Katherine, I will not allow you to marry me or

anyone else only because you feel terrorized by Lord Badham. That is my final decision on the matter," he informed her. "Pray do not raise the subject again."

She sat down, entirely crushed and defeated. She buried her face in her hands. "Yes, my lord."

"You will stay in this house until Pen and Pauline return to Kent," he stated curtly. "You will go to Sevenoaks with them. Until then, you will not leave this house at all, *at all*, do you understand? Unless I am with you."

He slammed out of the room and the house with nary a word to anyone, brushing past his sister and her husband without a remark.

Anna and Pen stared at each other as Quinn left. Anna finally broke the silence. "I have never before observed my brother to behave quite so badly."

"That is true." Pen nodded.

"He is usually the pattern-card of propriety."

"Yes."

"And congenial, besides."

"Yes, Quinn's a fine fellow."

"My brother has always been sweet-natured."

"Well, they must be in love," Pen said. "Only people in love argue so."

Kate felt like a prisoner in the Bruton Street house after only a few days. She heard news of the outside world from a distance as if she were Napoleon on Elba. She initially chafed at the isolation, as she was angered by Quinn's arrogant manner of arranging her life without so much as a by-your-leave. But later she found she didn't mind the seclusion, as it gave her an opportunity to think.

She spent many hours in the library or the back garden, pretending to read, while reliving the events of the day at Hampton Court.

His kiss had felt so good, and so right. Once committed, there was not a trace of reluctance in Quinn's hands or mouth; his skill had been a revelation to sheltered Kate, who had heretofore been the recipient of only shy pecks from her few male admirers. He was tender and sweet, yet as exciting as a summer storm.

Kate had surrendered completely, letting Quinn sweep her into previously unknown regions of bliss. She knew then she had been made for this man. Her mouth fitted his exactly, her body had slid onto his lap with nary a gap between them as they sought to grow closer. Shafts of exhilaration had shot through her being as he darted his tongue between her lips, over and over, in a seductive mirror of the mating dance. Kate's insides had melted as his skilled mouth beguiled her.

She remained confused and devastated by Quinn's rejection. His rebuff had come so closely on the heels of that scorching kiss, which had blazed a trail straight to her heart, while opening a whole new world of pleasure. Kate now craved his touch as much as her heart needed his love. The memory of his tongue easing into her mouth was enough to spark the most romantic dreams. Recalling his tender embrace encouraged yet bewildered Kate. How could he touch her in that manner if he didn't care? And if he cared, why had he become so very angry when she'd suggested marriage?

Katherine's early assessment of Devere underwent a radical change. Just as a child sees an elder only as an authority figure, she had not previously appreciated the depths of his character. She had viewed him merely as another amiable, good-humored fribble. He had taken care of her business by referring matters to his secretary, and gone about his fashionable life without a misstep.

The day at Hampton Court had been profoundly enlightening on several levels. Kate now understood a part of Quinn's intensity. There was nothing of the frivolous fop when he took her chin in his hand and claimed what was undeniably his. She vaguely understood that his code of honor prevented him from demanding more, even when it was offered freely.

She still clung to the slight hope he gave: There was no one else, and he was not sure if he wanted her or not; but, then, why had he kissed her? Maybe kisses were a cheap stock to milord Devere.

Kate rubbed the back of her hand over her lips, as if to erase her memory of the heavy, seductive weight of Quinn's mouth taking hers. She didn't succeed, couldn't succeed. He lived in her heart as though he were a tree which had taken sturdy root in a garden.

Ten

Two days later, the entire family went to Vauxhall Gardens, the last of the treats which had been promised to Pauline. After boating over the Thames, they met Devere and Hawkes at Vauxhall just as darkness fell. They arrived in time to see all the delights of the gardens at dusk, and then to experience Vauxhall at night.

Deliriously happy, Pauline sat in a box with her family, imbibing the Tyers' famous burnt wine and thinly shaved ham. Louisa and Kate were similarly diverted, but consumed with less abandon than did Pauline. The young women were occupied with examining the fashions of the throngs that crowded the famous pleasure gardens, and gossiped happily about the ensembles worn by the ladies who showed themselves off on the promenade. Quinn acted as host, genially ensuring that all the needs and desires of the party were met. He nodded and smiled at various passersby, as his acquaintance in London was vast, and he was well liked.

Pen and Anna kept a casual eye on their daughters and exchanged many speaking glances.

"Bring back memories?" Kate asked.

Anna smiled. "We did court here. There is something about the lighting at Vauxhall."

Kate gazed at the myriad tiny lanterns with which the trees and shrubbery at Vauxhall were lavishly decorated. "It is very romantic."

Anna eyed Sir Willoughby. "We shall have to watch the lot of you closely in Vauxhall."

They had seen the cascade, and eagerly awaited the fireworks, when Pauline groaned, clutching her stomach. "I am not feeling quite the thing," she whimpered.

Her mother examined her. Pauline's eyes were glassy and she swayed slightly in her chair. "How many glasses of punch did you take, my dear?" Lady Anna asked.

"I am not sure," whispered Pauline. "I was very hot, and now I'm tired and dizzy and sick and I want to go home!"

Her sister stared at her in dismay. "Go home! Before the fireworks! Whoever heard of such a thing!" cried Louisa.

Quinn took his niece's hand. "Pauline, dear, would you like to come up in my landau? Perhaps a spot of fresh air will make you right and tight again, hmmm?"

Anna said, "Thank you, Quinn. If she's not feeling better, mayhap you can take her home, and we will return after the fireworks."

Pauline's eyes teared. "But I so want to see the fireworks!"

"There'll be other times, I promise," said her father. "Just now, you should go home if you are not feeling well." He cast a worried eye over her flushed countenance and pressed a handkerchief to her forehead. She took it, dabbing at her tears as Quinn opened the door of the box.

"Do you want me to come with you, Paul?" Kate asked. She slipped her hand into the younger girl's.

"Don't you want to see the fireworks?"

"We'll come to Vauxhall again. I'm tired, too. I'll make you a hot posset when we get home."

Kate struggled to cling to Pauline's hand as they fought their way after Quinn toward the exit through the crowd. It seemed as though most of the visitors to Vauxhall were bound in the opposite direction, so walking to the exit put Kate in mind of salmon swimming upstream. Kate, who walked on one side of Pauline, felt Paul's arm slip from her grasp as she was jostled by the throngs.

Suddenly, Kate was alone. Where were Pauline and Quinn? They had been directly next to her, but now she couldn't see anyone or anything familiar.

Kate walked on, peering down this path and that, seeking her friends through the shrubbery. One passage looked greatly like another as the night deepened.

The fireworks were magnificent, and shortly thereafter, the Penroses returned to Bruton Street. After changing into her wrapper, Lady Anna went to Pauline's room to check on her welfare.

One candle was still lit in Pauline's cozy bedroom, hung with pink curtains and white lace. Her maid had changed Pauline into a night rail, and she lay in bed, drowsy.

Anna passed a hand over her daughter's forehead. "How do you feel, my sweetling?"

Pauline stirred. "Better. Where is Kay? She said she'd make me a posset."

Anna's heart chilled. "Didn't she come home with you and your uncle?"

"No. We supposed that she changed her mind and went back."

Anna raced to Kate's room, finding it dark and empty. Her scream ripped the night before she realized it had left her throat.

"Pen! Pen! Oh, my God! Kate!" Her husband rushed in and wrapped his arms around his trembling wife.

"Nan! Where's Kate?"

"I don't know! I thought Quinn brought her home, but she's not here."

Louisa, disturbed by the shouts, dashed into the room. "What is it?"

"We don't know where Kay is." Anna pulled from Pen's embrace and walked jerkily back and forth. The fine silk of her dressing gown crumpled between her fingers.

"Shall I send a message to Uncle Quinn's residence, or go over with a footman to see if he's home?" asked Louisa. " 'Tis just a few steps."

"No!" Anna screamed. She clutched Louisa's arm. "Don't any of you go out of my sight!"

Kate struggled to consciousness through wads and layers of fuzz, which seemed to have grown in her brain to vastly cloud her thinking. She heard voices, as if from a distance. As she came to, the voices sharpened until they seemed to pierce right through her mind.

The voices were male. Other sounds intruded:

coach wheels grinding on a graveled road, the shouts of a coachman.

The lurching of the coach made Kate sick and queasy, but she managed to sit up, rigid with outrage. She'd been caught entirely unawares and had taken a nasty cosh on the head. A foul-smelling rag clapped over her mouth and nose had completed the job. Ether, she supposed. *Thank God Pauline is safe with Quinn,* she thought. *But what on earth is this about?*

The coach rumbled to a stop. Its door opened, allowing a lantern's gleam to shaft into her prison. The light jabbed into her eyes. She rubbed the backs of her hands over them as they adjusted to the changing illumination. Her detestable Uncle Herbert pushed into view, accompanied by her Cousin Osborn.

Absence hadn't made Kate's heart grow any fonder. She looked at them with loathing. "I assure you, you'll catch cold if I'm not returned to London at once!"

Dressed in dark clothing appropriate for an abduction, the tubby peer smirked. "Talking tough now, Lady Katherine. We'll see how your tune changes when you're married to my son."

Kate remained untroubled by the threat. "I do not see how that can happen. I cannot marry until I am of age without my guardian's consent."

Herbert leaned back into the coach's tufted squabs. Kate noted irrelevantly that the leather of the seat was cracked and scratched. Mayhap it was a hired vehicle. Herbert said, "I think after this night's work you shall not hesitate to marry Osborn. Your reputation will be in tatters. No one, despite the size of your fortune, will marry spoiled goods."

Kate erupted into an angry tangle of fists and kicks. She shot out of the coach before either Herbert or Osborn could stop her. 'Twas still nighttime, and a soft rain fell. Kate tumbled out of the coach, landing ignominiously into a mud puddle. As resourceful as any heroine from Mrs. Radclyffe, she grabbed handfuls of mud and cast the muck into the surprised faces of her uncle and her cousin. As they shouted in pain—she had hit their eyes—she scrambled back under the wheels of the coach.

She hoped desperately that the horses would stay still, and that there would be an escape route on the other side of the coach.

Kate burst out from beneath the coach and ran. Muddy and bedraggled, she crashed full tilt into an older fellow dressed in rough clothing. Though he was a scarred, rascally looking chap, Kate was not inclined to be choosy at this time. She grabbed his sleeve. "Get me to London. My guardian will pay you well!"

He looked at her dispassionately, gripping her by the back of the neck of her gown. "I say, milord, I believe you've misplaced a certain baggage." Before she could run, he'd grabbed her arm to pitch her back into the coach.

"We'll have to tie her up." Osborn used a grubby kerchief to wipe mud from his face.

Kate didn't like the gleam in his eye. "Touch me and I'll kill you, you misbegotten, poxed whoreson!"

He laughed. "I'll enjoy taming you, darling Kate."

"I'm not your darling, and you can call me Lady Katherine."

"When we're married I'll teach you to keep a civil

tongue in your head. I'll put the crop to your back if I must."

"How dare you? You'll be dead first." Kate had no doubt that her guardian would find her. Her Quinn was more than a match for ten Herberts and twenty Osborns.

"I'll be master over my wife, I will!"

"You'll be master of nothing!"

Herbert intervened. "Tie her up and gag her, son. We'll be traveling through a few villages yet, and we can't have her crying out for help."

Thrusting the same muddy cloth he'd used to wipe his face into Kate's mouth, Osborn used his cravat to tie it around her head as Herbert and the hired tough tried to hold her down. Kate landed a solid kick in her uncle's substantial breadbasket. He fell back with an "oof," but her kicking and scratching were to no avail. In just a few moments, Kate, trussed like a bird destined for the oven, lay helpless in the hired coach.

Devere arrived on Anna's doorstep long after midnight, tortured by a devil's brew of guilt and fear. Where was his Kate? How could he have let her slip through his protective net?

The Penroses' house, brightly lit, shone like a beacon to draw him down Bruton Street at this late hour. Devere rapped at the door, which was answered not by the butler, but by Louisa, who flung herself into his arms. He hugged her tightly and kissed her on the top of her head.

"Come." She pulled him into the house. "We're all in the drawing room."

"Ah," said Pen, as Devere entered. "We wondered when you would appear. Tea?"

"Brandy," said Quinn, as he strolled to the sideboard. He couldn't stop a slight quiver from disturbing his hand as he poured. "Anyone join me?"

He looked 'round the room as he dabbed at his eyes with a handkerchief. Pauline huddled beneath a large shawl at one corner of a sofa. Anna sat nearby. Louisa and Hawkes decorously occupied wing chairs near the piano.

Quinn wedged himself between Anna and Pauline.

"I imagine that you've been sitting here, wallowing in guilt," he said to Pauline.

" 'Twas I who let her hand go," she whispered.

Quinn sighed. "This mull isn't your fault."

"What mull?" asked Pauline. "Everyone's been mysterious all night. 'Tis very rude."

Quinn wrapped his arm around his niece. "Pauline, I have a confession to make."

Pauline stared.

"Pauline, Kay isn't your cousin. She's my ward, Lady Katherine Scoville. She lived with you as our cousin at my behest, with your parents' full knowledge. I believe that tonight she was abducted at the order of her uncle, Lord Herbert Scoville, Earl of Badham."

"Good God, Quinn!" Anna gasped.

The males sat, unmoved. Apparently this possibility had already occurred to Pen and Hawkes, Quinn decided, for neither looked surprised by his statement.

Louisa, however, looked puzzled. "But I still don't quite understand. All right, I knew something was smoky as soon as Cousin Kay turned up in Kent, but why the abduction? Why the charade?"

"Well, it was the money, of course," explained Quinn. "Their part of the family spent all theirs, and they wanted Lady Kate's. They wanted to get it by marrying her to her appalling cousin. Her uncle imprisoned her, hoping I'd agree to the marriage. When she escaped, I hid her with us."

Louisa nodded with understanding, but Pauline had been glowering at her sister. "You knew? And you didn't tell me?"

"There was nothing to tell! I just suspected a hum, that's all," said Louisa. "You know how Uncle Quinn is with his jokes, and how often does he happen by with pretty girls on his arm?"

Pauline considered, her elfin face grim. "Never," she finally said. She looked around the room, surveying the faces of the adults, none of whom met her eye. "Do you mean to say I'm the only one who didn't know?" Her voice rose with outrage as she jerked away from Quinn and stood up.

Quinn spoke nervously. "Pauline, believe me, it isn't as though I didn't trust you, but I wanted to keep it as quiet as possible—"

Pauline continued as though Quinn had never spoken. "Well, that's just devilish fine!" She burst into tears and ran from the room.

Quinn rubbed his forehead. He'd rather shoot himself than hurt Pauline. "What a bloody awful mess!"

Anna rose. "Quinn, there's no use crying over spilt milk. What's done is done. It is clear you will be traveling on the morrow, so go home to bed."

"On the morrow? Absolutely not. I ride tonight. Hawkes, are you with me?" Quinn cocked his head at his friend.

"Certainly. But where will they have gone?"

"There are three possible destinations. Either they will take her to Gretna, to make a hasty marriage. Or they may take her to Wiltshire to find an unscrupulous cleric, possibly the one who owes his position at the abbey to Badham. The third possibility is that they will try to spirit Kate to France."

Hawkes stood. "I'll ride south. It's likely they'll try to get her out of the country, away from English law, at the earliest possible time."

"I'll ride north. I shall have to kill Badham, of course," said Quinn, in the same tone of voice he might use to discuss the weather. "I'll shoot the cub also, if I can find him. Pen, Hawkes, will you second me?"

"Of course." Hawkes said promptly.

Quinn tossed off the rest of his brandy. "Pen, will you send a footman 'round to Bryan St. Wills's lodging? I am sure he will wish to ride to Badham Abbey to find Katherine, if Badham attempts to take her there."

"I should go," Pen said.

"Not at all. Please stay in London and inform Bow Street of these events. Badham and his spawn bed at Limmer's. There is the chance that they remain here to obtain a special license so that cub can wed my Kate. It is improbable, but we cannot overlook any possibility."

The night, cool and clear, was perfect riding weather. *Perfect driving weather, also, blast it,* thought Quinn. He couldn't drag his mind away from a vision of his Katherine, hurt or raped by that pimply Captain Queernabs of a cousin. Rage coiled like a poisonous snake in his belly—an unaccustomed feeling, but Quinn found that it stiffened his resolve. He urged his horse onward, winding it, then replaced his mount at Barnet.

With luck he'd catch up with them at some time the next day. He assumed that Herbert, with his pockets to-let, couldn't afford the finest coach or horses. Badham therefore couldn't travel faster than five or six miles hourly. Quinn, with an abundance of ready cash, bespoke the fastest horse in every village through which he passed, changing mounts often.

The next day dawned warm and sultry. Quinn rode coatless, with his cravat undone; fashion be damned in his quest for Kate.

Beyond the environs of London, the country cleared and flattened into gently rolling fields, covered with grass and wildflowers. Sniffing the late morning air, Quinn cocked an eye at the sky. They were in for a storm. He hoped his horse, a chesty gray he'd rented in Huntingdon, wouldn't toss him off when the storm broke.

The first crack of lightning split the sky with a stunning white pitchfork. Rain began to fall in torrents. The skittish mount shied at the lightning and thunder, rearing. Clenching his thighs against the horse's heaving sides, Devere controlled its temper, then whacked the crop on its flank. The gray settled down into a steady, if swift, canter.

Kate realized that the close, humid weather had one great compensation: Both Herbert and Osborn preferred travel outside the coach, leaving her alone.

After she'd headbutted Osborn that morning when he'd tried to kiss her, they'd left her in peace. The sight of blood streaming down his face from his nose more than compensated for the lack of breakfast.

Hungry, but happy with the morning's work, Kate struggled to loosen the knotted rope confining her hands. Tied in haste, the knots would surely come loose. She hadn't dared to try last night, when Herbert and Osborn also occupied the coach, but she'd chased them away and had the day to free herself.

It was midmorning when her wrist tugged out of its bonds. Releasing the other, she tied the rope into two loose loops, sliding them back over her hands. Until certain of her escape, she dared not let her captors know she was free. She bent to untie her ankles as she heard the boom of summer thunder. The flash of lightning illuminated the interior of the coach through its spotted panes.

Rain thrummed, heavy and hard, on the roof as Kate pulled at the rope restraining her feet. The carriage lurched alarmingly, and its speed began to pick up. Good God! Had the coachman lost control of the horses? Kate had traveled enough to know the difference between a well-trained coach-and-four and a team that had kicked over its traces and was now bound hell-for-leather toward whatever fate might await it.

Kate clung to a strap inside the coach, praying. For one dizzy, nauseating moment the coach trembled, as if swaying on the edge of an abyss, then tipped and fell, flooding with mud and rainwater.

She cried out in fear, remembering her parents' demise. *Is this how it all ends, then?* Frantic, Kate tore at the rope binding her ankles, desperate to escape.

The cries of the tough who'd captured her could be heard from outside the vehicle, along with shouts and whines from Herbert and Osborn. Each seemed to be engaged in blaming the other for the accident.

She had to get out. This chance might be the only one. The rope around her feet came loose. Kate leaped for the door of the coach, then stopped. An inner voice counseled caution, so she peeked out of a window to make sure of an escape route.

Aha. They were, indeed, arguing amongst themselves. Even better, Kate could see the hireling on the ground, clutching his ankle as though he'd been hurt. The coach had fallen into a ditch, which accounted for the mass of mud and rainwater which drenched the floor of the coach. Kilting up her long, dirty skirts, Kate climbed out of the coach by way of the door, which now tilted toward the dark, wild sky. She crawled over the top and 'round the other side, away from the quarreling trio.

But which way? Keeping the coach between herself and her kidnappers, she set back down the road. Kate hoped that the way they'd come was the way she wished to go: back to London and safety.

A gray horse, shining with rain and exertion, came into view from 'round a curve with a rider on its back. Kate began to run. She didn't know who the unknown rider might be but she felt certain that someone, anyone, would be better than the company of Badham and his equally bad offspring.

She heard shouts behind her.

"Hi! Where are you going, you witch's brat!" Herbert screamed. "Osborn! Where's your pistol?"

"I'll beat you 'til you bleed!" Osborn cursed.

Kate ran faster, seeking to put the overturned

coach between herself and Osborn's pistol. The chap
on the gray pulled up his horse. Snorting, the beast
flung clumps of foam from its mouth. Clearly it had
been overridden, thought Kate critically. The poor
creature was completely blown. She hoped that its
rider didn't expect to go much farther that afternoon.

The outlines of the rider's whipcord body were exposed, the rain and wind flattening the linen to his
muscular torso. As he controlled his mount, he
reached into a saddlebag. Withdrawing a pistol, he
flourished it at the sky.

Dear Lord! A highwayman! Kate dashed to the side
of the road. Perhaps she could hide in the bushes.
With luck, he'd be after Herbert, and leave her alone.

But no luck. "I'll fetch you later," the highwayman
called to Kate before he rode toward the coach.

"Badham, you bastard, name your seconds!"

She knew that voice. For a dazed moment, Kate's
brain froze, then connected all the dots. It was
Quinn! His red hair, dark from the rain, clung to his
skull. He controlled his restive steed with one hand
while he threatened her captors with the pistol, looking more like a champion of old than the amiable
dandy she knew. Hatless and coatless, he bore no resemblance to the careless rake who'd haunted her
dreams these last months, but Kate had no doubt that
her guardian had come to rescue her.

Osborn's pistol banged, startling Kate, who
shrieked in fear and surprise. The gray reared,
screaming, and dumped Quinn into the mud.

Quinn twisted, lifted his pistol, and shot Osborn,
winging him through the shoulder. Kate could see
her cousin's body jerk from the impact of the shot,

then fall to the muddy road. Her uncle flung himself over to his son, attempting to support him as Osborn's shoulder bled, a bright patch of red in an otherwise somber, stormy scene.

His horse ran wild down the road as Quinn picked himself up and approached Kate. He tenderly flicked a strand of wet hair off her cheek. "Are you all right, sweetling?"

She nodded, not trusting herself to speak or move without bursting into tears from sheer fear, excitement, tension, and love. Grim-faced, he turned away from her and strode to Herbert and Osborn, tugging off a glove as his boots squished in the mud.

" 'Pon my word, Herbert Scoville," drawled Quinn. "Fancy seeing you. Taken to kidnapping helpless chits, have we?" He backhanded Herbert on the mouth. "Four days hence at dawn, Parliament Hill, Hampstead Heath. Name your seconds to Hawkes and Penrose."

Herbert coughed and spat teeth.

Quinn walked back to Kate. "The nearest village is a place called Cambermorne. I believe there is an inn. Shall we?" He offered her his arm.

Fortunately, the only inn in Cambermorne appeared to be clean and well run, thought Devere, as he and Kate trudged the last few yards of the quarter-mile between the overturned carriage and the Cambermorne Crossing Inn. He turned to Kate. Despite her hat, rain dripped off her nose. Her hair hung in sodden whips around her damp cheeks. Though wet and bedraggled as a drowned kitten, she still carried herself with aplomb, as if she were walking down Bond Street after a pleasant visit to the milliner.

"I'll bespeak rooms for the night," he said. "I'll send word to London, and they'll send a coach for us in the morning."

"Very well." Her voice was surprisingly calm.

He looked at her again. Water dripped off her bonnet. The hem of her dress was muddy from the walk. *Her silly little slippers are probably destroyed,* he thought. Still, he admired her for her fortitude. She had not once voiced any complaint. "Let's find you a hot bath."

They entered the small but well-appointed inn. Quinn arranged for a private parlor with two separate rooms flanking it. Darkness was falling. Quinn assured himself of Kate's comfort and sent messages to London before he took his own rest.

Eleven

Kate saw nothing that would cast doubt upon the claim that the innkeeper's wife had previously been employed as a housekeeper to a viscount in London. That dame took charge of Katherine's soiled dress and muddy slippers, saying they'd be dried in front of a fire, brushed, and returned to Lady Katherine in a trice. In the meantime, Kate relaxed in the hip-bath of hot water which was brought to her room. She found everything she needed for her comfort in the cozy lodging.

Shaky from lack of food, she welcomed the dinner of roast capons and a humble but hearty shepherd's pie of minced meat, vegetables, and potatoes. The unaccustomed exercise had engendered healthy appetites. Kate and Quinn washed down their meal with a couple of bottles of good burgundy.

Kate's hand quivered as she lifted her glass. "To you, dear guardian."

"My sweet Kate. You deprive me of my wine. Surely you are aware that it is the height of incivility to drink to oneself?"

She laughed. She'd been afraid that the circumstances would have shattered their easy camaraderie, but she couldn't remain nervous around Quinn. "To the destruction of bad Lord Badham!"

He lifted his glass. "May all scoundrels perish. Are you sure that you took no harm from this escapade, my ward?"

"Quite sure. Actually, the worst for me was the coach accident." She went silent, looking at the wine in her crystalline glass, lit to a brilliant ruby red by the fire.

"Why so?"

Tears prickled behind her lids. She blinked to dispel them. "Do you not know about my parents? They died in a carriage accident such as the one this afternoon."

"My dear Kate." Reaching across the table, he pressed her hand. "No, I wasn't aware of the circumstances of your parents' passing. My most sincere condolences. So, even climbing into a coach is, for you, a courageous act?"

She shook her head. "I know that such mishaps are few and far between, sir. But today . . . today, with so many strikes against me, I was sure all was lost. I knew from the condition of the interior of the coach that my uncle hadn't hired the best steeds or a sturdy vehicle. I feared the worst. And then you came."

"Just doing my duty." His voice was casual.

"I knew you'd rescue me. I told them you'd kill them, but they didn't believe me."

"They should have." Quinn's voice was grim. "But Katherine, I'm no medieval knight riding to your rescue. I made a terrible mull of it."

"I don't agree. All could have been lost. But we're here, we're happy and unhurt."

"It's like you to be generous, Kate, but please accept my apology. I discounted your concerns. It turned out that you were right."

Kate shrugged. It wasn't in her to press the point. "All's well that ends well, then," she said. She sipped the last of her wine, setting the empty glass onto the table. "Good night, Quinn."

After using the inn's small necessary, Kate retreated to her bedroom. The bed, covered by a clean, handmade quilt, was turned down invitingly. A fire blazed in the small hearth. After she changed into a nightdress provided by the landlady, Kate climbed into bed.

As tired as she was, sleep eluded her. After tossing and turning fruitlessly for what seemed like forever, Kate sat up. Wasn't there a decanter of brandy on the sideboard of their parlor? Perhaps a tot of cognac would soothe her nerves.

Kate fretted about her appearance, but concluded that even though she was clad only in a thin night rail, the odds were slender she'd meet anyone. She opened the door that connected her bedroom to the parlor.

The fire in the parlor had burned down low. The rain had stopped, and the open casement windows admitted silvery moonlight into the room. The round wooden table where she and Quinn had dined had been emptied of the remains of their meal and cleaned; nary a crumb interrupted its polished surface. A decanter of brandy sat on a salver on the table, but only one snifter was placed nearby.

Katherine trod quietly into the room. She didn't want to disturb Quinn if he had fallen asleep. She picked up the decanter. As she poured, the door to Quinn's room opened.

He stepped into the parlor with an empty brandy

snifter in his hand. He stopped short when he saw her, then put the glass down on the table.

He was clothed only in his breeches. His hair was slightly damp. She guessed he had removed his coat, cravat, and shirt before washing.

He was beautiful. The moonlight turned his shapely limbs into living marble. The chiseled white plane of his torso attracted Kate as though she were iron, and it a powerful lodestone. His flat male nipples were dark nubs on his chest, which was decorated with a wiry bed of hair, silvery in the moonlight.

Kate moved toward Quinn as though pushed by some mysterious, inexorable force. She slid her fingers through those fascinating curls, rubbing their coarseness between curious fingertips.

When he finally spoke, his voice was husky, as though his tongue were thick in his mouth.

"Kate. What are you doing here?"

She stroked her fingers in and out of the curls, then flattened her hand over his chest. The warmth of his flesh belied his resemblance to a perfect Greek statue. With tender absorption, she watched his nipples rise. She almost forgot to breathe.

"I wanted some brandy." She continued to caress his torso, watching it lift and fall as his breath quickened. "Why are you here, Quinn?"

He swallowed. She saw his Adam's apple bob convulsively as he sought the right words.

"I came to kiss you good night." He bent his head and touched his lips to hers.

With unspoken understanding, they both kept their eyes open as their mouths melded into one sensual being, with but one purpose.

Hot chocolate. Quinn's brown eyes were hot

chocolate, his mouth as sweet as the promise in his deep gaze. Their bodies merged, and for the first time, Kate felt her lover's manhood pressing hotly against her belly through the thin cloth of her nightgown. Her flesh leapt in response to his desire.

Quinn broke away. "Kate, I must know," he whispered.

She looked at him, her heart in her throat.

"Kate, are you sure?" He bent his burning gaze upon her again. "Are you sure you want this, want *me*, as part of your life, forever?"

She took his hands in both of hers. "Quinn—I'm yours. Forever." Would he ever understand the depth of her need for him?

He smiled at her suddenly, like the sunlight piercing through clouds. "Why, then, let's to bed." Taking her by the hand, he led her into her bedroom.

Kate did not know quite what to do with herself as Quinn went to the hearth and added a log to the fire. He used the poker to nudge the wood into a blaze. She sat on her bed and watched the ruddy light flicker over the play of muscles in his back, and then in his chest as he turned to her.

He swept her up into his arms, and Kate felt like one of the sparks crackling forth from the burning flames, free and flying high. Quinn's kisses were ardent and unrestrained as he unbuttoned her nightgown. He loved each spot of her skin he uncovered with his lips and tongue, brushing and nibbling as he explored. The little nips and bites he gave her served only to heighten the heat in her body as her smoldering passion flared into a blaze.

He stood between her legs as he held her breasts, one in each hand, and kissed her on the mouth again. He explored at his leisure, slipping his tongue deeper only when she let him in, allowing her to set the pace. She ran her hands through his hair and tugged him closer, exquisitely aware of every nuance of him, from his rapid heartbeat to his unique scent, which was an irresistible mixture of citrus, clove, and something else which belonged to Quinn, and Quinn alone. He plucked at her nipples and she shivered as the arousal in the sensitive crests ignited her entire being.

He pulled away from her only to tear off his breeches. His rod sprang forth. She couldn't restrain her surprised gasp.

It was utterly unlike anything she'd ever seen. The statuary she'd seen in museums showed only a small floppy thing, not this large, thick pole! Whatever was Quinn going to do with *that*?

Nothing yet, it seemed. Quinn pulled back the quilt and urged her into bed, then came after her. He covered them both by the quilt and wrapped her in his arms. He rubbed his body against hers, murmuring into her ear, "Want you, Kate, want you so much . . ." He kissed her again, sucking her tongue into his mouth, and gradually Kate's fear fled in the face of his wicked, wild onslaught. Passion pushed out doubt, even when his demanding hardness prodded her thigh.

She was wantonly curious about this particular part of Quinn.

As he cradled his head between her breasts, kissing the hollow, she reached down to explore with one hand. Heavy and hot, she thought it would burn her. She couldn't stop touching the silken, fascinating skin of his tool. She rubbed the sticky bit of moisture which appeared at the tiny slit at its tip; that was new, and interesting also.

Quinn groaned. She snatched her hand away. "Quinn, are you all right?"

"Oh, sweetling, I am so far beyond all right. God, Kate, I want you so much." He moved her hand back. "Please, don't stop." He moaned again as she clutched him, then pulled away from her to rest his head between her splayed legs.

He spread her legs wider and, embarrassed, she resisted. "No, love, let me see you. All of you. Ah, Kate, you are so beautiful." He bent his head to touch something warm and wet to Kate's flesh.

She squealed. "Quinn. *What* are you doing?"

"Loving you, darling, the best way I know how. Open yourself to me, like a flower to the sun." He slid his fingers through her curls to rub the heel of his hand against her mound, until she whimpered with her rising need and stretched her legs wider of her own will. He used his thumbs to expose her more fully, kissing her directly on the most sensitive spot.

Kate fell back on the pillows with a moan and gave herself up to Quinn's loving mouth. He pressed his tongue against her with firm little strokes, until she thought she'd go mad for release, but there was more. He slid one finger inside her, then another, and gently scissored them apart.

Kate would have flown off the bed but for Quinn easing his arousal into her. He lay his body upon hers as she screamed her ecstasy into his mouth. "Yes, Kate, yes, like that. Bend your knees, wrap your legs around my waist. Yes, darling, you are so good." Her hips tipped upward and impossibly, improbably, he slid even more fully inside her.

Kate must have emitted a small nervous squeak, for Quinn laughed tremulously. He rotated himself within her, and Kate felt him, large and round, in her tight sheath.

She gazed at him, feeling her eyes widen. They felt as enormous in her face as his manhood felt in her body.

"Yes, feel it, Kate," he hissed. His voice was almost triumphant, she thought, as he eased in and out of her. "Good or bad, feel everything. There's only one first time. It will never be quite the same again."

Kate gasped for breath as he gripped her hips, swiving her deeply. The sensation was like nothing Kate had ever felt. Big, hot, and hard, Quinn seemed to take over her body. Nothing existed but his bigness entering her, taking her, over and over again.

He sucked and nibbled her breasts as she writhed helplessly on the sheets. The fire in her raged out of control as he thrust into her. She found herself clawing his shoulders as his body rippled, then he collapsed upon her, burying his head in her long, loose hair.

After a few moments he shifted position so that they were lying side by side, still enfolded in each other's arms. He softly kissed her forehead, her hair, her eyelids, her lips. She floated on a sea of rapture. She never wanted this bliss to end.

When she awakened, she discovered she was a bit sore. She wanted to touch herself, but was shy about doing so in front of Quinn, who watched her with a small smile on his face.

"Well, darling?" He leaned down and kissed her swollen mouth. Her hips twitched. "Are you hurting, my love? I tried to be kind."

"I'm all right, if a bit sticky." Kate spoke hesitantly.

He chuckled. "This is all very new to you, isn't it? I'll get a woolly." He climbed out of bed in search of a damp washcloth.

Kate kicked off the quilt and looked down at the fluff of curls covering her mound. Strangely enough, her body appeared the same. It ought to look different, considering her maidenhead had been taken in a very thorough fashion. She stretched her arms above her head and arched her back, watching her breasts lift. The reddened peaks ached in a peculiar manner. She rubbed them, reliving the shaft of desire, almost painful, which had arrowed through her when Quinn had sucked them into his mouth.

Kate watched as Quinn washed himself at the ewer and bowl located atop the dresser in the room. When he returned, Kate saw that his tool, now smaller and softer-looking, was damp. He nudged her legs apart to gently press a cool cloth over Kate's tender female parts. She closed her eyes. While his touch soothed, she nevertheless felt intensely embarrassed at the unaccustomed intimacy.

"You're nicely formed, sweetheart," he remarked. "You touch yourself here, do you not?"

Kate's eyes popped before she covered her face with her hands. She was completely undone by his candor. "*Quinn*. The things you say—"

"Kate. Listen to me." He dropped the cloth and grabbed her hands, forcing them away from her flushed face so he could look her in the eyes. "Never be ashamed, never, about anything between us. You are a beautiful, passionate woman, and this"—he touched a finger to her swollen femininity—"God gave you this solely for your pleasure. So how could touching it be wrong?'' He bent his head to kiss her mouth again. Despite her shame, Kate quivered as the liquid heat began to pour anew through her body. He kept his grip on her wrists with one hand, alternately teasing her breasts and her bud with the other.

Kate abandoned control and let Quinn kindle her fires.

Katherine crashed onto a wooden floor. She whimpered in mingled fear and pain. She looked around, recognizing the ballroom of Badham Abbey, eerily lit by moonlight streaming in through the tall windows. The dust motes she'd raised by her abrupt entrance shifted like ghosts in the moonlight. The blood in Kate's heart froze solid. She did not understand how it still pumped, but pump it did, for she heard her heart's rapid thud, felt the fluid in her vessels as it raced through her body.

Quinn grabbed Kate as she sat bolt upright in bed, her scream halting in her tight, tense throat. "Kate, Kate, it's all right, I'm here, it's me." He enfolded the struggling, sweating girl in his arms as she whimpered. "You had a nightmare, darling, it's gone now." He continued to whisper endearments until she quieted and stopped trembling.

"Tell me about your dream, sweetling." He wanted to know everything that went on inside his Kate.

"It's nothing. Just—just—the night I left the abbey."

Fury sparked in Quinn's belly. *Damn and blast!* Nevertheless, he kept his voice calm and comforting. "It's over, love. I'll never let them near you again. I promise you'll always be safe."

"I know." She rubbed her face against his chest. "When did you decide you wanted me?"

"Hmm?" Quinn paused, surprised by the abrupt change in the conversation. "That's hard to say. I believe I desired you the moment you charged into my room, dressed in those outlandish tights." He kissed the top of her head.

"Really?"

"Umm, yes. And you?"

"I'm not quite sure, either. I knew you were interested by the way you looked at me, and somehow, that made me think about you in a particular way." She tipped her head back to look at his face.

His eyes were solemn as they met hers. "I did not intend to seduce you, Katherine."

"I know. Something about honor."

"Yes, something," he said drily. "I would not desire gossip about either of us." Quinn, more experienced than Katherine, knew gossip was the favorite food of the *ton*. Neither her birth nor her fortune would shield Kate from vicious tongues.

" 'Tis silly. Why let gossip keep us from happiness? I love you, Quinn, and I need you."

"And I need you, but there are those who will say I defiled my ward."

"I do not feel defiled."

"Just a bit sticky."

"Yes, quite." She giggled, and he couldn't help but take her in his arms again.

Twelve

Quinn, clad only in his trousers, yanked on the bellpull and shouted for his valet.

"Don't bring Malcolm in here!" Kate clutched the sheet around her shoulders. "Where is Bettina?"

"Both our servants have arrived, along with clean clothing. Shall I ring for a bath, sweetheart? We should be on the road to London as soon as possible."

"London?" Disoriented, Kate saw Bettina bustle into the room. The maid bore a salver with a pot of chocolate and a roll. The look Bettina shot Quinn reminded Kate of Bettina's attitude toward squints and wrinkles.

Quinn waited until Bettina left the room before replying, "I think you will agree that what happened last night requires our return to Town to marry as soon as possible."

"Why the haste? I want a proper wedding." Kate sipped her chocolate.

"The haste, my love, is due to the fact that you may now be carrying my child." He leaned over her, caressing her belly possessively.

"*Your* child, my lord?" Kate put down her cup with a snap.

"Our child," Quinn hastily amended his statement. "Are you always blue-devilled in the mornings?"

"I am not blue-devilled. Where is my wrapper, my maid, and my bath?" Kate swung her legs out of the bed, and gasped in shock when she sighted the dried brownish smears which stained her limbs as well as the bedclothes.

" 'Tisn't that much," said Quinn. "No need to be in a pother. However, I believe we both want a bath this morning, hmmm?"

He tucked the sheet around her, then tugged on the bellpull again. He opened the door and, in deference to Kate's need for privacy, stuck his head out. "Malcolm! Where is that bath!"

The visible evidence of her defloration startled Kate almost as much as the act. Quinn spared no time in repeating that act, giving Kate little chance to absorb the impact of the previous night. Frequency did not rob their lovemaking of its excitement, for Quinn invented variations which made Kate's head spin and her body quiver. The most commonplace event and situation seemed to hold erotic possibilities for Quinn, including the hipbath and the barouche. The journey back to London passed very quickly for Katherine, as she literally had her hands full of her creative, demanding lover.

A frisson of remembered pleasure ran through Kate's body at the thought. She suppressed her wanton longings and turned her attention to her surroundings.

Katherine's bedroom adjoined Quinn's, which augured numerous interrupted nights. Her dressing room was on the other side. The bedroom had a goodly view of Berkeley Square but was decorated in a manner which betokened vacancy for many a year, as the heavy puce hangings reflected a bygone era. Kate speculated the last tenant may have been one of Quinn's old mistresses or perhaps even his mother.

"M'mum's, of course," explained Quinn, as he escorted her down to dinner. They dined that night alone in Quinn's home in Berkeley Square. Quinn's white, starched shirt gleamed against his black evening coat; the ensemble was set off by a single ruby. He grinned at Kate. "After my father died, she needed to be close by. But now, she'll just have to become accustomed to the title of the Dowager Countess of Devere, and to the second-best bedroom!"

"I don't want to offend your mother," Kate said, sounding alarmed.

"Oh, no chance," Quinn said. "She's been pushing me to marry since the old man died. Protect the lineage, and all of that. She'll be delighted."

"Where is the countess now?"

"At Devere. You'll like the old country home, Kate. Lots of frogs and trees."

"I suppose I should begin to behave with more countenance, now that I am going to be a countess."

"You don't have much time. We will marry on the morrow. Shouldn't take more than an hour or two to get the special license."

Kate picked at her salmon as Bartram topped off her champagne. "Where shall we marry, my lord?"

Quinn eyed her with some concern. He had moved

an epergne full of white rosebuds off to one side of the dining table in order to scrutinize Kate more closely.

"I understand you attend St. Martin-in-the-Field, Katherine."

"Yes." Kate pushed her plate away.

"Will that church be satisfactory?" Quinn watched Kate over the rim of his champagne flute. Although she wore her white silk trimmed with blue velvet—an ensemble which was particularly flattering—she did not have the glow he had expected on this occasion. Quinn frowned. *What on earth did she want?* He'd spent most of the journey to London with his head nestled between her thighs. *She ought to be delighted!*

"Yes, my lord. It is very thoughtful of you to see to that detail." Her voice was listless.

"I see you are unhappy about all of this." Quinn waved his hand about.

Kate remained silent. Bartram carved her a slice of sirloin. The butler added green beans to her plate, then attended to Devere's dinner.

Quinn tried again to divine the cause of his Kate's megrims. "I am sorry we cannot wait until invitations are sent out or St. Wills returns."

A tear started from Kate's eye and coursed down her cheek.

Quinn promptly waved the servants out of the room. She wiped her face with her serviette, reaching for composure. "It is true I would have preferred some of my friends or family attended." There was only the slightest tremble in her voice.

"You have no family worth discussing," he said, hating the words as soon as they issued from his lips.

Quinn did not think of himself as harsh. "But Hawkes and Pen will be there, of course, to stand up for us."

"Sir Willoughby and Cous—Sir Pen will be our witnesses?" Kate's tone took on a happier bounce.

"Of course." Quinn smiled at his Kate and cut his meat.

"I thought Sir Pen would have taken Pauline back to Kent by this time."

"He did not. He stays in Town until I have met Badham."

"Met Badham?" Her voice sharpened. "Met Uncle Herbert where?"

Quinn realized he had misstepped, but couldn't see a way out. He chewed and swallowed as he considered his next words. "I thought you knew, sweetling. I challenged Badham to a duel on the occasion of your rescue. I thought it was necessary." He paused.

Kate went absolutely still.

"Hawkes and Pen are my seconds."

Her face was paler than the perfect roses in the epergne. "When?"

"In, um, three days."

Another pause. "And we marry on the morrow?"

"Yes, sweet Kate. You are in agreement?"

"Does my agreement matter? You are, after all, my guardian."

Stabbed to the core, he rose. "What are you saying? I was under the impression, Katherine, you love me and wish to marry me."

"Yes, of course I do. But do you not see how imperative it is for us to marry before you duel Uncle Herbert?"

Quinn threw down his napkin. "That is the plan. But good God, Katherine, what are you saying?"

"Quinn, if we do not marry before you meet Herbert Scoville, and you are killed, I am in his complete control," explained Kate urgently.

"And if I die, Kate plays the merry widow?"

"Hardly merry, my lord, but free!" Kate also rose, and frowned at Devere from across the table.

"Well, these are happy thoughts. Has it not occurred to you, sweet Kate, I might prevail?" He put his hands on his hips and glowered at her.

"I should hope you do, my lord, but that is hardly the point!" Katherine glared back at him.

"Well, what is your point?" He shouted at her from across the white linen, over the epergne filled with white roses.

"My point is that this is a bloody disaster, my lord, and if you had a pennorth of concern for anything other than your wretched *honor,* we would not be in such straits!" she flung at him.

"What straits, Katherine?" he demanded.

"Rapiers or pistols, my lord?"

"Rapiers, I believe. Does it matter?"

"Of course it matters!" she shouted. "Rapiers require skill. With pistols, any fool can make a lucky shot!"

"Are you calling me a fool?"

"Stop twisting my words!" Tears were running down Kate's face. "Quinn, I absolutely forbid you to duel my uncle!"

"What!"

"You heard what I said!"

"Katherine, you are in no position to forbid me

anything," he informed her curtly. "Good evening, madam." He stalked out of the room.

He slammed the door behind him. *What a fool I am!* He had actually let himself believe that Katherine wanted him, loved him, for himself. It was dashed ironic—women had desired him for his fortune or his title, but had never seen him as a romantic champion. Now one did, but he did not find the role at all to his liking.

Katherine, whose wealth and social status equalled his, wanted a knight in shining armor to protect her against her appalling uncle.

She didn't want a lover or a husband.

She didn't want to share his life with him, or bear his children, or be his friend and his companion.

His Kate's mind and heart were a tangled web, and overriding it all was a driving need he didn't quite understand. With a sense of stunned dismay, Quinn realized that she desired marriage merely to save herself from her wretched uncle.

She could hire a bloody guard, he told himself savagely. *But shouldn't she be happy? She'll finally be rid of the beast and his spawn!*

How could he have been taken in? He'd wager a stack of Yellow Boys that her climax, no, her several climaxes, were real. He knew the feel of a woman in orgasm; the myriad responses of her sweet furrow had become wonderfully familiar to his rod and to his fingers.

But it wasn't just that, for his Kate; he'd wager his last dace on it. She wanted him as passionately as he needed her. He was certain he had not mistaken her ardent acceptance of his lovemaking. Damn and blast! As angry as he was, he desired the perfidious wench still!

Quinn stamped upstairs to his room. The last thing he wanted now was to encounter servants. He slammed the door to his room closed, and then hauled it open when he realized there was nothing to drink in his bedroom. He jerked on the bellpull and shouted for brandy.

Kate remained in the dining room, numb. How could events have taken such a horrible turn? Why on earth was Quinn so angry? Didn't he understand he was her whole life, and that she couldn't bear to lose him, not after all the other losses she had endured?

Kate understood that Quinn's code of honor demanded a duel. Badham had abducted her, and Osborn had tried to shoot Quinn, hitting the horse instead. Those facts made Katherine deeply ashamed to be a Scoville. How could she be related to such villains?

If Herbert were allowed to survive, they'd never have any peace. The thought made her feel a bit better, though not much. It made sense, more sense than considerations of honor.

She pressed her napkin to her eyes until they stopped watering. Bad form to let the servants see her weep.

Kate left the dining room and retreated to her bedroom.

She stared balefully at the door which led to Quinn's room. No sound came from the other side of the door.

The bedroom was bleak and chilly. No fire burned in the hearth, as Bettina was not aware Kate had retired early. Only one lamp was lit.

The room had been dusted, and the bed linens were fresh. The water in the ewer on the dresser was cold, but adequate.

Kate undressed and washed and cried herself to sleep.

The next day dawned cool rather than sultry. Kate was glad for the change in the weather. Her nerves were stretched to their limits, and she did not know if she could tolerate another close, warm day.

Unsure of appropriate attire for a fallen woman who was about to wed her seducer, she opted for simplicity, selecting a plain, ice-blue sarcenet with a matching chip-straw hat. A frown creased her brow as she eyed the jaunty hat in the mirror. Shouldn't she hide her face? She told Bettina to bring her a bonnet with an exceptionally deep poke instead.

Thus attired, she met Quinn downstairs in one of the drawing rooms. This one was lined with books, its furniture upholstered in leaf-green brocade.

She looked at her intended. Quinn's eyes were as puffy as hers, and he seemed to have difficulty keeping his lids raised.

Crop-sick, is he? Serves him right! Somehow the knowledge that Quinn had had as bad a night as she did made Kate feel better.

Ashamed, but better.

They took the closed barouche to Doctor's Commons to procure the license, and were accompanied by Richard Carrothers, "who," explained Quinn, "is a dab with the details!" While Carrothers was in the edifice dealing with "the details," Quinn took Kate to a coffee house and poured cup after cup of strong brew down his throat.

The day dashed by. After a quick luncheon in Berkeley Square, Kate allowed Bettina to dress her again in her white ruched silk for the simple ceremony at the church.

Considering the hastiness of the wedding, both Kate and Quinn were surprised to see numerous equipages drawn up in front of St. Martin's. Several of the vehicles sported crests of the nobility painted on their doors. It was a Tuesday at three in the afternoon, an hour during which members of the *ton* normally visited each other and exchanged gossip.

Kate and Quinn entered the church by way of the main doors. As they trod the length of the nave, they were astonished to see that the dimly lit church was half-full. They stepped up to the altar decorated with flowers and greenery, looking for the officiant and the witnesses.

The cleric bustled forth from the chancel, where he had been instructing the choir in anticipation of the Sunday service.

"Well, well." He beamed at the two of them. "You are here, and eagerly anticipated, I vow. The special license?"

"Sir, what are all these people doing here?" Kate wanted to know as Devere removed the license from his pocket. "And where are Sir Willoughby and Sir Pen?"

The reverend raised his white eyebrows. "So impatient, these young ones," he murmured. "I believe your witnesses have arrived."

Sir Willoughby and Sir Pen hurried up the main aisle of the nave. Anna, who walked behind them, carried a bouquet of red roses. She handed it to Kate, then dabbed at her eyes with a handkerchief. "Weddings always make me weep." She smiled mistily at Kate. "Welcome to our family, darling Kate."

"Thank you." Kate could barely force the words out. Thank heavens for Lady Anna, who could make Kate feel cherished with a mere glance. "But who are all these people? And why are they here?"

Devere cast a glance over the room. "Quite a few familiar faces, what?"

"No," said Kate. "I've never seen any of them before."

"Ah, but we have," said Sir Willoughby. "The pink of the *ton* have decided to grace your wedding with their presence."

"I don't want them here!" exclaimed Kate.

"We can't toss them out, Kate, it's a church!" Quinn pointed out.

"I don't even know them. How can they wish me happy?"

"They don't. They are merely curious." Sighing, Quinn glanced at Anna. "Can't stop the servants from talking, can we?"

"So that's it?" asked Kate.

"Almost certainly," Quinn said. "I am familiar with my neighbors. Virtually everyone here lives in the vicinity of Berkeley Square, or is acquainted with someone who does."

Hawkes looked out over the throng. "Good Lord," he murmured. "There's Staveley."

Kate frowned. The name rang a tiny bell in her muddled brain.

"You're joking." Devere raised his lorgnon.

"Weren't you lurking about her for awhile, Quinn?" Pen asked in a soft tone.

"Yes, but that was before I met Kate."

"Whatever for? Widows, however wealthy, aren't your style," Anna said.

"Staveley's all right. Got brats already. Proven breeder and all."

"A proven breeder?" Kate was outraged. "Let me see that!" She snatched at Devere's eyeglass.

He evaded her grab. "See here, Kate, you mustn't stare! You're causing a scene!"

"I'm causing a scene? Tell me, my lord, is this why you're marrying me? To breed? Aren't you taking a bit of a chance? After all, I am not a proven breeder!" She made another attempt at the lorgnon.

The group at the altar was about to break into an unseemly scuffle when Kate heard the soft slap of running feet clad in slippers. She turned to look down the nave. A small figure fashionably dressed in rose-pink sarcenet dashed toward the altar, bearing a bouquet of pink roses. She was followed more decorously by a servant.

"Ah, so she made it," said Quinn, with satisfaction in his voice. He cocked his head to Katherine. "I did arrange for one of your friends to attend, Kate."

Lady Sybilla Farland reached the altar, puffing in a manner certain to draw censure from the watching biddies. "Oh, so you already have flowers?"

Kate squashed the bouquet against her friend's chest as she ruthlessly hugged Sybilla without a care for the condition of the sarcenet. Sybilla squeaked, then hugged Kate back, and whispered in her ear.

"I just received Lord Devere's message. You sly

minx, I had guessed after that day at Hampton Court, but I didn't know!"

"I didn't either. It all happened so fast! We can talk about it later."

"Where is Mr. St. Wills?" asked Sybilla. "He's your oldest friend. Didn't he come?"

"Ahem!" the cleric coughed for their attention. "If I may begin?"

Katherine examined Quinn as the reverend's sonorous voice lulled her through the wedding service. Her lover, dressed in his finest for the occasion, had become more lively as the day had progressed. Kate became aware of Quinn's scent, his newly trimmed hair, his shaven chin. She watched his mobile lips as he gave the proper responses during the service. She remembered how those lips felt sucking on her breasts. Distracted by Quinn, she stumbled over her words.

She came apart when Sir Pen withdrew two rings from his pocket and presented one to each of them.

"Robert's ring," she whispered. Tears came to her eyes. She held the heavy signet in her palm, remembering the last time she had seen it. The ring had adorned her grandfather's hand as he lay dying. Bennett, Kate's father, had worn this ring, and it had been returned to Kate's grandfather when Bennett had been killed.

"Who's Robert?" asked Quinn, sotto voce.

"Robert Scoville was the first earl," murmured Kate. She sniffed, then handed her bouquet to Sybilla. She hunted in her reticule for a handkerchief. "Henry the Eighth gave that ring to Robert along with the earldom."

"And this one?" asked Quinn, holding aloft another ring for her inspection. It featured a large cabochon sapphire set in gold.

"That one's almost as old," said Kate. "It's the countess's wedding ring. My mother wore it." She blotted tears from her eyes and nose. "From where did you get them?"

"Ahem!" The cleric interrupted their quiet conversation. "If I may conclude?"

"Ah, yes. Quite. Sorry." Quinn favored the officiant with a brief smile.

"With this ring, I thee wed," instructed the minister.

"With this ring, I thee wed," sang out Quinn, slipping the ring onto Kate's finger.

"With this ring, I thee wed," murmured Kate.

"You may now kiss the bride!"

Quinn pulled Katherine into his arms and kissed her thoroughly and possessively. He whispered into her ear, "Everything will work itself out, sweet Kate, you'll see!"

She hugged him back and burst into tears.

Thirteen

A bit embarrassing, her conduct at the church. Quinn knew her tears had sprung from her tender heart, but he had also heard the whispers that had flowed in their wake as they walked back down the nave and climbed into their carriage for the short ride to Clarendon's. *She doesn't look happy. . . . did you know she's his* ward? *Devere's married an underage chit with the wealth of Croesus . . . understandable, I'd do it myself. . . . probably a pretty creature when she isn't imitating a watering pot! No one knows her . . . of course not, she isn't even out yet! He does prefer virgins . . .* He hoped Kate hadn't heard that last. His affection, no, his *adoration*, for his wife far exceeded anything he'd ever felt for the other women he'd used for his pleasure in the past.

He glanced at Katherine, who sat a few inches away from him in the barouche. Too far. He slid next to her, and slipped his arm around her shoulders. She turned her face up to him, accepting his kiss. He didn't release her until the equipage stopped at Clarendon's for their wedding feast.

The conversation over the meal was also lively but general. No one mentioned the forthcoming duel. Sybilla again asked about the whereabouts of Bryan St. Wills.

"We don't know!" admitted Quinn. "I hunted for Kate along the Great North Road, and Hawkes went south to Dover. We asked St. Wills to go to Badham Abbey, in Wiltshire. I sent a message there, but I'm not quite sure what's happened to our friend."

"I am quite troubled," said Kate. "Bryan is so very reliable."

"P'raps I'll ask my father to check on it," said Sybilla. "What's the use of having the ear of royalty if you can't use it once in a while?"

The chef at the Clarendon, who had served Napoleon, outdid himself, but Quinn couldn't taste a bite. His sole desire was getting his lovely wife back into his bed.

His *wife*. What a wonderful word.

He'd missed her last night, but felt he needed to prove a point, to himself, if not to her. Neither of them had spoken of their quarrel all day, but it was there, like a half-healed bruise. 'Twas only a matter of time until one or the other pushed on the spot to see if it still hurt. He guessed it would be Kate, especially since he planned to go to Signor Angelo's on the morrow to practice. He also knew she was too honest to make love with him if she were angry, and he'd be damned if he'd force her.

Quinn opened the door adjoining their rooms, attired in a nightshirt. Kate was seated in front of a vanity as Bettina brushed her hair out. He caught her eye in the mirror.

"That will be all, Bettina," he said, keeping his voice low and soothing. He noticed the servant did not leave until Kate nodded.

"Well, Countess Devere, my bedroom or yours?"

"This doesn't truly feel like my bedroom."

"If the decor is not to your taste, you may of course change it in any way you please," he said. "Perhaps we shall visit a draper's on the morrow to purchase new fabric for hangings and bedclothes."

Kate's visage brightened. "I'd enjoy that, my lord."

"I'm your husband now. No more 'my lord' except in public." The conversation was stilted, but Quinn had no idea how to put Kate at ease. Dash it, they should be more easy with each other now that they were married, shouldn't they?

Perhaps Kate would not feel truly married until they shared a bed. Yes, that was it. A good bout of sex would surely improve her mood. It always made him feel better. Why should she be different?

"Come," he said, taking her arm to lead her to his room.

She pulled away gently.

"I'm sorry, Quinn, but we really have to talk." Kate's voice had only the merest hint of a tremble.

He smiled as he took back her arm, kissing her on her forehead. "Are you still upset about the duel?"

"Very much so, my l—Quinn." She sat on her bed.

"Some actions cannot be ignored, sweet Kate."

"I know." Her voice was miserable as her hands twisted in her nightgown.

"I thought you would be relieved to be rid of your detestable uncle and his whelp." He sat next to her to cover her hands with his own.

"I will be. Are you also going to duel Osborn?"

"I am not sure. It would be unattractive for me to kill an underage child, especially since I have already wounded him."

Kate rubbed her face against his arm. "My lord, please call off the duel."

"*No.*"

"Oh, God, Quinn." She turned her face into his chest and cried without shame or restraint.

He took her in his arms and waited out the flood. It was shorter than forty days and nights, but no less damp. When she lay against him, quiet, limp, and weak, he pulled back the covers and put them both into her bed. He found her a handkerchief.

"I'm sorry. This is our wedding night, and I'm spoiling everything." She blew her nose with a small but appealing honk.

He kissed her moist cheeks and her forehead. "You're not spoiling anything, sweetheart. We'll have many nights together. But I must say your attitude does not betoken much confidence in me."

"I hate to take any chances. He's so absolutely wicked, Quinn. What if he arranges to stab you in the back, or something like that?"

"I hardly think that is a possibility, Kate, but I shall arrange to, er, watch my back." He cuddled her close. "I say, would you like to come to Signor Angelo's fencing establishment with me tomorrow? Then you will see that I'm not so helpless."

"I'd like that. Will they allow me in?"

"I'll arrange everything. Not to worry."

Reaching over, she stroked his shaft. "You're so thoughtful."

"Hmph."

"And very sweet."

"Hmph." *What the devil is she planning?*

"Quinn, darling, may I go to the duel?"

"*What?*" He sat up.

"It just seems that I'm quite involved. What harm would it cause?" She continued to touch him through his nightshirt.

"It would be entirely unsuitable, Kate." His rod twitched and rose.

"Oh, nonsense. We are married now. What do we care what other people think?"

"Hmph." He was very hard. With some shock, he realized she was seducing him. This was not the plan.

"Say yes, darling Quinn." Her hand wrapped around his tool, which was as hard as a tree trunk.

He groaned. "Kate, you minx."

"You cannot stop me, you know." *Stroke, stroke.*

"You will not step foot out of this house on Thursday morning without my say-so!" He jerked away from her.

She giggled. "What's wrong, Quinn?"

"You know very well what's wrong! From where did you learn this scandalous conduct?"

"I thought you liked this. You liked this on the way back to Town."

"I don't like it when you're asking for something outrageous. I will not be bribed!" He jumped out of bed.

"If you don't like it, why are you so—so—so—"

"Ready?" He loomed over her.

She grinned up at him saucily. She leaned over and flicked at the tip with one finger, which tented his nightshirt. He'd had enough of her teasing, so he leaped upon her and started to tickle her. She squealed and tried to roll away, but became entangled in both the bedclothes and her long nightgown, laughing helplessly.

"Stop, Quinn, stop!" Kate tried to wipe the tears from her eyes while squirming away.

Laughing, Quinn continued to scrabble with his fingertips up and down her sides while Kate wriggled and writhed. He slid down the bed as she struggled in the opposite direction. She gasped when he grabbed her ankle; she tried to pull away without success. He laughed harder as he mercilessly scratched the tender underside of her arched foot.

He nibbled on her big toe.

"*Quinn*. What on earth are you doing? That's dirty!"

"Your toes had better not be dirty. You got from your bath into this bed. If the carpet is dirty, one of the housemaids will be sacked." Quinn bit gently. Kate squealed and jerked.

Quinn let her go only because he wanted to keep his teeth in his head a while longer. He slid up the bed until he was level with her. He slipped a hand between her legs while he smiled into her eyes.

She felt luscious and ready, so he pulled up his nightshirt and lowered himself into her with more abandon than at the inn, where he'd had to be concerned for her welfare. This time he could take what was his with no restraints.

He swived his wife with a sense of primitive male satisfaction, prolonging the act as long as he could, drinking in each of Katherine's moans and whimpers with far more abandon than he'd eaten their wedding dinner.

Quinn lusted for Kate's body and wanted desperately to fill her with his children. Imagining her belly full and rounded with his baby only served to make him even more eager. He flooded her with his seed, hoping again she'd be pregnant soon.

Lying beside her after their love, he wondered about his peers. The married ones complained about their state while the bachelors slandered a condition about which they clearly knew nothing.

Marriage is grossly underrated. . . . If I'd known how good it was to make love to one's wife, I might have married before! But in his heart, he knew there was only one woman for him—the one he'd waited for. The one who cuddled beside him in their marriage bed. Katherine, Countess Devere.

Kate awakened with a sense of delightful lassitude as the first rays of the sun struggled past the heavy dark hangings of the Dowager Countess's bedroom. Her mood abruptly evaporated as she realized she was alone.

Damn and blast! Quinn had sneaked out, the wretch, without waking her up for the duel. Kate leaped out of bed and yanked on the bellpull, screaming for Bettina.

Katherine fumbled through her belongings for her oldest gown and blucher boots. As on the day before, her relationship with Quinn had led her into a social situation for which she had no idea of proper attire, but she assumed a dueling field was no place for flimsy muslin or silk. She pulled on her stuff gown.

"Has he been gone long?" Kate demanded of Bettina when her maid bustled in, tray in hand.

"I beg your pardon, my lady?" Bettina stared at Kate as though she were a Bedlamite.

"Devere. When did he leave?"

"*Leave?* The earl? At this hour? Are you feeling quite the thing, my lady?" Bettina put the salver down on a dresser and advanced toward Katherine, hand outstretched.

"Tell me, at once, Bettina, where the earl is at this moment."

Bettina touched Kate's forehead with a reflective look on her face. "No fever," she muttered.

Kate pushed her maid's hand away. "Of course I am well! Where is my husband?"

"I do not go into the earl's bedroom, my lady," said Bettina stiffly, "but I believe my lord is there. I don't mean to be saucy, but I hope you do not ask me to check!"

Kate stared. "Yes. Quite. The duel is tomorrow, is it not?"

Bettina reached for the fastenings of the stuff gown. "Yes, my lady. It's to be at Parliament Hill at dawn. Tomorrow." The maid pulled the gown off Katherine's shoulders. "I am sure it will not be necessary for you to wear this dress." She put it back in the press, nose wrinkling with disapproval.

"You're quite right, Bettina." Kate spoke meekly. "Please get me my wrapper."

Kate tied the strings of her dressing gown and regarded her maid, who was still busy at the clothespress.

"Bettina."

"Yes, my lady?"

"I have never asked you to do anything which would endanger your position." Kate sat on her bed and poured chocolate from a silver jug into a china cup.

"Thank you, my lady."

"Tomorrow may be an exception." The cup was decorated with red roses painted around the gilded rim. *Very tasteful,* thought Kate.

Bettina turned. "Is that so, my lady?"

"Please be assured that you are now my employee, not the earl's. I will not allow you to be sacked."

"Thank you, my lady."

"I wish to attend the duel on the morrow."

"Of course, my lady." Bettina went to Kate's dresser. She began dusting the bottles and brushes which were set out.

"The earl does not agree."

"I understand perfectly, my lady."

"Is there a stable boy or cook's helper whose clothes can be borrowed?"

Bettina's busy hands stilled. "That should not be necessary, my lady."

"How so?"

"Simply follow in a carriage, my lady. No need to be uncomfortable."

Kate considered. She tipped her head on one side. "I do believe you are correct. I had thought to disguise myself as a tiger and travel on the back of my lord's equipage. But that is sadly melodramatic and unnecessary, is it not?"

After she finished her chocolate she tiptoed into Quinn's room. She wondered why he'd deserted her in the middle of the night, but couldn't help feeling grateful as she stood by his bedside, listening to him snore. She slipped under the quilt to catch an extra nap, but his sonorous breathing made it impossible.

She jabbed him in the side with her elbow. Snorting, he rolled over onto his stomach. His breathing quieted. She curled in the crook of his arm.

She awoke later to find her husband smiling down at her. "Awake at last, Quinn?"

He kissed her on the forehead. "You made it very difficult to sleep, sweetling."

"I didn't mean to disturb you. I thought it might be nice to wake up together." Her hand slipped down the length of his torso.

"It is nice." He cuddled her closer, caressing her breast.

"Why did you leave my bed last night?"

"Couldn't sleep."

"Is there something wrong with the mattress?"

Quinn squirmed. "No."

Kate eyed her husband, determined to discover the problem she sensed. "Well?"

"It's just that—well, sweetheart, you—you sleep rather loudly," he said, sounding lame.

"I beg your pardon?" Kate was almost affronted. *What on earth is he implying?*

Quinn's discomfort visibly increased. "Your breathing. Is loud. When you sleep."

"Do you mean to say, my lord, that *I* snore?"

"Well, er, yes."

Kate was speechless.

Quinn hastened to add, "I wouldn't have said so, 'tis ungentlemanly. But yes, Kate, since you raise the question, you do—snore. A bit. A very little bit."

He patted her on the head. "It would be better to say that you—sleep loudly. Yes, that's it. You sleep loudly. I felt you would be less disturbed if I slept in my own bed, you see."

Kate wasn't fooled. She whacked him on the head with a pillow. "You are saying that I snore? Sir, you sound like a company of elephants taking a bath in a rushing river, and you have the gall to tell me that I snore!" She bashed him again.

"I do not snore!" He grabbed the pillow out of her hands and hit her back.

"I apologize for differing with you, my lord and master, but you most distinctly do snore." She used another pillow to smack him in the chest.

"No one else has ever told me that I snore!"

Kate gasped. That was a foul blow. "No one else has been honest with you, my lord. I assume your other bedmates were either hired or earnestly seeking your affections for reasons known only to themselves." *Whack!*

He raised his brows. "Do you not desire my affection?" *Whack!*

"I'm married to you. I don't have to scheme." Kate waved the pillow at him threateningly.

He grabbed it as he clambered out of bed, retreating to a safe haven behind a table set near a window. "Peace, peace!" He waved the pillows. "I have the weapons, sweet Kate, so you'd best make peace before I overwhelm you!"

She grinned at him. "Overwhelm? That sounds fun. Come and overwhelm me, my lord!"

Quinn, true to his word, took Kate to observe him at fencing practice at the establishment of Signor Henry Angelo.

After removing his coat, Quinn, dressed in cross-braces and tight-fitting breeches, fenced with Signor Angelo as Katherine watched. Kate had to admit her husband handled the rapier well, and surely would best Uncle Herbert if Badham were so foolish as to choose rapiers rather than pistols. Her concern regarding firearms remained.

Her thoughts were interrupted by the strangest sight; another woman in the exclusive environs of Signor Angelo's! Kate knew that Devere had used persuasion as well as outright bribery to bring her in; but here was a lady, bold as brass, swaggering into the room as though she belonged here.

Quinn finished practice and came to stand near her, wiping his face with a towel.

"Quinn!" Kate hissed, sotto voce. "Who is this lady?"

"That's no lady, that's Madam Cain."

The woman picked up a foil and tested it, swishing it through the air.

"Is she going to fence with Signor Angelo?"

"Most likely."

"Quinn, I would like to fence also. Would you fence with me?"

Her husband's shoulders gave a sharp jerk upwards. "I am not a fencing master," he said in what Kate recognized as his most repressive tone of voice.

"I don't require a teacher, just a partner. I already know how to fence. Please, Quinn. I didn't realize ladies were permitted to fence in London. Now that I know, please may I practice a bit? I'm sadly out of trim, but I promise to be entertaining."

"You know how to fence?" Quinn recoiled in horror.

"Of course. And how to ride, hunt, and shoot, and many other useful skills. What do you think I learned in school?"

His mouth made a tight line. "What other 'useful skills' did you learn at that school in Bath?"

"Oh, ever so many! Too many to recount. Languages, of course, and everything one needs to know about the proper maintenance of a household and its accounts, dancing, music and art, well—everything! And Miss Telmont said many times that I was one of the top students," Kate assured him. "So, may I fence?"

"Absolutely bloody well not!"

Kate drew back, astonished at her husband's unusual display of temper. "Well—well, *she* is!"

"Madam Cain is very bad *ton!*"

The woman looked at Kate and smiled, but did not approach.

Kate said, "Well, so am I!"

"You are married to me. You are therefore very good *ton.*"

His arrogance both silenced and infuriated Kate. What the devil was wrong with him? She struggled for a suitable rejoinder while her husband dictatorially laid down the law as he saw it.

"While it would remind me most pleasantly of our childhood follies, sweet Kate, I'm afraid I must decline. A gentleman does not fight his lady." Quinn shrugged back into his coat of navy superfine. "Shall we be off to the draper's?"

Kate was about to argue when she remembered that she had never won an argument with Quinn by conventional tactics. She deliberately softened her tone. "Yes, my lord." She hoped she looked submissive as she followed him out of Signor Angelo's.

* * *

As he handed her up into his barouche, Quinn shuddered at the thought of Kate fencing. Kate with a pillow was discomfiting; Kate with a rapier in hand would be a force to be feared. He climbed in after her, saying, "You seem to have great respect for Miss Elizabeth Telmont."

"Yes, she's been very good to me. She was very kind after—after my parents went." The equipage started to move.

He pressed her hand. "I'm glad you had someone there to support you at school. It must have been a very difficult time."

"Not really. I've heard others complain about their schools. I was fortunate."

"How so?" He was curious about how Kate's mind worked. Most people would be sad or bitter about the loss of their entire family.

"I've actually been rather lucky. I may have lost my parents, and have just that appalling uncle of mine left, but I have good friends. Like Anna and Pen and Bryan." A cloud passed over her pretty face.

Quinn guessed she was worried about St. Wills. "Don't worry, sweet Kate. I'll take care of this small matter of Bad Herbert Badham in the morning before Bettina's even brought in your chocolate. Then we'll be free to see about Bryan St. Wills, hmmm?"

Her eyes were soft and sparkling. "I have wonderful friends, but I have the *best* husband!"

He shot her a suspicious glance. "Yes, as long as I am dancing to your tune, what?"

"I don't know what you could mean, Quinn." Kate opened her eyes very wide.

"Hmph. As if you don't now how to get what you want."

"You don't seem terribly unhappy about the way matters have unfolded."

"I'm not. But you may cease managing me this instant."

"Hmph." She said it right back at him, the saucy baggage, and laughed at the silly look he knew adorned his face. "I'm your wife. Does that not mean I'm yours to command?"

Quinn frowned. He was determined not to be outmaneuvered by this determined female. "Let's see what we can find for your room," he said as the barouche stopped at the draper's.

They retired early, directly after dinner. Kate surmised that Quinn wanted a good sleep after exhausting them both in bed.

He made love to her with more than his usual fervor, she believed. The thought did not sit easily with her. Did he imagine he'd meet his Maker on the morrow?

Kate couldn't sleep. As Quinn snored—sleeping loudly, as he'd put it, that insulting wretch—she got out of bed and went to her own room, now hung with white Battenburg lace. She wondered what life would hold for her the next day. Her mind ran 'round and 'round like a mouse in the wainscoting. If Herbert lost—well, who would care? Certainly not her! Another rat killed, and one more to go.

If Herbert won—Kate's mind shied away from the consequences. Having been wed to Devere, Kate didn't have a care for her own fate. She knew that, as a wealthy widow, she'd be able to gather the shreds

of her life and weave them into something meaningful.

But Quinn had been her lodestone for months,
her rock and her stability. She'd come to depend
upon him for everything. Yes, as the Countess of
Devere, she'd be financially secure and in control of
her own fate. But everything Kate truly valued: love,
husband and family, would be gone . . . again.

To lose Quinn was unthinkable. She pressed one
hand to her stomach. Quinn was right. She could be
carrying his child. To bear his heir and raise the child
to adulthood without a father might be beyond her
capabilities.

Kate closed her eyes and silently beseeched whatever God was in the heavens to protect the life of her
husband.

Fourteen

Quinn arose early. The day looked as if it were going to be unseasonably gray and cold. Without Kate in his bed, he was chilled as he swung his legs out onto the floor. Sleeping separately was both a blessing and a curse, but today he wasn't displeased to find himself alone. She'd gotten a maggot in her head about the duel, so he was just as happy that she slept in her room. Avoiding the fifth board from the wall—the one that creaked—he tiptoed over to the door connecting their rooms and listened, just to make sure.

Silence.

Good. Quinn stole to the door to the hallway and opened it. He gestured to the footman stationed outside. Quinn put his finger to his lips before the fellow started to speak.

"Bring Malcolm," he whispered. "Quietly. Don't disturb Lady Devere, or there'll be the devil to pay for all of us."

Nodding, the man slipped away. Scant minutes later, Malcolm appeared, along with two other servants. One carried hot water for Quinn's wash. The other had the tea tray.

Malcolm shaved Quinn, then the earl and his valet selected clothing for the engagement. Quinn didn't

know if Badham would select pistols or rapiers, but
he'd take no chances. If they shot at each other from
twenty paces, he wanted to blend with the foggy
dawn. If not, well then, he'd be pleased to run Badham through in any clothing.

A gray coat with brushed silver buttons. Trousers
the color of mist. A gray, curly-brimmed hat to cover
Quinn's reddish locks.

Suitably attired, Quinn exited his room, Hobys in
hand. He dared not clatter down the hall lest he
rouse Kate.

As Quinn had predicted, the dawn was misty and
gray. Light came reluctantly to Parliament Hill despite its elevation. The horses stamped and fretted in
their traces as they waited.

Almost everyone was there who should have been
there: Quinn and his seconds, Pen and Hawkes.
Hawkes had brought the required sets of weapons.
Pen had even engaged a sawbones if things went
wrong and Badham was only injured, not killed.

"Where the devil is he?" Quinn tried not to whine.
It was not enough that the blackguard had abducted
his wife and had gotten him up out of his nice warm
bed before dawn, but the rotter had to be late on top
of it all! Quinn felt most unjustly put upon.

"Don't fret, Devere, this must be him!" Hawkes
laid a calming hand on Quinn's sleeve. "Now you'll
have at him!"

Pen squinted through the mist. "I say, Quinn, that
barouche looks mighty familiar."

Quinn strode to the crown of the hill. He frowned.
"Damn and blast!"

The barouche was indeed familiar. Bloody hell, that was *his* crest on the door, and the woman getting out of it was his wife! "Katherine!" He barreled down the hill to her side.

Kate released the hand of the coachman who'd assisted her as she alighted. She greeted Quinn with her most brilliant smile.

"Good morrow, my lord!" She surveyed him from top to toe, nodding with approval. "You appear to be quite untouched. Is Herbert dead, then?" she inquired, a hopeful note in her voice.

Quinn shook his head. "Blighter hasn't shown up."

Kate's face fell. "But there's still time, isn't there?"

"I don't know. He was supposed to be here at dawn." Quinn pulled off his hat and ran his fingers through his hair. He crammed the hat back on, dismayed. *Mustn't go about with messy hair,* he thought in horror. *What am I thinking? Malcolm would be appalled!*

His wife continued to regard him, looking pleased. "You do look smashing in that hat, Quinn. Gray does become you, you know."

Quinn was not diverted in the least. "Why, thank you, Katherine. Now would you care to explain what you are doing here?"

Kate smiled up at him, attired in a blue walking dress with a paler blue spencer. The short, tight garment drew attention to her generous bustline. *And well she knows it, too!* Quinn groused silently. He wondered what kind of monster he'd created as Kate fluttered her long, dark lashes over her sparkling blue eyes.

He was enchanted, as always, and could refuse her

nothing. Though he'd try. He was not going to be managed by her for the remainder of their lives.

"Come." Taking her arm, he escorted her up the hill. "Greet Pen and Hawkes, and have a coffee."

Kate raised her brows. "Coffee?"

A servant stepped out of Hawkes's carriage with a hamper. He opened it to reveal a silver coffee service.

"Had we known of your attendance, my dear, we would have arranged for chocolate," Quinn said sardonically. "As it is, you will just have to make do. Napkin?" He handed her an embroidered linen square.

The servant poured and they waited. They spoke desultorily about the weather and the time.

A half-hour passed.

And another.

Finally, Kate spoke. "I say, Quinn, wasn't the engagement at dawn?"

Quinn nodded.

"At Parliament Hill?"

Quinn nodded again.

"Hampstead Heath?"

"Umm."

Kate looked around, twitching with agitation. "Did we *all* mistake the day? P'raps it's tomorrow!"

Pen spoke. "It's today, to be sure. The bounder's cried off."

Kate gasped. "You mean he's not coming?"

"Apparently not." Quinn spoke calmly, but his blood boiled. "Hawkes, who were the seconds?"

"His son, of course, and some sharp calling himself Captain Grayned."

"Hmph. Captain. Not bloody likely! I'll stand you a guinea, Hawkes, the blackguard's made a run for it!"

Hawkes laughed. "I'll stand any wager for a guinea, Devere!"

"Yes, well, I'm a married man now. Can't fling around the Yellow Boys the way I used to. I say, shan't we go over to Limmer's? I am really quite anxious to conclude my business with Badham and his spawn."

"As am I," said Kate.

Quinn looked around. "Dash it, Kate," he complained. "We've too many carriages here now."

"Well, I told you I was coming," she said. "You chose not to believe me. Did you think I would sprout wings and fly up to Parliament Hill, my lord? Of course I took a carriage."

"I asked you to stay home," Quinn said.

"No, you told me to stay home. There is a rather large difference."

Coughing, Hawkes nudged Sir Pen. "I say, we are rather *de trop* here, old boy. We'll meet you at Limmer's," he called to Quinn and Kate as he hastily climbed into one of the four carriages parked at the bottom of the hill.

The doctor cleared his throat. "May I assume, my lord, you will have no need of my services?"

"Not this morning," Quinn replied gloomily.

"I'll send the bill." On that note, the sawbones departed.

Two carriages were left. Sir Pen said, "I'll take your landau and meet you at Limmer's."

"Hi-ho," said Quinn to Kate. "Looks like it's just you and me, old girl. Let's go see if we can roust Badham and his brat from their midden!"

* * *

Bettina sat in the carriage, glowering at Quinn as he climbed in. He asked, "Bettina, what are you doing here?"

Kate raised her brows. "Surely, my lord, you didn't expect me to go out alone?"

"I didn't expect you to go out at all. This is your doing, isn't it?" he addressed Bettina, who answered with frost edging every syllable.

"The countess planned to disguise herself as a postilion or a groom, my lord, and to attach herself to your equipage. I persuaded her that dressing as befits her station and taking a carriage was more appropriate."

Quinn was mollified. "Very good, Bettina. Remind me to increase your salary."

Kate interrupted. "Bettina is my servant, not yours, my lord. It is not your place to berate or reward her." She turned to Bettina. "Remind me, if you please, to raise your salary."

"I beg your pardon?" Quinn looked down his nose at his pert young wife. He glanced at Bettina. "Katherine, we will continue this discussion of your illusions elsewhere."

"Illusions, my lord?" Kate looked miffed.

Quinn put his finger to his lips, then turned to Bettina again. "I have noticed that the countess tends to be abominably blue-devilled in the mornings, Bettina."

"With all respect, I must disagree, my lord. My lady has generally been cheerful at all times—until four days ago." The maid's voice was heavy with reproach.

Quinn sighed, closing his eyes. He leaned back against the squabs, weary resignation weighing down every bone. "The both of you are blue-devilled in the mornings!"

* * *

Snores filled the carriage. Kate glanced at her maid. "Bettina, you are my witness that Lord Devere snores." Removing her bonnet, Katherine handed it to her maid, then settled herself back against the curve of Devere's arm for a short nap.

As the carriage entered busier precincts of London, the early morning noises of hawkers, coachmen, and others who were abroad roused Devere from his slumber. Blinking sleep out of his eyes, he glanced down to see his wife cuddled next to him. He smiled. He adored the managing wench, even when she snored.

"I say, Bettina," he whispered. "Don't mention it to her, but you will please note that the countess snores."

"Very good, sir."

The coach pulled up outside Limmer's Hotel with a jerk. Quinn thrust out an arm to keep Kate from falling off the seat. Clinging to him, she blinked drowsily. "Are we there yet?"

"We are. This is Limmer's Hotel," he said.

She peered out of the window. "What a grubby, gloomy spot."

"It is. Very bad *ton*, caters primarily to country squires, racetrack touts, and people who don't particularly care what they eat. Stay here," Quinn ordered and, for once, it seemed that his Kate had no particular desire to argue with him. Opening the door from the inside, he jumped down to the ground without the aid of the retractable steps or the coach-man.

Entering the dim lobby, he encountered Hawkes and Pen. Pen looked angry, but it seemed Hawkes was on the verge of amusement.

"Bad luck, Devere, the bird's flown!"

"*What!*" Quinn stared at his friend.

Hawkes gestured at the clerk behind the polished wooden desk. "This chappie tells me that our friend Badham and his puppy paid their shot two days ago and haven't been seen since."

Pen glared at Quinn. "I thought you had the Bow Street Runners on their tail."

"I did. But after I called him out, there didn't seem to be any need." Quinn turned to the clerk, who shuffled his papers. "Is there any rumor or clue as to Badham's destination?"

"There is, sir."

"My lord," corrected Hawkes.

"Don't worry about that," Quinn said. "Out with it, man!"

"When Badham signed the final bill, he used the name Scoville and indicated he had a forwarding ad-dress of Boston, in the Americas. See?" The clerk waved a scrap of paper.

Quinn took the paper and squinted at it. He could sense Pen and Hawkes hovering over his shoulder. "That certainly seems to be the case. Boston, in the Americas, not Boston in Lincolnshire." Frustration built in his chest. He felt like a cat waiting at a mouse hole, unaware that the prey had scampered out of a different crack in the floor. "Damn and blast!" Quinn slammed his fist into a nearby wall, smashing through the cheap wainscoting.

"Here, here! There'll be none of that!" The clerk rushed out from behind his desk. "Lord or no lord, you'll pay for the damage, sir!"

"Of course." Quinn massaged his hand after he pulled it out of the wall.

Pen removed a wallet from his coat. "If it weren't you, it would have been me, brother," he remarked to Quinn as he passed a few banknotes to the clerk.

"What next?" Kate asked, as the footman deposited another slice of carved beef onto her plate.

Light shafted down into the dining room of Quinn's Berkeley Square house, where the party had repaired for a bit of sustenance and to discuss their next move.

Her husband considered. "I'm not sure. P'raps I'll have the Runners and my man of affairs make some inquiries."

"I think we should go to the abbey," Kate said. "I don't quite believe in this Banbury tale of Herbert and Osborn going to the Americas. They're nothing there, while here, he's an earl, even if everyone cuts him."

"On the other hand, if they'd sold the abbey, they might have a spot of money to start over with," Pen said. "They must have known that we'd never rest until they were dead. The only way to keep their shabby skins whole was to go very far away." He glanced at Quinn. "With you married, they must have known that we wouldn't pursue them to America."

Quinn emitted a snort of laughter. "Quite right about that. I, for one, have no desire to visit the benighted place, even for the pleasure of killing Herbert Scoville."

"Whether or not he's gone, I want to go to the abbey." Kate waved at a servant to serve another bottle of burgundy.

"Why, Kate?" her husband asked. "You cannot have happy memories of the place."

"I don't, but if they're gone, it's now my property," she said. "And if they've sold it, I want to talk with the new owners and ask if I can retrieve some family heirlooms."

"I doubt if they'll allow you to take anything very valuable away," Quinn said.

"I don't want anything very valuable. I want to inquire about the disposition of some of the family portraits. After all, they're paintings of my family, and no one else's. Surely the new owner can't care about them as much as I do."

"The child has a point, Quinn," Pen spoke. "You can also take the opportunity to see if Badham and his whelp are lurking in the vicinity. Two birds with one stone."

"The new owner might also grant me access to my parents' graves." Kate cut her beef.

Quinn raised his hands in defeat. "Very well, I am persuaded that a journey to Wilts is the right course of action. Kate, you are very persuasive. And we have the opportunity to find Mr. St. Wills."

"Bryan *is* a concern," Kate said. "I feel responsible because he did ride east to find me. You've heard nothing, from anybody?"

Quinn shook his head.

"People don't just disappear off of the Great Western Road," Hawkes objected. "It's a bit wild along

Bagshot Heath, isn't it? Did the Runners search the place?"

"They did," Quinn said. "Didn't even find his horse."

"Sounds like a dead end," Pen said.

What a frightful turn of phrase. A shudder ran through Kate. She gestured for the footman to close the window. The sunlight pouring in through the glass panes didn't affect her chill. "Well, if we're leaving Town soon, I must see about packing."

"Cannot your maidservant see to that task?" Quinn's lazy gaze went from her hair, down to her bosom, and back up again to meet her eyes. He smiled.

She warmed beneath his heated glance. His intentions were as clear as a bright summer day. "Er, no," Kate said. "As I have married, I must bespeak more suitable attire. It will not do for me to continue to wear white and pink. Most inappropriate."

"That is so." Rising, he offered her an arm. "I should have liked to accompany you, Katherine, but I fear that I must meet with Carrothers if we are leaving Town again."

"I understand, my lord. I shall take Bettina or perhaps meet Sybilla Farland at Grafton House."

Unfortunately, Sybilla would not meet Kate, claiming indisposition. Kate suspected that the prospect of shopping bored the intellectual Miss Farland. Sybilla had never seemed interested in frills and furbelows like other girls. Kate sighed, wishing that Louisa, who loved to shop, still lived in Town, but Lady Anna had taken the young women back to Kent for a rest after the excitement of Kate's abduction.

Kate, followed by her maid, first visited Grafton

House to buy fabrics, then directed the footman to take her purchases in Quinn's barouche to Madame Mirielle's establishment off of St. James Street. Kate would walk. The activity was perfectly unexceptional at this hour, and other shoppers thronged fashionable Mayfair.

After luncheon, Kate knew, St. James Street, with its wealth of gentlemen's clubs, would become a male domain. Any female seen there between the hours of two and six risked gaining a reputation as fast.

"Oh, let's stop here," Kate said to Bettina, who carried smaller items—trim for the blue zephyr gown that Kate planned—in a basket. The caricatures in the window of Mrs. Humphrey's Print Shop had caught Kate's eye.

She giggled at one of Prinny—no, His Majesty—which showed the monarch in a costume which more closely resembled a striped balloon. George IV had fancied himself a dandy. Ha! King or no, he couldn't hold a candle to her husband, thought Kate with pride.

Other pedestrians stopped to look at the drawings as Kate's gaze passed over to a cartoon of an interior of a church, which depicted a stringbean of a man with an exaggerated long nose, holding fast to the arm of a silly-looking chit with big eyes, a bosomy body, and a mooncalf smile. His other hand lifted her skirts, exposing one garter, tied around her plump knee.

The hair of the man was colored red, and the blue-eyed wench looked at him with the expression of a lovestruck fool. With shock, Kate recognized herself and her husband on the occasion of her wedding, just a few days before. She tore the cartoon off the window to peruse it closely.

The title of the drawing was *"Ton* Manners and Morals."

Kate covered her mouth with her fist. She couldn't breathe.

The dialogue in the bubble above Quinn's head read, "Having bedded her, I'll marry her and take all that is valuable from her. What else shall an honorable guardian do?"

The words from the simpering girl's mouth were no less humiliating. "My dear lord, how lucky I am to have such an attentive swain!"

Two people in the background said to another, "And she isn't even *out* yet!" His companion responded, "Milord has a preference for virgins . . ."

Kate bent over from the waist, gasping for air, the vicious caricature crushed in one clenched hand. She heard Bettina's voice as though it came from far away.

"My lady! My lady!"

Kate straightened with an effort, hoping that she hadn't attracted the attention of any passers-by. She heard laughter. Blinking back tears, she turned to see two young bucks chuckling at another cartoon. She felt ill. What if they'd seen the caricature she now held, and identified the chit in it as her?

Worse, the drawing wasn't an original but an engraving. Dear God. There could be thousands of copies of this mean, hateful rubbish distributed all around London. Kate leaned against Bettina, closing her eyes.

"My lady! Are you unwell?"

Kate pressed a hand to her lips, from which her lunch now threatened to issue. She gulped. "Yes, I am most unwell, Bettina. Let us proceed to the barouche with all haste. I must return home at once."

Kate reached for the veil adorning the poke of her bonnet, tugging it down to conceal her face. Leaning on Bettina's arm, Kate staggered down St. James Street. She reached the haven of Quinn's carriage none too soon.

Bettina turned to the door of the dressmaker's establishment, but Kate called her back. The maid looked astonished.

"We shall attend to clothing another day, Bettina." Kate ordered the coachman to return to Berkeley Square, then collapsed against the squabs. She closed her eyes, willing her tears to disappear until she had reached the safety of her room.

Slamming the door in her maid's astonished face, Kate flung herself across her bed. Sobs racked her body. She curled herself around a pillow and wept.

How could she face her husband and his sophisticated friends after this humiliation? Is this what people would think of their marriage, that it was a sham, so Quinn could take her virtue and her fortune?

Pain stabbed Kate deep in her soul when she remembered that Quinn had never told her that he loved her. Dear God. She'd given a heartless man her heart. He'd said he needed her, but it was well known that a man did indeed require a well-born wife, to give him heirs and to use for his pleasure. And Quinn was very, very adept at using her for his pleasure. He'd desired another woman because she was a proven breeder, and seemed most concerned about leaving his seed in her body at every opportunity.

Worse, it seemed that the entire world knew that the charming dandy turned into an insatiable beast behind closed doors. *Milord has a preference for virgins* . . . Is that all she was to her husband? A suitable vessel for his use?

Kate sat up. He wouldn't win. She wouldn't let him.

Fifteen

Where on earth was his Kate? After returning from an afternoon at White's, Quinn prowled the house, which seemed strangely large and empty, despite the hordes of servants crowding the manse. Darkness fell, and still Kate shopped? Most peculiar and absurd, but both Kate and her maid were absent, as was his barouche.

Worry stung Quinn's mind. What if Badham and his noxious offspring had taken her yet again? Seemed unlikely, with Osburt wounded and the both of them out of the country, but odder events had transpired since she had entered his life.

Approaching Kate's bedroom, Quinn hesitated. He did not like to intrude, but this room was the only place he hadn't looked for his wife. After opening the door, he gasped in shock. The room looked as though a high wind had swept through. Every drawer had been opened, and the doors of the clothespress were flung wide. Few dresses remained therein, and no shoes. Ribbons and bows lay scattered over the dressing table. What the devil was going on? Where the hell was Kate?

Quinn grabbed the bellpull and shouted for Harper, embarrassed to hear the sharp edge of panic in his voice. Surely the chit hadn't run! Why would she?

Everything was wonderful. Herbert was gone, and they loved each other. Didn't they?

Quinn couldn't help the suspicion that roared through his mind. With Badham gone, the danger in Kate's life was over and she . . . she didn't need a protector anymore. Damn her. She'd hinted that she needed a champion, and he'd been there for her. She'd used her lovely body to get what she wanted: a marriage of convenience to protect her from her wicked uncle. And now that Bad Uncle Herbert was gone, well, Kate was also. Or so it seemed.

Quinn seethed, anger heating his blood. How dare she? She belonged to him, and he'd have her back. She could be carrying his child at this very moment. Did she think she'd steal his heir?

Harper entered, the picture of calm in her neat gray dress and ruffled cap. "Yes, my lord?"

"The countess. Did she return from her shopping expedition?"

"Yes, my lord, but set out again thereafter."

"Where did she go?"

"I do not know, my lord, but I was under the impression that you were aware of the journey. The countess left quite openly, taking several portmanteaux." Harper withdrew a flint from her pocket to light the lamps and candles set about the room, eyeing the dishevelment with a frown.

"Damn and blast! Did she go alone?"

"No, my lord. Accompanied by her maid, she left in the barouche. Is there a problem? I thought that you and the countess had planned to leave London for Wiltshire and understood from Bettina that you intended to travel separately."

"Yes, there is a problem. We had no such plans,"

Quinn said through his teeth. He'd have to whip her when he found her. He did not like to think of whipping Kate, but he could not tolerate a willful and disobedient wife.

Rich with fragrant summer greenery, Wiltshire delighted all Kate's senses. The grounds of Badham Abbey were no exception. Kate cast her gaze over the wide swards, now busy with gardeners repairing the evidence of Herbert's neglect. She sat at a table near the balustrade she'd climbed months before during her escape from her uncle, listening to the current owner of the abbey.

Randolph Gillender, a stout fellow of perhaps fifty years, spoke as a servant poured afternoon tea. "I remember your mother, my sister, quite well. Fine lass she was."

"I remember her also. Not a day goes by that I don't miss Mama." Kate wished she knew how to fill the hollowness in her heart.

"Of course." Leaning over the table, her uncle pressed Kate's hand. "You are not much like her. You seem to have the look of the Scovilles."

Kate stirred her tea, bending her head in shame. "How you must hate us."

"No, never! I could never hate Margaret's child."

"But my grandfather forbade all contact between our families." She lifted her head to look again at her jolly, kind uncle. "Can you imagine? I never knew you existed until this day."

"That was part of the marriage contract." Uncle Randolph settled his bulk deeper into his chair. "Bennett and Margaret were wild for each other, but your grandfather, the old earl, wouldn't allow the marriage unless we Gillenders had no contact with the Scovilles. Called us Cits, he did."

"Well, he wasn't too proud to take your money." Kate couldn't help the bitterness in her voice and soul. She'd admired and loved her grandfather, and had believed that the old earl had cared for her. But he'd deprived her of the one thing most important to Kate: family.

"Ah, the old earl was rich as Midas, but he always wanted more. He would have disowned Bennett otherwise. Margaret couldn't bear for Bennett to lose his title. She knew it meant everything to him. And she wanted to be his countess, and to make certain you could marry well." Randolph sighed. "It was hard, very hard, giving her up. She was the youngest, you see, the golden girl of our family. Mum and Dad fair doted on her."

"She was beautiful, wasn't she?" Kate hoped she wouldn't start to weep, shaming herself in front of Uncle Randolph. Despite his kindness, he was still a virtual stranger.

Sorrow pervaded her. She'd been disillusioned about her grandfather, her Uncle Herbert, her husband—was there no one upon whom she could depend?

"Aye, your mother was lovely. And you have her sweetness of temper and high spirits. Never think you aren't a worthy daughter, Katherine. Have another berry tart, and don't be blue-devilled." Her uncle smiled at Kate, placing a pastry on her plate. "All's well that ends well, what?"

She tried to shake her foul mood. Her uncle didn't deserve to share her megrims. "It is grand that you now own the abbey and the title. The Gillenders deserve it."

"Yes, we do, don't we?" Randolph said complacently. "Now all we need is for you and your husband to mend your fences."

"I don't know if that's possible." Kate fiddled with the napkin in her lap.

"Best consider it, Kate. I don't know many earls, but I can't imagine that a peer would take too kindly to his wife running out on him. Humiliating." Randolph stirred his tea.

"I'm the one who was humiliated!"

Her uncle shrugged. "Gossip's the wine and bread of the *ton*, niece. In a fortnight, there will be another scandalbroth to amuse the quizzes, and no one will remember Kate Tyndale's hasty marriage. Don't refine upon it."

"He doesn't love me, Uncle. Whatever shall I do?" Despair sat in the pit of Kate's stomach.

"What's love got to do with it? You rubbed along rather well, didn't you, before you saw that wretched cartoon?"

"Well, yes." She ran a finger around the rim of her teacup.

Her uncle scratched one of his chins. "Care for your own happiness, not the scoffs and scorns of others. Do you think I care a dace for society's good opinion? Would I have bought the title and the abbey if I did? I know what they'll say. The *ton* gossips will unsheathe their claws and label me a pretentious upstart, a pert mushroom—all of that. It doesn't matter. My children will be presented at court, and they'll make good marriages. That's what matters."

Kate picked up her pastry fork. "I want a marriage like my parents had."

"Ah, Bennett and Margaret, they were quite the pair. Once they laid eyes on each other, nothing could keep them apart. You wish for a rare kind of love, Katherine. Best make do with what you've got."

"What I've got is nothing." Kate poked at her tart.

"And whose fault is that? You ran out on your husband. You'll be fortunate indeed if he does not take a cane to your back."

Kate bit her lip. She knew that few husbands spared the rod, but couldn't picture sweet-natured Quinn wielding it. But he'd shot Osborn, hadn't he? He'd seemed eager to kill Uncle Herbert. Quinn did indeed have a violent side to his nature.

"Papa! Papa!" Lydia Gillender, a sparkling sixteen-year-old, burst through the open French doors onto the balustrade. "There's an assembly!"

"An assembly?" Randolph asked his oldest child.

"Yes, in Salisbury two nights hence. We can go, can't we?"

Randolph glanced at Kate. "Yes, if the countess will stand as chaperon while your mama is in London."

"Oh, please, Cousin Kate! 'Twould be quite unexceptional!"

Kate smiled. She'd missed her share of parties in her abbreviated maidenhood and wouldn't deny herself this pleasure. Perhaps the dance would help her forget her troubles. And she knew Lydia, in the two years before her presentation in London, would benefit by attending a few small gatherings in the country. The poise gained would assure the diminutive Lydia, blessed with the unusual combination of blond hair and dark eyes, entree into the *ton*'s most exalted circles, for she was a diamond of the first water. "I should be delighted to attend."

Dressed in her white and blue, Kate sat down after a country dance and fanned her heated face. "La, Bryan!" She laughed up into the face of her friend. "I fear this dance has given me a jolly great thirst!"

Bryan St. Wills picked up his cue immediately. "Shall I procure you a lemonade or perhaps champagne, Kate?"

"Thank you." Kate snapped her fan closed, then looked around the ballroom. All of fashionable Salisbury had turned out for this assembly. Country matrons herded their chits, dressed in their best, into the room to be partnered by the blushing sons of the local gentry. Older personages indulged themselves in a dance or two as they chaperoned the young folk.

Bryan returned with champagne for Kate, who sipped it while chatting with him and watching out for Lydia Gillender. She needn't have worried, for Lydia was a hit. Dressed in lemon-yellow sarcenet and lace, she hadn't sat down for two hours as her attentive swains made certain that the soles of her dancing slippers would be worn through by midnight.

Kate leaned into her chair, tipping her head to address Bryan. "A lovely evening, is it not?"

Bryan, however, didn't return her comment. Instead, he seemed intent upon someone, or something, taking place across the crowded room. Kate turned to see what phenomenon had caused the normally polite Bryan to ignore her.

An exquisite of unusual height and striking mien had entered. Kate's breath caught in her throat.

Taller than the other gentlemen by at least a head, the dandy's shoulders, sheathed in impeccable black superfine, filled out his superbly cut jacket as though the garment had been molded to his masculine body.

The severe black-and-white of the Corinthian's evening dress was relieved only by a large ruby in his cravat. He advanced, parting the throng with more panache than Moses dividing the Red Sea.

He drew closer. Long, elegant hands, immaculately gloved, were half-covered by a luxuriant fall of lace from the wrist—an unusual, old-fashioned touch. Clearly this beau wasn't afraid to defy or create fashion at his whim.

Kate couldn't breathe. Her head swam.

"St. Wills." Quinn nodded at Bryan.

Bryan inclined his head. "Devere."

"A pleasure to see you, sir. We had quite lost track of you after you set out to retrieve Kate." Quinn's voice was silken. Reaching down, he lifted one of Kate's hands off the arms of the chair she clutched. He caressed her palm as he smiled down at her, mischief infusing his gaze.

She closed her eyes. She hadn't known what to expect when next she saw Quinn, but flirtation in the midst of a crowded assembly hadn't been in her plans. A trembling heat captured her lower body.

"I didn't find Kate at Badham Abbey and continued on to Somerset to visit with my parents," Bryan explained. "I wished to apprise them of my pending nuptials."

"Then congratulations are in order. Lady Sybilla Farland?"

"Yes."

"A charming girl. It is to be hoped that the four

of us see each other frequently in the future. We have so much in common."

"Thank you." Bryan cleared his throat. "I understand from Katie that you all experienced concern over my whereabouts. Please accept my most sincere apologies. I did send a message, but the post in some areas of Somerset is not what it should be. I shall speak to the Home Office about the matter."

"Quite so." Quinn paused. "My wife."

Kate opened her eyes and raised her gaze to Quinn's. He seemed amused at her discomfiture.

"Will you allow me this dance?"

She swallowed. "Yes, my lord."

The small orchestra struck up a waltz. Quinn slipped one arm around her waist as he took her hand. Holding her in a close, possessive clasp, he whirled her into the throng.

The room spun. He pinned her gaze with his. The fiery heat in his brown eyes seemed to consume her every thought. She knew that this dance could have only one end. Did she welcome or fear it, or both? Would she come meekly to heel, or would she run?

Why should she not leave? He didn't love her. She was merely his possession, and he'd come only to assert his claim, to take her back to London and a life she couldn't face without the comforting bulwark of his devotion.

She didn't need him. Though her property became his upon their marriage, she had found a refuge. Uncle Randolph would take her in for as long as need be, although he didn't approve of the break between Kate and her husband. For the nonce, she ignored the void in her heart she'd felt without Quinn.

He twirled her out of the room into a darkened hall, then into a small quiet chamber hung with the cloaks and pelisses of the assemblage. He kept hold of her hand as he tossed a coin to the servant in the cloakroom. "Make sure no one enters."

The woman nodded and left.

Kate gasped with surprise. "What on earth are you doing?"

He pressed her against a paneled wall. One hand, still clasping her wrist, raised it high above her head. His other hand explored her, long fingers stroking her throat, then dipping lower. His body caressed hers. She moved her free hand against his chest, needing some room. His hips pushed against hers.

The carved trim of the wall rubbed against her buttocks. The sensation wasn't uncomfortable, but stimulating in a way that Kate didn't want to experience at this particular moment.

"That's precisely my question to you, wife. What did you think you were doing when you left our home so suddenly?"

"I—I—I—" Kate couldn't breathe, couldn't think, couldn't explain. How could Quinn, so full of masculine confidence and assurance, possibly understand? "It's not my home."

"Everything I have is yours, and you are mine, Kate. Mine."

"No!"

"Yes." Quinn bent his head toward hers, seizing her mouth in a savage kiss. Hard and demanding, this was the kiss of a conqueror, an invader, and it ravished her to her soul. His hand eased into her low-cut bodice, taking her breast. A gloved thumb passed back and forth over her nipple, igniting her.

She whimpered, opening her mouth to his. He stroked her tongue with his, then released her hand, which prickled as the blood flowed into it anew.

"Mine." His voice was a guttural growl against her lips. He tugged her bodice down, revealing both breasts, and palmed them. Her nipples tightened into sensitive cones beneath the stroke of his gloved hands.

She tore her mouth away from his. "Stop it, Quinn!"

"Why?" He lifted her skirt, sliding one hand up to her knee. He untied a garter.

Horribly reminded of the dreadful caricature, Kate struggled for freedom, but failed as Quinn shifted his weight to crush her against the wall. His strength outstripped hers. She moaned. She didn't understand his mood. What would he do to her? He'd never forced her before . . . never had to.

He didn't have to this time, either. With despair, she felt her traitorous body respond to his nearness, his masculine power. Her muscles loosened, becoming pliant under his touch.

"That's better, sweet Kate." Quinn loosened his pantaloons, rocking side to side until he stood between her spread thighs. With one hand on her breast, he pushed her skirts out of the way and hooked his other hand beneath her knee, lifting it.

He'd made her completely accessible and available to him. She felt herself redden, sensed the rush of blood through her body with every quick beat of her heart. She couldn't stop him. She didn't want to.

Quinn filled her, thrusting with a steady rhythm. Gasping, Kate clung to his shoulders. Her slipper fell off her foot as she put her leg around his waist for balance. Her standing leg began to tremble as she became a slave to his passion, and her own.

With both hands, he pulled her down off the wall and lay with his back on the floor. She drew in a surprised breath as his thick, hard erection slid to its full length inside her.

"*Quinn.* What are you doing?"

Laughing up at her, he rotated his hips. She moaned, feeling him swirl inside her. Her knees were bent on either side of her body. She planted her hands on each of his shoulders to keep her balance as she learned to move with him in this variation of the ancient ritual of loving. Arching as she rode him, she threw her head back.

Exaltation and delight overwhelmed her as Quinn's laughter turned to groans of arousal. Kate bent down and kissed him, darting her soft, hot tongue inside his mouth while she rocked herself on him in the ways she discovered would pleasure her the most. She stretched, offering her breasts to his mouth, moaning as he suckled her. Roles blurred as Kate took her husband down the magic road of desire to fulfillment. Who was the possessor and who the possessed?

"Kate, ah, Kate, don't leave me again. I love you, Kate."

"Oh, Quinn." Kate's body seemed to explode in a cascade of glittering sparks. She collapsed on his chest, kissing him wildly. "I love you so much. I'll die without you."

They lay together on the floor in a tangle of limbs and clothing until Quinn stirred. "Why did you leave, love?"

She gulped. "It—it—I—I—"

"Was it this?" He reached into a pocket of his coat and removed a twist of paper.

Kate's stomach began to churn as she recognized the hateful caricature. "Yes," she whispered.

"Poor darling Kate. So young to experience your first taste of the *ton*'s cruelty. Where did you get hold of this bit of poison?"

"I—I—saw it in the window of the print shop on St. James Street."

"Why did you not come to me?" The reproach in his voice knifed her to the heart.

"I couldn't face you. I couldn't tell you that I—I can't share your life, Quinn." Kate slipped off him and stood, adjusting her clothing. Tears pricked her eyes. She'd told him the truth. She hadn't the slightest idea how she'd live without him, but she knew that she'd never be happy as part of the *ton*.

Rising, he took a handkerchief from his pocket and handed it to her.

"Thank you." She dabbed her eyes, then cleaned herself.

"You're welcome to anything I have. Kate, I don't understand. You're the one who's always saying that you don't care about the foolish opinions of others. Why turn tail at the first sign of trouble?" He buttoned his pantaloons.

"I don't like it." A sudden anger flooded her. "I don't want to be the target of gossip. I don't like people constantly watching me. And, quite frankly, I don't like London particularly. Being back here made me understand that I'm really just a country girl at heart. I want to go back to my home in Somerset and forget that the last eight months happened."

Quinn began to laugh. Kate stared in astonishment.

"My darling Kate. We don't have to live in London if society pleases you not. In fact, I spend most of my time in Surrey."

Hope leaped, matched by curiosity. "Surrey? What on earth is in Surrey?"

"Devere is in Surrey. My horses are in Surrey, and you and I and our children will live in Surrey. One doesn't raise children in London, sweetheart."

"Oh." Kate, bewildered by this surprising turn of events, repeated Quinn like a numbwit. "Surrey?"

"Yes, Surrey. We'll go there after you've finished visiting with your uncle and his family."

Epilogue

Devere Manor, Surrey
Eight years later

Kate sat on the lawn, an open picnic basket nearby. A sumptuous repast, half-eaten, was spread out on the blanket bedside her.

The delights of potted ham and strawberry tarts had given way to the more interesting pastime of badminton as her son and daughter strove to best their father. Quinn, his cravat untied and face red with exertion, dashed after the shuttlecock hit by Margaret, their seven-year-old. He whacked it firmly with his racquet. Kate watched it sail into the branches of a large oak.

"I'll get it!" she called. Standing, she brushed crumbs off her skirt.

"You will not!" Quinn strode over.

"Please, don't tell me to keep my dignity here in the country!"

"Where we are has nothing to do with it. You are a good eight months pregnant."

She covered his mouth. "Quinn, the children,"

she murmured. "And really, it's more like seven months."

"Kate, you are not climbing into that tree."

"Mama! Papa!" Bennett shouted.

Turning, both parents gasped as their four-year-old swung from his knees upside-down from one of the old oak's limbs.

"Bennett! You will get out of that tree this instant!" Quinn shouted, leaping over to the tree.

Bennett grinned and threw the shuttlecock down to his father. "Catch me, Papa!" He dropped, hitting Quinn in the chest and knocking his father to the ground.

Quinn untangled his limbs from his son's. "Pestilential imp." He glanced at his wife. "But I must say that he comes by his climbing skills honestly."

Kate smiled. "To be sure, they may come in useful in the future. Who knows when he may have to climb out of a tower prison."

Quinn frowned. Bennett squirmed, and Quinn let his son go. The children ran off to continue their game.

"My darling Kate. I had hoped that after all these years, you had forgotten that terrible episode in your life. You have not had nightmares for a good many years."

"No, no more bad dreams, but I haven't forgotten. How could I?" Kate scooted over to nestle her head into the hollow of his shoulder. "And why? After all, it brought me to you."

Author Notes and Acknowledgments

Regency devotees will remember that Rowland-son's caricature of Madam Cain at Signor Angelo's predated 1820, and I have indulged in a little artistic license in its regard. The presence of the actor, Kean, in a production of *Macbeth* was similarly invented; this is, after all, fiction.

No book is written in a vacuum. Judy Dedek, Constance Robinson, Dianna Garbett, Luann Erickson, Louise Pelzl, Judy Myers, Brenda Novak, Sara Myers, and, most importantly, Caroline Cummings, read and helped me with this work. The contributions of Dee Hendrickson, the *Regency Plume,* and Patti Berg are also acknowledged, as is the generosity of Kensington Books, a marvelous organization which has given so many aspirants their start in the publishing world.

ABOUT THE AUTHOR

Susan Swift divides her time between her homes in California and Maui, Hawaii. She lives with two retrievers and her real live hero of a husband. Her hobbies are hiking and kenpo karate, in which she has a second-degree black belt.

Visit Sue's website at: www.bigfoot.com/~brusan